Bird magic

Bird magic

A. C. Smith

NATIONAL
LIBRARY
OF AUSTRALIA

A catalogue record for this
book is available from the
National Library of Australia

ISBN: 978-0-6454900-0-8

Cover design and illustration by: Bridget Acreman

For those whose dreams are flowerless,

and for those who watch them glow.

Book one of the Iwizadi Trilogy

Prologue

The ancient people could talk to trees and animals. That's what the stories said: in every tale from the old-days there were people talking to animals. That just seemed to be something normal for them, something they accepted without question. There were stories where people talked to birds and learned to fly. There were stories where men became rivers and women transformed into wind.

Aisling knew that these were just stories, but she loved to listen to them whenever her dad or one of the neighbours told them. There was an art to storytelling, something that Aisling had not yet been able to grasp. She didn't understand the nuance of foreshadowing or how to build suspense. At five years old, the way her dad wove words into stories was a magic of its own, even when she had heard the same story one hundred times.

Her favourite story, like most children, was the one where the wizard Iwizadi was captured and then escaped from prison, and the people lost their magic. She asked her dad to tell it to her over and over again, which he did without argument, just like his parents had done with him. Time with his daughter helped Peter cope with his loss.

According to the story, a very long time ago in a wealthy city, in a wealthy country, there lived a man named Iwizadi.

Iwizadi was a well-liked teacher, and the most capable wizard anybody had ever known. The city was called Libalele and was said to be perfectly clean, and the buildings covered with a magic paint that shone so brightly that you could see the city's shiny glow in the sky before its outline appeared on the horizon. Travellers making their way down the mountain road into the Lele Valley always felt excited to see the shine as they made the final ascent and crested the rim of the valley. From there, the road wound down into the ancient crater where the city was built, passing lush fields and the clear, crisp water of the Liba. The people at the time believed an even older civilisation carved the valley from the stone using a long-forgotten magic.

The story begins shortly after Iwizadi had discovered a new and powerful type of magic that allowed him to turn into stone. Of course, the other ancients already had magic that allowed them to turn into animals and birds and fish, even trees for those who could master it… but turning into stone was never seen before. It was something the ancients always thought possible but until then nobody had achieved. Iwizadi became a celebrity and very wealthy. People begged him for his secrets, and his classes were always full.

But some other wizards became jealous and fearful of Iwizadi's discovery; fearful that he would become too powerful and discover new evil forms of magic and use them against the people. They hatched a plot to capture him and steal his secret new magic, which he kept locked up in his classroom, recorded in his journal. The journal, when it was not with him, was sealed with a protective spell that would only allow the right person to see its contents.

Leading the conspiracy was Iwizadi's younger brother, Umwahu, who had always been jealous of Iwizadi's advanced ability and too impatient to study magic like his big brother. Umwahu had no fear that Iwizadi would control the people with evil magic; he knew his brother would always do good for the people and had no such ambition. But Umwahu also knew that fear could be used to control people, and started to spread rumours that Iwizadi had discovered another new, evil magic that he would use to put thoughts in others' minds.

Umwahu's plan worked, and it did not take long before Iwizadi was arrested. While working in his classroom, Iwizadi was shocked when the king's guardians burst through the door to bring him to justice.

"There must be some mistake!" he protested.

"There is no mistake," The tallest soldier Heykel answered, "The king has issued a warrant for the arrest of the dark wizard Iwizadi, for the crime of treason. Your workbooks and materials will be taken as evidence." Aisling didn't fully understand things like warrants and treason but she knew it was an exciting moment in the story.

Then Iwizadi was led through the streets in a cage. Any time a wizard was arrested, a magic cage was the only way to safely contain them. Without it, the wizard could escape. The youngest and shortest of the king's guards, Cesaret, did not say a word through the arrest and the transport. He looked uneasy about the whole situation, himself having studied magic as a child under Iwizadi. Cesaret could not believe the rumours, knowing Iwizadi as a patient teacher. But if he did not do his duties as a king's guardian, he knew it would be him in that cage.

The ordinary city people whispered and pointed, and sent messages to each other using the birds, who could be trusted more than people. Bird magic was the oldest form of magic, and most Libaleleans knew how to use it. Sending messages over long distances was what made the people rich and powerful, and Libalele's people fiercely guarded their secrets.

Iwizadi was imprisoned for life, while his brother Umwahu began working as the king's personal wizard. He gained power and influence but remained a mediocre wizard and never improved his abilities. In the city and beyond, people began to distrust wizards. It started with the grander displays of magic like transformation, but eventually spread to even the way people used magic to light their homes. When someone was seen using magic they were threatened to be locked up with the 'evil' Iwizadi. People were arrested on Umwahu's orders, but eventually released after promising to denounce others they saw engaging in suspicious activity. Remarkably quickly, people only used magic in secret. Even the harmless Bird magic drew too much suspicion and people hesitated to use it. The birds, confused at the sudden silence, moved out of the city unnoticed. People also left, and there were rumours that a new colony was established far in the West beyond Umwahu's reach.

It was a heavy story for a young child, but Peter always told it in such an exciting way. He knew his daughter didn't understand all of its themes, so he emphasised the bits about magic and embellished the role of the birds.

"But those are only rumours," people would say about the new colony.

"Those people are traitors."

"Good riddance."

The city went dark, and a new generation of people grew up without magic. They were the first children not to talk to birds since anyone could remember. Talking about magic became a crime too, but still some people who knew Iwizadi believed he was innocent, and carried on in secret teaching magic to their children.

Meanwhile, Iwizadi appeared to live through his prison sentence without any trouble. This was for two reasons. Firstly, Cesaret, his former pupil ensured a comfortable situation for Iwizadi with good food and anything else he asked for, and secondly, Iwizadi was still able to use his Stone magic, despite his anti-magic cell. You see, every anti-magic protection corresponds to a specific type of magic, and since only Iwizadi knew how to use Stone magic, nobody knew how to stop him.

So Iwizadi turned into a statue whenever he was alone, only ageing when in human form, and all the while devising new types of magic that would keep him alive forever. And in this way, over the decades of his prison sentence he hardly aged at all. This enraged Umwahu even further, who had already spent years trying and failing to understand his brother's Stone magic, and was starting to show signs of ageing.

Eventually, after many more years, the king died and Umwahu claimed the throne through violence and threats and blackmail. He was now the most powerful person in the city, having already made magic illegal among its citizens, but secretly acceptable for the ruling class. All the while he kept using his own magic to influence others and plant unwanted thoughts and doubts in their minds. But Umwahu could never understand Iwizadi's Stone magic, no matter how hard he tried, or how many people he employed. This only made him angrier, and he was a cruel leader who arrested many people based on nothing but hearsay and mistrust.

Umwahu lived to the age of one hundred and forty, dying in his sleep an angry and unjust leader. Hope spread through the people, the oldest of whom had not forgotten the old times, and could even remember the days where magic lit up Libalele, and the city was the envy of the world. Some people cried with grief and others with hope. Iwizadi continued patiently waiting in his cell, turning to stone whenever possible, barely more than fifty years old after spending nearly one hundred years in prison.

Umwahu was replaced by his grandson Isiko, who had seen different types of magic and wanted it to be available to the people. His first act as king was to make magic legal again, but it would take time before the people could relearn to trust each other, and already a lot of magic had been lost when children were not taught by their parents under Umwahu's reign. Many people had never seen magic at all and would never learn to use it. It was a dying artform.

So Isiko asked Iwizadi to teach the people. Iwizadi gladly accepted, and went back to his old position teaching magic at the school. But something was different. Four generations he had been in prison, and the world outside had changed. Few people knew any magic at all, and those who did were reluctant to use it, accustomed to persecution and fear.

During the time that magic was illegal, the people were forced to discover new ways to do things that had traditionally been done with magic. That's when Noi was first used to light peoples' houses.

Noi was amazing in its own way, but it was not magical. Iwizadi learned everything he could about Noi, but he could not accept that it would ever replace magic as an energy source. There was no way, he thought. It was too clunky, and it ran out and needed to be replaced every few weeks, and it left ugly scars on the earth. No, in Iwizadi's opinion, magic could not be replaced and he made it his mission to teach everyone.

Iwizadi was said to have written everything in his journal and volumes of all known magic that he used for teaching. Nobody knew what happened to these books after he died and it was rumoured that they were buried with him, even though nobody knew where he was buried.

But fewer and fewer children came to his classroom as the years went by. Their parents thought that magic was old superstition and that instead, Noi was the future. Huge companies were established that sent teams into the mountains to mine for Noi, leaving destruction and piles of dangerous garbage when they had finished digging. Rumours spread that Noi was turning the rivers strange colours and poisonous to drink.

"But that's another story for another time," Aisling's dad always said when he got up to that part. She always begged him to tell her more, but she was sleepy and as soon as he continued to talk about Iwizadi's struggles, she would fall asleep and dream of magic, never knowing what happened to him in his fight against Noi. If she were older, she might have noticed Peter's emotions clouding his storytelling, and perhaps his personal judgements slipping into the characters.

One night after this story when she was still very young, Aisling met Iwizadi in a dream. They were in his classroom. She knew it was him immediately even though she could not see his face: the harder she concentrated on him, the more transparent he became and she kept forgetting what he looked like. He was holding a thick book under one arm that was covered with ornate decorations and hypnotic patterns. She looked around at the room and saw his desk in the corner covered with papers. She saw the students' desks arranged in a semi-circle, and the plain wooden floor decorated with an elaborately woven rug with a pattern that looked like the Milky Way. Pigeons were on every windowsill and she noticed that they must have been up several stories high. Iwizadi stood by the open door, facing her. She couldn't see his expression but she felt safe.

"Can you show me magic?" She asked innocently.

"This is magic already," he answered, and seeing that she was confused he added. "How else do you know what I look like?"

And in that confusing way that dreams change details of the world, Iwizadi suddenly looked just like her dad. His buzz cut and stubble and thick eyebrows were exactly like the ones she knew. But his eyes were not. Her dad had grey eyes, but Iwizadi's were black, ringed with yellow, like a solar eclipse.

"That's not you, that's my dad," she said, still confused but not scared.

Iwizadi then changed again and Aisling saw herself. She laughed when she saw her goofy smile, missing the two teeth she had recently lost.

"That's not any better!" she protested with a short-lived childish grumpiness.

"Alright, fine," Iwizadi said slowly. "I will show you. Are you ready?"

Then the dream changed and she could not see his face clearly. She felt herself waking up when the wizard's voice very clearly came to her. "It was a good start, Aisling," he said.

Chapter 1

In a small room at the government headquarters in the Capital, Jack Hargreaves sat at a utilitarian desk, surrounded by crumpled maps and official documents stained with various liquids. His office was always a jumble of papers, and was always poorly lit no matter how many times he asked maintenance to replace the burnt-out globes. It was usually stuffy, because a crow had decided to nest at his window and he couldn't open it. Maintenance hadn't done anything about that either.

With great care, but a sense of urgency, he selected the Leader's personal pen and slowly traced the Leader's elegant signature onto the page in front of him, careful to get exactly the right slope of the letters, the right height, the right curve on the *B*…

And a minute later he had made a perfect copy. He had to hurry. Forging the Leader's signature was a serious crime. If anyone saw him, he would be in serious trouble, possibly life in prison. He stuffed the forged letter into an envelope – one of the Leader's personal envelopes stolen during last night's excursion – and quickly stored it inside his jacket pocket. Peter could not refuse him this time.

A tap and a scratch at the window made him jump. He cursed himself for panicking, because it just the crows. The mother had returned to feed its babies.

"I thought I told you to move out," he muttered, collecting himself. It was already dark, so he would have to hurry and leave now to make it to his brother's house and back before dawn. It wasn't unusual for him to be working late at night. He grabbed anything he might need - keys to the Noicar, coat, government badge – and strode to the elevator. It glowed blue like everything else powered by Noi. It wasn't so long ago that the elevator was installed, and Jack remembered walking up endless flights of stairs to get to his small office.

"Soon it won't be like this," he thought. "Not after I secure that huge Noi deposit under Peter's house."

The elevator opened to the garage and Jack exited briskly, fixated on the Noicar. He had to get out and back before anyone saw. They would surely question him being there without an official reason for using the Noicar.

On the way out he stopped to see the garage attendant, Gansuil.

"Nice warm night, Mister Jack."

"Indeed."

"Have your papers?"

Every employee needed approval to use a Noicar. Jack handed Gansuil an envelope with a few bills inside. Gansuil, unflinching, peeked inside. The two men said nothing for a moment.

"Everything in order?" Jack asked.

"Seems fine, Mister Jack," Gansuil answered. This was not his first bribe, nor Jack's. It was an open secret that anything could be procured for a price. The price of borrowing a Noicar without approval was one day's worth of Gansuil's pay. The garage door opened, gliding silently on its tracks into the ceiling, powered by Noi like everything else. "See you back tonight then."

Jack approached the driver side of the Noicar and it responded to the proximity of the key. Blue trucks lit up its undercarriage, like a predatory animal about to pounce. He sat inside and started the ignition. A low hum was all that told him it was ready to go. The older models had used a louder engine, but this was the latest prototype. It used a new type of engine that treated the Noi more gently, and was not only quieter, but more efficient and cheaper to run. The government loved it. Jack loved it. There were few feelings like driving one of the new models, especially at night, silently stalking through the empty city, feeling powerful compared to the random old vehicles that the public used.

He slinked out of the garage and sped off into the city. It was a long drive to Nelasive, but at that time of night the roads would be clear.

"Why didn't he leave that stupid town?" Jack wondered out loud. He often talked to himself while driving: it was the best time to think because he was really alone. "He could have had a great job, a prosperous life, here with me. Too late now. He could have been a level nine. I'll be level ten after securing the deal. Or higher."

But he knew it wasn't so simple, hence the need to produce the forged letter. Peter never took Jack seriously and had fought every attempt to relocate him. But this time he could not refuse. A direct order from the Leader could not be ignored, even by Jack's anarchist brother. Even he knew the consequences.

When Jack had reached the far side of the city, he saw the expressway open before him. It was the best in the country and he had played a large part in its development, even if people didn't recognise his achievements. Even the Leader had downplayed its significance in order to gain political points. Jack should have been promoted for it, but instead he was moved into that tiny office on the top floor with barely a window. And crows. Bloody crows. If it wasn't for those rumours about his past. Of course, he had an excuse and he could deny them, but they were after all true. But in the end, the expressway got built did it not?

Small lamps powered with Noi placed along the roadside lit the way for the next two hundred kilometres before Jack reached his turnoff towards Nelasive, his birth city. They created a never-ending spaghetti of cables that littered the expressways around the whole country, connecting every lamp to a power source. But the smaller roads in the cities were not so thoroughly developed. It was another half an hour along dark and eerily deserted roads before reaching Peter's quiet street. As expected, nobody was out. It was after midnight. Doorsteps were illuminated by faint blue glows of weak Noi lights, some flickering. They were too expensive to maintain for most people, so they put up with the poor quality.

It was an old area of the city, made to look new again some forty or fifty years before. That's when their parents had moved in, following the promises of prosperity and the hype generated by the press. The old foundations were still in place for most of the buildings, but their facades were renovated and looked fresh. Some buildings maintained their original plumbing and had frequent problems. A faintly metallic smell lingered everywhere. Jack hated being there, but he only visited on business now. Since their parents died, he had no reason to, not even to visit Peter. He had seen Aisling only a few times in her life. She looked too much like her mother.

It was the promises. Fairy tales, Jack called them. His

parents heard the rumours that the town was at the site of a huge Noi deposit and everyone raced to buy the houses quickly before they became impossibly expensive. It was supposed to be a big operation and all the new occupants could get rich. They thought they were making a wise investment.

But there was some scandal, Jack vaguely remembered. When he was young, before he could properly understand, his parents were talking anxiously about leaving. His mother wanted to move back to the city where she was originally from. His father continued hoping the Noi operation would start soon. Eventually, with no jobs and no money, his mother left, and so did half the town. Eventually his father followed her back to the city, and Jack and Peter grew up in the Capital.

"Everyone can be convinced if the price is high enough," Jack thought out loud.

Now in the present day it still hadn't begun. That's what Jack had come to change. He was going to try and override fifty years of protests and red tape with the forged signature. By removing Peter, he could finally secure enough land for the government to start drilling in that part of the city.

Why suddenly all this concern with the environment? The people needed Noi. How else did they expect to get it? With all these delays the price had steadily increased over the years, leaving many families worse off as supply diminished and demand increased. Jack was helping people. He wanted to help.

The radio in the car was tuned to a late-night talk show, and a croaky woman sleepily intoned: "Magic is the topic this hour. We have with us tonight Dr Wanda McCullough, expert in Noi extraction technologies."

"Good evening."

"And Jonathan Prince, spokesperson for the Ministry of Energy."

"Thank you for having me, Linda."

"Wanda, the first question from our listeners is for you: What possible benefits are there from other experimental forms of energy currently in discussion?"

"That's a great question, and before going into the specifics, it's worth mentioning that Noi extraction methods are under continuous review to improve safety standards, but it is ultimately a very clean source of energy that produces only a minimal amount of by-product-"

"By-product?"

"-that we can quickly and cleanly dispose of and put to use in other areas of research. These other sources as you say, are purely conjectural. There is no evidence so far to suggest that something such as magic, the hot topic on everybody's lips, could ever replace Noi, let alone be reliably performed. The science of magic is still out in any case, and it is not available to essentially one hundred percent of participants in our research."

"Have you seen successful magic yourself?"

"Not successful as such. I've seen one of the refugees from Blue Island walk into a room and dim the lights as he did so, but that can hardly be considered magic per se, and there is nothing to suggest that it was him that caused the lighting to dim." Hearing this, Jack scoffed.

"Jonathan, what does the Ministry have to say about such forays into research and development, when there is still no strong theoretical basis for magic? Is it a waste of tax dollars?"

"Well Linda, the Ministry does believe in fair economic competition and as such feels it necessary to explore all possible alternatives, even if such routes lead to dead ends and confirm that Noi is in fact the superior form of energy in this world."

"Some tax payers would disagree."

"Some tax payers disagree that we should be funding a military, when this country has not seen war in generations, but I ask if that logic is sound. Could it be that we haven't seen war because of a strongly funded military?"

"That's going a bit off topic, isn't it?"

"Hardly Linda. You know taxes run this country, and research from the Ministry of Energy have application in all other Ministries, including Defence."

"Jonathan, are you suggesting the military is applying findings from the Ministry of Energy's research into magic as an energy source?"

"Magic that isn't even confirmed as a viable energy source?" Wanda added.

"No, not at all. I never said that. All I'm saying is that if one Ministry succeeds, it shares its successes with other government bodies, that's a general fact."

"So, no one listening needs to put on their tin foil hat and get into one of those novelty *anti-magic* containers?" Linda gave a laugh like a frog.

"Absolutely not. Wanda, back me up on this: The Ministry can't even confirm the existence of magic at this point, let alone build magic weapons and give them to the army."

All three laughed. Jack did not. Jonathan could ruin everything if he didn't keep his mouth shut.

"Absolutely not."

"So," Linda continued, "Wanda, is the future of the Noi industry threatened like some claim?"

"Not at all. We as humans will likely be using Noi until the end of time. Rest assured, for those tens of thousands of people working in the Noi business, those jobs are safe, some of the safest jobs in the world."

"Isn't that reassuring for our listeners? Now you mentioned that it was a Blue Island refugee who caused the magic? How fascinating."

"It could hardly be called magic."

"Jonathan, does Wanda's experience help direct your Ministry's research? For example, using more refugee participants? Should the public be worried about magical refugees? Is their supposed magical background cause for concern and the reason they've been declared illegal immigrants?"

There it was, thought Jack, smiling, good old-fashioned right-wing racist talk-back radio. He loved it.

"Well Linda, I don't think it's fair to say that refugees from Blue Island are inherently more magical than any other race of people in the world, but from a scientific perspective it's worth investigating whether there's any truth to such a claim. But overall, no, the public don't need to worry about magical immigrants invading the land, and I refer all such concerns to the various Ministries associated with such issues: The Ministry of Home Affairs, Ministry of Defence, Ministry of Housing, and so on."

Jack turned the radio off. That was close. A good deflection, but close.

Peter's house was the same as all the others, but Jack hated it more. It was the house they were born in. It was Peter's now since their dad had died, but soon thanks to Jack it would belong to the state, and he could secure a share of the profits from its valuable Noi deposits. The man in his dream convinced him it was necessary.

The Noicar glided stealthily through the dark streets of the suburb. It came to a stop in front of a small two-bedroom house. There was a waist-high fence at the road, enclosing a small patch of grass in front of the house. The paint was chipped and peeling on its walls, and the door was a faded shade of green. Jack remembered the pride their parents used to have for the house. The gate squeaked as he opened it, and he hesitated slightly before knocking on the door. There were shuffling sounds from inside.

"Dad!" Aisling called out after waking from a dream, but her dad wasn't inside. She listened for a moment then heard his voice coming from outside, soft and muffled. She opened the window so she could see what was going on and looked out through the iron bars that were common in that part of the city. Her dad was outside. It took her a moment to recognise the other man, but eventually she realised it was her uncle. Her dad had his arms folded and stood blocking the doorway. It was a hard conversation for her to follow, but her dad was angry at her uncle. They talked in low voices but it was just loud enough for Aisling to hear some of the conversation. Her Noiclock told her it was after midnight. Jack only ever visited late at night.

"Can't I come visit you, brother?" she knew her uncle's voice even though she had only met him once or twice. It was a weird voice she thought, not like the people she knew. It was high pitched and always sounded like he had a cold.

"What are you really doing here, Jack?" her dad's voice was much warmer. It made her feel safe. She didn't remember her mum's voice at all.

"You were always so direct," Jack paused and smiled smugly. "You know what I want here."

"And you know you can't have it, Jack. I've already told you the answer is no."

"So stubborn as always, little brother. But you don't have

a choice this time. I have instructions from the Leader himself." Jack picked up the official envelope from the inside pocket of his coat and withdrew the forged letter.

"Let me see." Peter reached out to take the paper from Jack, angrily and with a small hint of fear.

"Look with your eyes." Jack snatched the paper back away from Peter and held it where he could read it, like a spoilt child who doesn't like to share.

"This doesn't convince me."

"The Leader owns this land now. So, you and the girl have to leave. You don't have a choice." Jack took out another page and thrust it into his brother's hand. Jack also reached into his trouser pocket and found a gold coin to give Peter. "For your trouble. The coin is my personal gift."

"I don't want your money. I want my home." Peter threw the coin at Jack's car, where it echoed with a loud pinging noise and left a mark. Jack watched calmly and turned slowly back to his brother, shrugging his wide shoulders.

"Oh, Peter. Silly move. I'll send you a bill for damages to the car. Probably worth more than just that gold coin, so you'd better pick it up before it gets too dirty. The coin isn't the real price, however. You will see on that letter that you are to be recompensed with a small portion of the profits should this site prove valuable. Go ahead, read it and sign. See you soon." He finally gave Peter the letter to keep.

Then Jack got into his car and drove away. Peter spat after the car and tore the paper he was holding in half. He watched as Jack's car disappeared into the night, quietly gliding down the road past his neighbours' houses, and ran a hand over his fuzzy scalp. Everything was bathed in blue from the street lights that stood at regular intervals. The miracle of Noi. Peter turned to go back inside and saw some movement at Aisling's window as she quickly closed it and pretended to be asleep.

"We're going to have to move," he sighed and said the words quietly to himself. He went inside and leaned against the door, feeling powerless. He held the pieces of the torn letter together and read them carefully.

Aisling was confused about what she saw during the night. When she woke up and saw her dad the next morning, he said nothing about her uncle's visit but looked like he hadn't slept.

"I have another wobbly one." She pointed at her mouth. This seemed to break Peter out of his trance, and he smiled and picked her up. She chattered at Peter while he made her breakfast and got ready for the day. It was a Wednesday, but instead of going to work Peter said he had some important errands to run.

Whenever Peter went to work, Aisling went next door where the Fidelis lived. They were too old to work, and loved having her over. Aisling loved it too because they spoilt her with attention and food. Peter dropped her off there at the normal time.

"I'll be back tonight," Peter kissed the top of her head and she ran inside to say hello to the cat. "Be good for Mr and Mrs Fideli."

"Okay," she called back, stroking its soft fur.

"She always is," Mr Fideli called out from the other room, where the volume from the radio threatened to drown him out. He had some hearing damage from working in the mines in the old days before anyone took safety seriously. The news report blared out something about the recent influx of refugees and the government's efforts to prevent them arriving. Someone was being interviewed and was fearful that all the refugees were witches. The government couldn't stop every refugee from arriving, but it could label their immigration a crime.

Peter hated listening to the news. Ever since the government bought the broadcast rights to every radio station, the news had become less of a common service and more of a propaganda machine. The current enemy of the state was illegal immigrants, who were accused of witchcraft. Every day Peter heard that the Leader was a great man who gave Noi freely to all his citizens, and outsiders were trouble. There was never news about the other countries in the world. As a supposed source of information, it just raised more questions: Why was the price of Noi still rising? What was happening overseas that made refugees want to come? Could it really be worse than here? That was the one question Peter didn't know if he wanted answered.

"She's a cheeky one," Mrs Fideli laughed and said goodbye to Peter.

"I might be later than normal today."

"Don't rush. She's very welcome here."

Peter sometimes got the feeling that Mr and Mrs Fideli wanted children but got too old. He sometimes thought he could detect some sadness in the old couple, but they got on very well with him. If it weren't for them, Peter might have already left the city. He got in his Noicar and tried to think. They were being made homeless. Where would they go?

Refugees. Refugees from Noi.

The radio blared through the open living room window: "In other news the government has begun its ambitious project to search for alternative energy sources. Critics say the project is poorly conceived, and question the logic behind it…" There were rumours of a new technology that could transmit moving images just like the radio, but nobody Peter knew had ever seen proof.

Peter started his car and headed north on the forest road, past the city limits where the road suddenly deteriorated and was more of a suggestion than a defined route. The Leader hadn't managed to touch the land in that direction yet, and that's where Peter wanted to go.

Chapter 2

The first time Aisling saw magic she was six years old, days after moving to a small settlement with her dad and some refugees from Blue Island, which was somewhere in the sea to the north-east of her hometown. It was hard for her young mind to understand the huge distances involved whenever they tried to explain it. She thought the day she spent travelling with her dad to the refugee settlement was the furthest journey in history.

Altogether the community consisted of about eight or nine families and was only a few hours' drive from where the Leader has claimed her dad's land. At first, she was scared when her dad led her to the large, round tent he had built in the style of the Khun. They looked different to the people she knew from Nelasive and people on the news called them witches. They were broader and had wide faces, but she saw him shaking hands with them and felt better. A few of them approached her and smiled, saying something in their language. Some of the Khun followed Peter inside. Most of them didn't speak his language but they liked him all the same and he kept practising the little he knew of theirs.

Her dad had visited the settlement many times after discovering it by accident while tracking a deer, and gotten to know a few of the Khun. He decided to build a house with them the day after Jack visited, reasoning that it was in such an isolated place that there was little risk of harassment. Over the coming years, their humble tent would become a warm and inviting home, large enough for a family. Peter helped renovate all of their homes.

"Very sad, but you live here now with us. It is much better for you both." An enormous Khun man named Chuluun was talking to Peter as they sat down together next to an ornately carved chess set in Chuluun's home. Aisling sat close to her dad, admiring the little pieces. Chuluun moved one of the white pawns forward two spaces.

"I can't believe he would go through with it. His own brother." Peter moved his own pawn. "And for what?"

"Noi," Chuluun answered, taking Peter's rhetorical question literally and looking at the old generator he had hooked up to everything in the room. "Everything is Noi." It was not the first time Peter had wanted to vent his anger about the situation. Chuluun and the other Khun all knew their story.

"Fucking Noi," Peter echoed disgusted, moving his knight. "As if they didn't have enough to last a thousand years already. They had no need, and no right to take my land."

"It was personal." Chuluun offered his knight in exactly the same way.

"You're damn right it was personal. Jack always wanted what I had. Since we were kids." Peter got up angrily and found a bottle of wine in his bags. He poured two cups.

"He don't want any refugees. The government calls us illegal immigrants," Chuluun said with good humour almost laughing at the absurdity and changing the topic, gulping down the wine.

"Suppose not." Peter took a sip.

"You are a refugee now too. What have you got that he don't? A daughter?"

Peter sat back down and stared at the pieces. "I guess it's the only thing I have that he doesn't, unless there's something I don't know. She calls you Bluey; says it's more friendly than Khun. Cuter."

"We like it. I am the cutest of us all, it is true." They laughed. The sun was going down and some insects had started making noise outside as the temperature dropped slightly. "Why do you still use Noi?" Chuluun asked while pouring another cup of wine.

"What choice do I have?" Peter asked, confused. Noi was the way society operated. Noi made all their things work; it powered their homes.

"Peter, we are friends, we are family now. I don't like to use Noi but we have used it since you came here. I think you are ready now. All Khun agree it is time for you to know if you are going to live here. I will show you the Khun way." Chuluun looked very serious all of a sudden and seemed to radiate an inexplicable kind of energy. The other Khun nearby stopped talking as if they had been waiting for this moment, and Aisling stared at Chuluun, unable to move. "You are the only man from this country here talking with us like humans. Nobody else wants us in this land. You live here now like we do. Watch. No more Noi."

Aisling watched. She saw Chuluun fixated on her dad, still as a boulder, one scarred hand on his lap and the other on his cup of wine. Nothing happened for a few seconds, but suddenly Aisling noticed something like a static shock in her fingertips and saw that a lamp on the table was lit. It was impossible. Nobody had moved, and the lamp wasn't even connected to her dad's small Noi battery. But there was light. The signature blue glow of Noi was lighting the room.

"How did you do that?" Peter stood up, without taking his eyes off Chuluun, and taking Aisling's hand. "How does it work without Noi?" There was panic and curiosity in his voice. He suddenly trusted the Khun less and wondered if it was the right choice to build a home here with them.

"Let me show you." Chuluun still had not moved, and continued to stare at Peter. Aisling struggled free from her dad's grip and sat opposite Chuluun in the seat Peter had abandoned. Her dad put his hands on her shoulders and they watched Chuluun, waiting for him to show them how the lamp was working. Chuluun's son, Khuch Chaddhal came into the room holding an old book. He placed it on the table in front of Aisling. It was written in the Khun language so Peter and Aisling couldn't read it, but they could see it was illustrated with strange pictures of people doing impossible things.

"The Book of Boloi," Chuluun said in a voice much softer than normal. Aisling got the impression that it was some kind of holy book. "It is our Magic book."

"Magic?" Peter felt unsure. He was taught that magic wasn't real. The stories about ancient people turning into animals were just stories, he thought. It wasn't possible that magic existed in the distant past, or that what he saw now was magic. It was just not right. "Magic isn't real."

"Yes, it is, dad. I heard it on the radio at the Fidelis' house," Aisling squirmed in her seat. If that's what witches were, they weren't so scary.

Chuluun laughed like a power saw and pointed at the lamp, which was lighting the room perfectly well, and without the annoying flickering that sometimes came with Noi lamps. He picked up the lamp and handed it to Peter. "You test it. Take it. Walk outside. You will see it still works.

No Noi."

Peter did as he was told. He took the lamp outside into the warm night air with Aisling. The light followed him; it was definitely coming from the lamp.

Impossible. It isn't connected.

Peter continued a few steps away from his now dark house before a shiver went through his body. "Aisling, what is this?" But he already knew. Aisling had already accepted it. It was the magic she had been hearing about her whole life. Peter wished he was a child again.

Without saying anything else, they walked back inside, lighting the way as they went. Chuluun sat contentedly in his loose shirt and pants and carelessly poured himself more wine, not caring when a few drops splashed onto him. "Magic" he said with certainty.

"Magic..." repeated Aisling, remembering the story of Iwizadi. She had heard it a hundred times before. For her, the idea that magic could be happening in front of her was not so hard to believe, but for Peter it was confronting.

"How am I supposed to feel about this?" he blurted out, "We hear on the radio that you are witches. But until now I thought it was all lies."

"You are scared?" Chuluun asked compassionately.

Peter looked at Aisling, who had already accepted the magic. He didn't want to admit it in front of her.

"No," he said. "Just confused."

"It is okay. It is normal to be confused." Chuluun moved his queen across the board and proudly announced checkmate.

After the initial shock, Aisling and her dad quickly settled into the Bluey camp in their first few weeks living there. The Khun easily adopted Aisling's word in place of their own native demonym because they liked her that much. They were relieved to be able to go back to using magic after a few days relying on Noi.

It was a comfortable life for them and they never struggled for food or water- the Blueys had a large communal farm that seemed to never not have food, presumably due to some magic that Peter couldn't understand yet. They had erected their large sturdy tents in two rough rings around a central fire pit. Their tents were lined with various furs and were unbelievably warm and windproof inside. It was a simple construction that they could quickly move if they ever needed to. Peter vaguely knew that in their homeland, Blueys rarely lived in one place for more than a few years at a time, except for in their single large city which was the exception to the rule. The camp was also kept very clean and ordered. Their abundant food stores were somehow never victims of vermin, despite their rudimentary storage techniques. Peter supposed this was also due to magic.

The camp was located just inside the north-eastern boundary of the expansive Mishkash Forest, close to the coast where they had first arrived. The forest covered a huge land area in a sweeping arc across most of the eastern half of the country. It had boundaries close to Nelasive, and almost every other own and city between there and the Capital.

Most of the other refugees had attempted to settle closer to the Capital, but found themselves treated harshly and moved from one temporary camp to another whenever the government said so. They had no rights in their new country, and many simply disappeared. The Blueys living near the forest had heard about the treatment of their friends and relatives back before they braved the journey from their homeland. They risked finding another route across the sea, before arriving at their current spot. They had already lived there many years by the time Peter and Aisling joined them, losing contact with all other groups of refugees over time. Even the birds were not much help in keeping contact.

Thanks to Light magic, there was always power, and Chuluun took it on himself to show Peter and Aisling how to perform the most essential spells. Peter struggled at first, because his mind had been closed to magic for a long time. As an engineer, he liked to know how things worked in technical detail, but that was not possible with magic. Aisling on the other hand had no trouble picking it up, and a few months after that first time Chuluun showed them, she was as competent as any of the Blueys at making light. Peter did learn but he was never quite as adept as his daughter. His mechanical mind was good at the process on creating magic, but he longed to understand it better, and that hampered his ability.

Peter was however, very good at learning the Blueys' language, which he used to study the Book of Boloi with Chuluun. A few months after moving, while Aisling was still six, Peter was sitting with Chuluun late at night in Peter's home. Aisling was put to bed some time earlier. Remnants of their cooking were piled next to the sink and there was still a smell of garlic wafting through the tent. They had some homemade wine in front of them that tasted like plums but stung like nettles.

"There are many different kinds of magic," Chuluun explained, his grasp of Peter's language improving rapidly since Peter and Aisling moved in. "This one here is Light magic."

"The one that makes the lamp work."

"Yes. We can also use Light magic for other objects.

Persons too." Chuluun pointed at a section of the text and an image of a person with a halo. "Watching now."

Chuluun sat perfectly still, as he always did when performing magic, unblinking. Sometimes Aisling thought he looked dead. He raised his hand with the palm facing Peter, when suddenly a light began to shine from it. His hand was creating light. It was not a strong beam, but more of a cosy glow. And not blue like Noi, it was bright like daylight.

"Incredible…" Peter said, unable to look away. Up to that point he had only been able to make the lamps work when he concentrated intensely. It made him feel tired in a way he never had before, and didn't quite know how to explain it. Chuluun only ever had one expression, so Peter didn't know if the magic made him feel tired in the same way. Chuluun's face was wide and dark, and very wrinkled. He looked like he was made of stone, as Aisling said once. Aisling sometimes smiled when she thought of how ridiculous they looked together: Peter was thin and strong, and his face very expressive. His eyebrows had a mind of their own. Peter and Chuluun looked like a buffalo with one of those little birds that hitches a ride.

Khuch was like a more handsome version of his dad, Aisling thought. He was agile, but still stocky and strong. He had at least three different facial expressions, compared to his dad's one. Khuch could easily pick up Aisling, as she was small and energetic like her dad. But her face was shaped differently to his: like her mum's she was told. She was blonde and with a pointy chin whereas Peter had dark hair, permanent stubble and a small squashed face. She had his grey eyes at least, and the same expressions.

"This one is more advanced. You try it now, you are ready," Chuluun instructed, and Peter read the section of the book with some difficulty, Chuluun offering hints when he got stuck on the ancient words. It sounded easy enough in theory. Peter focused very hard on sending magic to his hand. After a minute of concentrating, he managed something like a spark to fly out from his palm, but felt suddenly so tired he couldn't continue. Chuluun handed Peter more wine, which was gratefully accepted. "Takes practice. Patience. Have some rest." He winced as the wine burned his throat, but felt his energy coming back.

Aisling was peering sneakily past the partition to her bedroom when she saw Chuluun use Light magic on his hand. She looked at her own hands, still small, the scar on the back of her left hand still ugly from where she had tripped in the kitchen when she was a baby and broken a glass. She looked at the lamp, at Chuluun, at her dad, and suddenly both of her hands were glowing. She quickly shook them frantically as if trying to shake off a spider web, and the light went out. She ran back to bed, too excited to sleep, and under the covers played with making the light in her hands turn on and off.

Every day since living with the Blueys she had seen magic, and it felt like she was living in one of her favourite stories. She thought about Iwizadi again, who she had seen again and again and again in her dreams ever since she could remember, even though his face was always forgotten in the morning. He always started the same way, in his frustratingly hard-to-define shape, then looking the same as someone she knew, like her dad, or Chuluun, or Khuch Chaddhal, before transforming into a misty, shimmering man she couldn't see properly. And he always said the same thing: that it was a good start. One time he also said he was trying.

A few months after learning to make his hands glow, Peter had become quite adept at making his hands or other objects light up, and he was thrilled. Magic opened up so many possibilities, and was so much more convenient than Noi. The battery he originally brought from his hometown was growing dusty and sat unused in a corner, when once upon a time it had been a cumbersome but necessary tool that occupied a place in the centre of any room. One night, Chuluun was at their tent again, patiently teaching Peter more uses of Light magic, and Khuch Chaddhal and Aisling were playing a game that involved running frantically through the tent and hiding behind random objects. He was only a year older than her but seemed much older than that. Whenever she found his hiding spot and they laughed, various objects, or his hair or his hands would glow, almost as if he radiated magic.

A pigeon rapped at the window and Chuluun stopped moving. So did Khuch.

"No magic now," He ordered. "Quickly plug in the battery."

"What's going on?" Peter asked, concerned.

"No time. I will explain later." Chuluun rushed to bring the battery to the centre of the room and attach the lights in the customary way. He quickly brushed off the dust that sat on top. The cables were stiff and hard to position. Once connected, he grabbed Khuch, roughly in Peter's opinion, and said something very fast and very quietly in their own language. The two of them froze and stared at the book. Aisling stared too, and suddenly it vanished.

"Where did-" Peter began, but was cut off by a knock at the door. He went to open it and found his brother Jack on the threshold, his Noicar parked some distance away where the road stopped at the entrance to their settlement. The Khun had all gone inside, but Peter knew they would be listening, even those who couldn't understand the language.

Jack looked around disapprovingly at the camp and it was Peter who spoke first.

"How did you find me?"

"Not without difficulty," Jack extended a hand but Peter didn't shake it. "I asked around. Some old friends of yours in Nelasive said you came this way when you left town. I didn't realise you'd be living in such appalling conditions."

"What do you want?"

"I came personally to deliver you the good news, brother," Jack announced, anticipating Peter's questions. "The site of your old home-"

"Our family home"

"-has successfully yielded a great wealth of Noi."

"You came here to gloat?"

"I came here to tell you," Jack strained through a fake smile, "that you are now incredibly wealthy. Now, where's that contract you signed? I would be happy to give you a small fortune if I see it."

"I told you last time, I don't want your money."

"So, you didn't sign it? Well, isn't that a pity. I suppose that money will go to the state. Which is just as well," he added, looking around, "as this dump could use a bit more investment. Unless, of course, these people are here illegally?"

Peter stood silently but firmly, his pose not giving any answers, until Jack decided it was time to leave.

"You should replace those old generators, they look hazardous. Even prehistoric hippy communes like this need Noi. And an unused generator is a danger. See you soon, Peter. Always a pleasure."

Jack strode towards the Noicar, drawing fearful stares from all the Blueys who were peering out from their tents. Peter continued to stand still like a statue as he watched Jack drive away, as if to make sure he was really gone. The flickering blue light coming from the other houses told him that everyone had connected their Noi batteries and turned off their magic while a visitor – an intruder – was around. He realised he was once that same intruder. A huge hand came to rest on his shoulders, leading him back inside. Chuluun said something in his language, which Peter thought sounded like "is he gone?", and the pigeon flew away.

"We can use Light magic now," he told the room, and in front of Aisling sitting at the table with Khuch, the Book of Boloi reappeared.

"The same thing happened to us," Chuluun said to break the silence. Peter poured them both more wine. "The state took our home for Noi. Blue Island, you know is the source of much Noi in this world. But most importantly it is our family home."

"You said there was a war," Peter said, realising that he did not know much about the Blueys at all. They didn't usually offer information freely. He felt violated, uncomfortable that Jack had found him.

"Yes. There was the War for Noi. Excuse me for not telling you about it earlier. Your language was hard for me before. Now it is better, and I can tell the story." He sat down, and the chair groaned like it always did under his bulk. He was a very solid man. "You call us Bluey. In our language we are called Khun. We are Khun. In our language it means simply 'people'. Blue Island we call Gazar.

"All of this happened before I was born. A long time ago, everybody used magic. Light magic. Bird magic. Fire magic. All kinds of magic. We had a big city in Gazar called Khot, you know. Thousands of people lived in Khot. It was full of Khun who gave up travelling. Khot was bigger than your big city Capital. And it was more beautiful. Our government cared about the city and the Khun. But the government changed, and the new leaders made magic a crime. All types were banned and only some of us kept using it in secret. So, the Khun found a new power, you call it Noi. Some Khun used magic secretly. Including my ancestors.

"But everyone used Noi. Slowly, very slowly, Noi replaced the magic we lost. Magic was not allowed so Noi was used for everything. And because it was so useful, Noi became very valuable; more valuable than gold. The government wanted the control of all Noi, and it made lots of money. It made lots of money from selling Noi to other nations and from taxes, but people got poorer and poorer. And they forgot all about magic. Their spirits were poor too. All of life was Noi, Noi, Noi. My family kept magic secret for many long generations.

"The government was destroyed one day after much violence and another new government took over. People were happy at first and magic came back, but the new government was just the same, and all they wanted was money. They sold parts of Gazar. They sold our land to rich kingdoms across the sea. The government got rich but did not share its wealth with the people. New people arrived from the rich kingdoms and helped to destroy Gazar. So much destruction. All of the beautiful city Khot was dirty. The mountains were dirty, the grass was dirty. The birds already abandoned the island long before. Gazar is still blue now, however. Gazar still has the most Noi in the world, but the government sold the same land to different kingdoms at the same time to double its profits. This was in my lifetime when I was a small boy.

"Now, the kingdoms of Nyika and Naha in the east, the kingdom of Arazi in north, are all claiming the same land on

Gazar. Our land. All for Noi. Nyika, Naha, Arazi all brought soldiers. They don't care for us Khun. They only care for Noi. Some Khun left but we stayed, as long as possible. Only the Khun with magic stayed. I had my son, and a wife. Soldiers killed her, so I left. I came here with baby Khuch Chaddhal and all the other Khun in this camp. Five, nearly six years, we were alone here. Then you visited, and at first, we were scared, but we are alright now. We will go back to Gazar when the war is finished."

There was a long silence before Chuluun spoke again. He drank a cup of wine in one go.

"We saved magic when we came. Khun are being killed on Gazar. If we didn't leave, magic would die too. Many Khun have fled, saving magic but it is spread throughout the world and we are losing each other. Now you are magic too: you are Khun. We are the only people in this world who don't need Noi; only Khun know freedom." He looked around and reflected on the paradox of freedom and the necessity to stay hidden.

"I never heard about that war," Peter admitted. "Except for the refugees that they call witches."

"Not reported," Chuluun replied, matter-of-factly. "Why would your Leader need to report the War on Gazar? The Leader has Noi here, on this land. Gazar is none of his business."

"How much don't I know about the world?"

"I will show you more tomorrow," Chuluun answered cryptically and stood up to go home. "Now I am tired."

He left without saying goodbye, as they Blueys – the Khun – often did. Peter thought it was rude at first, but he had gotten used to it.

"It is getting late, Aisling. Time for bed," Peter said to his daughter.

"Look at the owl, Dad. Isn't he big?" she pointed at an owl using a glowing finger and a thin beam of light showed Peter exactly where to look. "His name is Bu."

Impressed, but not surprised with her command of Light magic, Peter picked her up and took her to her bed, even though she was getting too big for that.

"How do you know the owl's name?" he asked, tucking her in.

"He told me."

"I see, of course he did. And what else did he tell you?"

"He said we can't trust pigeons because they forget things."

"Okay honey. That's enough talking to owls tonight. Time for sleep."

"Okay," she yawned. "Dad? Does Chuluun know Iwizadi? Maybe he can help with the war." She was very serious about the idea.

Peter had to laugh at this, "No honey, Iwizadi is just a character in a story," but he doubted himself after saying it. "Now close your eyes."

Don't trust the pigeons, he thought. Bird magic. Aisling had picked up the Light magic so easily, it was possible she already learned Bird magic on her own. It was a question for Chuluun the next day.

The Khun knew about Iwizadi of course, though Aisling was surprised when she learned that they had a slightly different story about him. Storytelling it seemed played a large part in their culture, and most nights they would collectively conjure a magic fire that radiated the perfect amount of heat and light but needed no fuel. The fire always waned when one of the Khun turned away from it, and if Peter stared at it long enough, he felt that it warmed him better than any fire he ever knew.

In the Khun's version of the story, Iwizadi was more complicated. He made mistakes. He experimented with risky spells. He made enemies. In their version, Umwahu was not evil. It wasn't his fault that people stopped using magic: when Noi was discovered, the people naturally wanted to use it. They thought it had greater potential than magic and they slowly forgot as Noi took over their lives. Iwizadi was frightened for the future of magic, and in his fear took greater risks to create spells. After an accident where he turned his assistant to stone and could not change him back, Umwahu decided it would be safer to keep Iwizadi somewhere he could not hurt others. The part about magic being made illegal was the same, but not for the same reasons. Umwahu outlawed magic after seeing its potential for destruction. Noi was safer for the people even with its flaws.

Umwahu's successor, his grandson Isiko, had been influenced by Iwizadi and released him. Isiko was a good ruler and sought to do good for the people, leaving Iwizadi alone to continue experimenting with new types of magic.

The Khun's version ended with mystery. One day, Iwizadi just disappeared, leaving no trace and taking his books with him. Some people say that he had perfected a dangerous type of Spirit magic, or Death magic. Others say he was captured by more enemies. Nobody really knew.

Most of their stories revolved around memories of Gazar, and Aisling loved hearing about the different types of magic they used. The adults stayed up late and Aisling was usually one of the first to go to sleep, where her dreams were frequently visited.

But she was not alone. Ever since arriving on the continent, Chuluun had had just one dream: every night, he was in a stone tower, watching the birds on the window ledge, when suddenly a terrifying presence made him turn around. A man was there but he had no face, and whenever Chuluun tried to focus on him the dream ended. The space where his face should have been was like a deep feeling of nothingness and dread, and Chuluun couldn't stand it. Through repetition he learned that he could extend the dream by refusing to acknowledge the man, despite the fear he felt. Chuluun found that if he continued to think about the birds, he could almost hear them interpreting the fearsome man's words into their strange chirps and warbles. But in the peculiar way that dreams warp reality, their sounds never meant anything, despite Chuluun being adept at Bird magic when awake.

But after a lifetime of trying to find his way through this dream, he still could not understand the words the birds spoke. He found that if he concentrated on the birds' voices, he could stand to look at the man for longer. And the longer he listened to them, the more it seemed as though the man's face tried to take shape, though it only ever looked like a smudged oil painting, all the colours and edges blending into one hideous shape. The only thing he could focus on was the book in the man's grip. He assumed it had something to do with the Book of Boloi.

Chuluun had consulted the other Khun about his dream, but he learned very little. Despite being a magical race, the Khun were anything but superstitious, and refused to speculate aimlessly on what things could mean. They were a people who believed in what they could see and feel. No Khun had been known to create Dream magic, so they all dismissed the possibility. Nowhere was it mentioned in the Book of Boloi either, as far as they could interpret its esoteric pages. Chuluun had tried to invent Dream magic himself, to test whether it was possible or not. After getting no results he agreed with the others that Dream magic was probably not the reason for his haunting, and instead chose to believe that there was no message hidden in the recurring dream.

Yet every night, his unconscious mind attempted to probe and prolong the dream, hoping that he could one day see the man clearly, and hear the words he spoke through birds. The other Khun reminded him that birds can make mistakes when communicating. Tesver, his old friend and the strongest user of Bird magic among them, was particularly troubled by the dream. According to him, no Bird magic had ever been known to behave in that way or have that effect on a person. He reasoned it was not Bird magic at all, and perhaps something darker. Chuluun was not reassured.

The years went by happily. Peter never took Aisling back to their old home in Nelasive. As far as he was concerned, that town was swallowed by corruption. Besides, the longer they lived with the Khun, the more they learned how to use magic, the less use they had for their old life. In fact, after a few years both Peter and Aisling realised they did not miss it at all.

Aisling's appetite for magic was enormous. Whereas Peter would spend hours thinking about whether a spell was possible or not, Aisling would just try without thinking and deal with the consequences later. It was the same with the Khun's language: Aisling acquired it effortlessly by spending time with the other Khun families who could not speak her language, whereas Peter learned it through concerted effort and long patient lessons with Chuluun. While he learned to speak it perfectly well, he did not have the same ease of expression as his daughter. Watching her and Khuch Chaddhal one night playing a game where they created floating globs of multi-coloured light while babbling away in Khun, Peter felt a mixture or pride and envy, followed by shame. Ashamed of the envy he felt towards her. He didn't want to be that person anymore.

Peter and Aisling's difference in magic ability was similar to their different approaches to language. Aisling could manipulate magic to perform anything within her repertoire, combining spells with ease, as if she did not need to translate magic into words. Peter used magic like he used Khun: deliberately and accurately, but rigidly. He was competent with magic, but was always amazed at how fluidly his daughter could link and combine different spells.

Even though they never returned to their old home, they still occasionally heard news. The Khun seemed to have a never-ending supply of up-to-date and accurate news. Peter and Aisling knew it was the birds, but even after a few years of living together and learning magic, all the Bird magic they had learned was limited to that one night early on when Aisling had talked to an owl by chance. *How many different types of magic are there?* Aisling wondered often.

Tesver was the favourite of all the birds who visited. Aisling thought Tesver's long nose and black eyes made him look a bit like a bird of prey, and was scared of him at first, until Chuluun introduced them. Tesver did not address her directly, and waited a long time before saying anything, as if he were trying to hear something distantly.

He whispered something to the crow resting on his shoulder. Aisling saw the crow nod, and Chuluun led her back home. Their new home was all she knew, and even though she didn't miss their hometown, she was curious about it. She wanted to see the house she could only distantly remember, and it was a long time before she found the courage to ask her dad to show her.

One day when Aisling was sixteen years old, she awoke feeling worried. Not knowing why – she slept without dreaming – she ignored the feeling and went about her ordinary routine. She went to the kitchen and used a spell she had been practising unsuccessfully for years. Staring at a clean glass and standing perfectly still for a few moments, she then gently raised her left hand to the rim of the glass and held it there, as if trying to stop it from trembling. A few drops of water started to flow from her fingertips, then a steady stream erupted, which she then aimed at the glass as best she could. The glass filled quickly as the stream grew stronger until the glass overflowed. Aisling ran to the basin and aimed her gushing torrent of hand-water down the sink.

"Shit! Shit!"

Peter sleepily entered the kitchen at that moment and saw Aisling panicking over the sink with her relentless supply of water. Half crying and half laughing she called out:

"I can't turn it off!"

Peter laughed and held out his own glass.

"Thanks. I was thirsty."

Aisling laughed harder and the water stopped. Peter laughed too. After nearly ten years of living magically, Peter was extremely pleased to find that Water magic was an area where he could outperform his daughter. He learned early on that when Water magic was performed, it clung to you, like surface tension, and the way to stop the spell was to think about something else, to get distracted and break the tension. And he was often distracted. Aisling on the other hand focused on her magic whenever she did it, and found it harder to turn off the Water magic.

It was a long time since Peter heard that his brother Jack had succeeded in finding the enormous supply of Noi underneath their old house, but only recently had he heard of any progress extracting it. He marvelled at the extremely long delays involved in any government operation. Why couldn't they have just got on with it ten years ago when they kicked him out and found the deposits? Why had it taken so long? Never mind, he thought, they got what they wanted. If they'd done it fifty years earlier, their parents' lives would have been better, too.

"Joke's on them though," he explained to Aisling when he heard the news. "We don't even need Noi now, and our life is better than ever."

Aisling, who was too young to remember her first home when they moved, couldn't compare her life at the Khun settlement to anything else.

"What was so bad about it?" she asked earnestly. Peter answered a little too quickly:

"Our whole lives were about Noi. Everything. Where we could get more. How much we had left. Would we run out? How much it cost. And all our neighbours were the same, just constantly worried about Noi." He then effortlessly performed Water magic to fill a coffee plunger with hot water, impressing Aisling. "And now ironically after trying to ruin our lives, we live free from all that worry about Noi, and with magic that we never imagined could exist."

"Don't you miss the people there?"

"Yes, the Fidelis most of all. And the guys at the garage," he paused. "But I wonder if we ever knew them as people. All they talked about was Noi and what they heard on the radio."

"I get it."

"It's hard to explain."

"I know. Like how the Blueys always talk about Gazar," she wondered if she should ask, but decided anyway. "Can you show me the town?"

"Okay."

"You don't have to."

"No, no… We should go. You should know where you came from."

"It might be different now, though."

"Definitely. Since they destroyed our home."

"It'll be weird."

"I know. We can go today if you like."

"Really?"

"Yes," Peter looked seriously at Aisling then added, "And do not use magic."

"Of course not," Aisling answered as if it were obvious, but realising that she had not given it a thought. There had been the rare occasion when an outsider visited the Khun settlement – a lost hiker here or there – and the whole community hurriedly turned on their antique Noi generators, hiding all traces of magic to avoid suspicion. To the rest of the world, they were a forgotten and neglected group of refugees living in squalor, with a father-daughter pair of hippies. It looked as if the government couldn't be bothered persecuting their undocumented status, but they always maintained an underlying level of fear and readiness for the inevitable.

"I mean it. Who knows what will happen if outsiders see us using magic?"

"I get it. It's fine. I won't use any."

"Okay. Can you be ready in half an hour?"

"Yes."

Outsiders. Aisling thought about the word her dad had used while she got dressed and prepared some food to take. Were they really insiders? She spoke Khun with her neighbours and had learned their magic, but was she really fully inside their culture? They still seemed so secretive, she thought. Even Khuch. He was only one year older than her and they had grown up together, but after he turned thirteen and had to go through with his ritual rite of passage as an adult, he had seemed more distant. Was she excluded from adult Khun life now? It didn't seem fair. It wasn't her choice to live there, even though she was glad they did. She couldn't imagine a life without magic. Even the thought of visiting her hometown and hiding her magic for a day made her miss it. She had not been outside the Khun settlement since arriving and realised she was very anxious about leaving it.

As they approached their bikes, Peter asked Aisling a little hesitantly:

"Are you sure you want to go? It's a long way." It had been many years since they abandoned Peter's Noicar. Its pieces were used in various projects he was tinkering with.

"I'm sure," she answered. Peter tried to not look worried. "It's okay Dad. It will be fine."

"I hope you're right." They got on their bikes and pedalled towards the one road leading out of town and through the forest. They rode side by side.

"Dad?"

"Yes?"

"Do we belong with the Blueys?" She still sometimes called them that. In fact, the Khun thought it was endearing and even translated the word into their own language where it had extended to mean something like dear or honey.

"What do you mean?"

"I mean… You said before 'outsiders', when we were talking about other people from the country. But it's our country where we were born. How can they be outsiders?" She added after a breath, "And sometimes I don't feel like we should be there in the village."

"That's a lot to take in. Let me try to answer." They rode

along in silence, obviously thinking hard. Impatiently Aisling pressed Peter to say something. "I think, sometimes we are put in situations where we have to choose where we belong. A long time ago, the Leader made it clear that people like us don't matter. We were lucky, because at that same time we were forced from our home and the only place that made sense to go was with the Blueys. They welcomed us and they call us part of their community."

"But don't you wonder if you're missing out? Like you can never fully be one of them?"

"I did. At first."

"What happened?"

"I talked to Chuluun." Peter suddenly laughed. "And he was insulted. He thought I was insulting him for not making us welcome enough."

"That sounds like him."

"It was absurd! I told him because I couldn't do magic properly, because I couldn't speak Khun properly, because I didn't understand all of their culture and hadn't been through the initiation that I felt like a stranger."

"That's what I worry about too."

"But this was nearly ten years ago! You know what he said to me?"

"What?"

"He said, 'Peter' you know, in that serious voice he has and with his face… you know that face he does when he says something serious…"

"I know the face," Aisling snorted.

"He said, 'Peter, you live with Khun, you are Khun' and that was it."

"They make everything so simple."

"Because it usually is."

"But-"

"*Tsenkher*," Peter used the Khun word for Bluey, "most complicated problems have simple answers."

"I want to do the initiation," Aisling confessed, without thinking, then added softly, "like Khuch."

"We can talk to Chuluun tonight about it. For now, let's just think about where we are going."

"Okay." Aisling was satisfied. She smiled lopsidedly and her dimples exaggerated themselves.

They rode on in silence for a while, deciding that even though the forest road – if it could be called a road – was almost always empty, it would be too risky to use magic on their bikes to get there faster. It was frustrating not to use any magic. The road was in bad shape, after years without use, and a few times they had to push their bikes across some difficult terrain. It was eerily quiet the whole way through, except for one moment where Aisling thought she could hear an owl hooting distantly.

Eventually, a short time after lunch, the trees thinned out, and a few minutes later the road became more defined, and suddenly they burst forth from the forest and could see a town past the next hill. Looking back, Aisling was astonished to see how tall and thick the forest really was. She had no idea it was so big and shivered when she thought how easily they could have gotten lost in there. She had already lost sight of the road they followed to pass through it.

The going was much easier then as they rode into the outskirts of the town. A simple sign marked the Nelasive town limits, and was signed with the Leader's crest and smiling face. *This Noi project brought to you by Abe Brown. Making lives better.*

Looking around at the streets, the buildings, the people as they rode in, Aisling could not believe Noi was making lives better. Making whose lives better? It was a shocking realisation that her dad had not been exaggerating about his old life. He might even have been downplaying it. She felt miserable as soon as they entered Nelasive, as though a heavy weight was driving her into the ground.

Everything glowed a hypnotic blue, and she felt like some of her strength was leaving her body. Some of the people had faint blueish glows permanently emanating from their hair due to working in the nearby Noi mines, and they all wore a look of resignation. There were signs that the town was functional, sure: they passed a supermarket, various shops, a small medical centre. But Aisling could not help but feel like there was no life there. There was no soul. Not having seen so many people and buildings since she was five years old, she felt glad that Peter was there. It was a bit overwhelming.

"One more street," Peter told her, slowing down. "Just around this corner-"

And as they turned the next corner they came to a stop. A road block was set up about a hundred metres away, beyond which they could see a tall mound of dirt and a strong blue glow. A sign ahead advised the area was restricted to employees only and beyond that they could see some serious machinery.

"Our house was just over there," Peter said, pointing up the road. "Number twenty. Of course, we had half the road to ourselves because people kept moving away."

"Where to?"

"Don't know. They were bought out by the Leader." They stood there and looked at the mine in the distance, not knowing how to feel. A lady in a uniform opened the door to the roadblock office up ahead and started walking cautiously towards them.

"Let's go," Aisling said. "I don't like this place."

"Me neither," Peter agreed, and they rode away before the lady came within earshot.

Some buildings nearby were plastered with posters advertising some kind of political movement. Maybe a rally, it was hard to tell. There was graffiti on the side of what looked to be a government office that read *No Water No Life*. Realising how thirsty she was, Aisling reached for her water bottle, only to find that it was already empty. Peter offered her the last mouthful of his. Being inexperienced in living without magic, Aisling suddenly realised that she didn't bring enough water to get home, having automatically relied on Water magic for so long already.

"Have we run out completely?" Peter asked, with a hint of panic. Aisling nodded guiltily. "Shit. We're going to need some for the ride home. The water here is no good. Noi poisoning. Maybe we can buy some."

He fumbled around in his pockets for some coins, hoping that he had enough for at least one large container. He didn't know how much it would cost after having been away for so long. They reached the supermarket that they saw on the way in and pulled over in front of it. A few Noicars flitted past, making their signature quiet humming sound. Aisling notices the roads were damaged in many places.

"I'll go in and get some. You just wait here and watch the bikes. I won't be long."

And Peter really wasn't long before he came out holding two satisfyingly big containers of drinkable water. But in that short time, Aisling had gotten into a lot of trouble. She thought it would be a nice idea to surprise her dad by replenishing their water on her own, since they didn't earn any money living with the Khun.

Checking that nobody was watching, she held her bottle

close to her body inside her open jacket, and held one hand over its rim. After a moment, a few drops started to collect inside, and then a small jet came from her index finger. She glanced around again to double check she was alone, and realised with fear that a man could see her from a window across the street. She wasn't sure if he was looking or not.

Trying not to worry, she held still and concentrated on finishing. The jet grew in size and a few small streams of water began to dribble down the bottle. That was the moment Peter exited the supermarket and saw what was happening.

"Stop it now!" he hissed at her, but knew that it was a mistake. Aisling concentrated on stopping the Water magic, but that made it stronger. All she could think about was water: The water she wanted to drink; the water Peter had bought; the water poisoned with Noi; the water now streaming from her hand uncontrollably.

"I can't!" she cried.

Peter knew he had to distract her so he got on his bike and told her to start riding. The action of riding a bike should be enough to distract her.

But Peter didn't see the man in the window, and Aisling in her panic was too scared to tell him.

They left quickly, trying to look casual, and the water stopped after a few moments. Most of the attention in the town was focused on the Noi mine and the roadblock, so there was little danger of running into police or being stopped on their way to the forest. Peter was anxious not to spend much time there lest he be recognised.

And he wasn't. They made it past the town limits and as they approached the looming wall of trees that marked the start of the Mishkash, Peter glanced behind him a few times to check if anyone was following.

It was not a crime to live at the Khun settlement, since Peter and Aisling were citizens and had the right to live anywhere in the country. But it was suspicious at least. And it was a crime to harbour undocumented residents. Most people were unaware that anybody at all lived in their direction, let alone a camp of magical refugees. The local government would be interested to know Peter and Aisling's address so that they could impose taxes on them. It was a miracle that Jack hadn't told anyone, but Peter supposed he had more important things to think about. Or perhaps he had told, and it just didn't matter. Peter didn't know.

The government too, Peter worried, might question why they almost never bought any Noi. Sure, it wasn't unheard of for people to live a life unplugged, but the people who did that were usually fairly vocal about it and wanted everyone to hear about the evil and destruction that Noi had brought to society. Those sorts of opinions were usually silenced pretty fast after garnering brief attention on the Leader's news broadcast: "A man living near county West has renounced Noi in favour of a simple, prehistoric lifestyle." The news always made those people sound mad.

"There's no way we could explain our survival," Peter whispered to himself, thinking that neither of them would know how to live without neither Noi nor magic.

When they were approaching their home late in the afternoon, a low vibration filled their bodies. They stopped pedalling. Looking up, Aisling and Peter saw the distinctive blue of Noi as a government craft hovered over the canopy going the same direction as them. It floated ominously ahead of them and the vibrations ceased.

"That can only be bad news," Aisling stated.

"I hope the birds gave them enough warning."

Never in their ten years living in the camp had they seen

a flying craft, and they were scared. They pedalled faster, not knowing what they would find when they reached home. About ten or fifteen minutes later they saw the craft returning, circling. It was clearly scouting the area for something.

They arrived home to a flurry of activity. Everyone was dismantling their tents and homes and packing up what they could carry. Aisling looked around and saw Khuch packing all of his cooking supplies into a bag. He did not look as worried as the others, maybe he was too young the last time they were forced to move and couldn't remember it. Couldn't remember the violence when they fled Gazar.

"You saw it," Chuluun greeted them, straight to the point the way he always did. "We will go deeper into the forest now. Refugees are not welcome in this country."

"Do you know if they saw you?"

"Definitely."

"We'll go with you."

"No, you stay. This is your home."

"Our home is with you."

"No time for argument," Chuluun shut Peter down. "You have documents. You have time to think. It is better for you not to know where we are."

"You're right."

"We will go now."

Chuluun saw that all of the refugees, all thirty-six of them, Aisling's friends and neighbours, were standing nearby wearing large backpacks hastily stuffed full with what they could carry.

It was twilight now, but the usual vibrancy of the setting sun was slowly being overpowered by the soft blue glow of Noi as several craft approached.

"This is not goodbye," Chuluun said calmly, and turned

to lead his people somewhere hidden in the forest.

Peter and Aisling started to run inside their home but Aisling felt a confident hand on her shoulder. She turned to see Khuch. He stuffed some paper into her hand, then slowly touched her nose with his, and his forehead with hers. A powerful feeling of belonging spread through her whole body, and she smiled, and felt like she could never smile big enough to express herself.

"Khuch," Chuluun's voice carried over the air and sounded like he was standing right next to them, even though he was already half hidden in the thickness of the trees. Khuch and Aisling separated and looked at each other for a short moment, before he turned around and ran to catch up with the others. Aisling looked at the scrunched-up ball of paper in her hand. Unfolding it caused a horribly loud crackling noise she was sure would draw unwanted attention, but she then realised she was alone with her dad and the vaguely threatening blue of Noi coming from vehicles somewhere nearby. The craft couldn't hear paper.

The paper was simple and clear, exactly the way the Khun preferred to communicate. A pigeon with its beak open. It was drawn in a rush but Aisling understood. To anyone else it might look like a picture drawn by a child, but she knew what Khuch wanted her to do. She felt comfortable with many types of magic already, and could combine them in ways that impressed even Chuluun once or twice. But she knew then that it was time to learn something more advanced. Something she had until then been unable to do. Something that caused her to feel a nervous excitement mixed with fear. This would be the rite of passage she wanted, what she would have to do to finally belong with the Khun.

Bird magic.

It must have been Jack. But it didn't make sense. Jack knew about Peter's home for years and never acted. Why now all of a sudden? Why crack down on immigration now, years later? It didn't make sense to Peter, but he was panicked. How could he explain that they lived without Noi? How could he explain why his neighbours had vanished? But Aisling feared it was worse than that, that the government wasn't just looking for illegal immigrants. She barely spoke a word as they went inside their home.

"We should go too," Peter finally decided, turning his panicked energy into action.

"But they're looking for illegal immigrants," Aisling returned, trying to convince herself. "We're allowed to live here."

"That is true. But can you describe how we supposedly live without Noi? Can you explain why the other tents are abandoned? It's clear that there were more people living here than just us." Aisling looked at the remaining material of dismantled tents that the Khun couldn't carry, and then at the hyper-productive vegetable patch.

"No, but-"

"I know it's hard to say it but we have to go."

"I know, but…" Aisling hesitated, "what if they aren't looking for illegal immigrants?"

"What are you talking about?"

"The government already knew they were here. Remember how uncle Jack came one time, a long time ago?"

"Yeah."

"So, what if they want something else…" Peter then knew that Aisling was talking about magic.

"Nobody saw you in the city, right?" he questioned, fear rising in his voice. "Right?"

"I don't know."

"Did someone see you?"

"Maybe!" Aisling blurted out.

"And they must have seen us go into the forest."

"I saw a man. In the window across from the supermarket. But I don't know if he saw the water."

"But magic isn't a crime," Peter thought out loud. "Most people don't even know for sure if magic exists. Why would people follow us? Suppose he saw you making water pour from your hands… if he reported it, who would believe it? Why would they send scouts after us?"

"It doesn't matter, Dad," Aisling mumbled. "We committed a crime by not reporting the Khun."

"You're right. If we stay, we'll be arrested for one thing or another. We have to go." They looked sadly at each other for a moment. "Bring only what you can carry, we'll go to the Capital together through the forest. I know people there."

Aisling recalled the Khun disappearing to the north: away from the Capital.

Outside, the night was illuminated blue as a craft drifted directly over the camp. Shadows moved through the house and Peter and Aisling remained motionless until the darkness resumed. She shoved a few belongings and some leftover food into a backpack and was ready to go within two minutes. A clean shirt and underwear, a toothbrush, her journal where she kept track of various magics that she learned, a tin cup, half a loaf of bread, a bag of dried tea. Peter was ready a minute later and they stood just inside the front door, waiting until they felt that no craft could see them running through the camp into the dense part of the forest where there was no path.

Aisling's heart was pounding as they waited there, watching as the blue glow came and went, casting spooky shadows that moved across the walls of their home. The tent-house Peter built. The home where she grew up. The home where she had spent hours playing and learning magic, where fairy tales started to come true.

"After this one, we run straight across the camp, okay?" Peter decided. "When I say go. And if you get there without me, don't wait. Just run."

It felt like forever. Waiting there, hoping that everything would be okay. Aisling imagined herself tripping over as they ran. She imagined that they got the timing wrong and they were seen leaving the house. She imagined that she couldn't turn off the Water magic and drowned the whole world. Peter had already opened the door and they could see one of the two crafts floating away, the darkness growing behind it, always creeping closer. The darkness that would either help them or harm them, they were not sure which.

"Now!" Peter yelled in a whisper, and together they bolted out the door. But Aisling had barely taken three steps when she remembered Khuch. She turned back and ran inside to get the paper he had given her from where she left it on the table and stuffed it inside her journal. Peter, who was first out the door, did not notice that Aisling was not with him until he reached a thick bush. He turned around and looked back panicked, to see Aisling still at the door, waiting for another opportunity to run. He could see men entering the camp through the main path. That opportunity would never come.

Hidden in the trees and the darkness, Peter watched as Aisling misjudged the craft's movements and attempted to run towards him. The light from the craft bathed the camp in blue, and the men were surrounding her in a second. That was it. What could he do? There were six of them he counted, and maybe more hidden nearby. He was scared to make any noise moving, and wide-eyed watched as the craft moved low over the camp and opened up. The men took her backpack and moved aboard, leading Aisling, one on either side grabbing her arms. Seconds later, the craft was gone, the light it emitted retreating into the night, leaving only darkness as Peter collapsed to his knees where he was, unsure what to do.

Chapter 3

Aisling knew she could not fight the group of armed men who surrounded her, and immediately surrendered, allowing them to confiscate her backpack and lead her onto the Noicraft. They did not have mean looks on their faces, in fact a few of them looked scared, and like they didn't want to be there at all. It was only after she had been brought aboard and ordered to sit on a chair in a bizarre clear case that she understood what was happening.

"Sir, we have the witch," one of the men spoke into a handheld radio. Aisling had seen these before: her dad had built lots of things using the parts cannibalised from his old Noicar. "Bringing her back now."

A witch? Did they really think she was a witch? She had never thought to use that word but supposed it was true. She and Peter only rarely listened to the news: Peter thought it was too politicised and inaccurate. Too biased. They were only vaguely aware of the searches for alternative energy and the persecution of refugees being labelled illegal and witches.

Two of the men sat and talked quietly and shuffled a deck of cards, another of them watched her silently, and two others went to another section of the craft, including the man who spoke on the radio. It was unclear if any of these men were in charge. One of the men was emptying her belongings onto a workbench. The Noicraft moved so smoothly she could barely even tell they were in motion at all. He piled her clothing on one side, and her food on the other. He picked up the journal and leafed through the pages, revealing the paper from Khuch, and tossed it aside, thinking it was just a picture of a bird. She winced when she saw him doing this and regretted bringing her journal at all.

The man flicked through some of the pages before taking Aisling's journal into another room. He was expressionless as he did so, but she felt a sense of foreboding. Aisling noticed a faint smell of bleach in her case and sat still, not daring to move or to ask the men what was happening. She was scared, but not so scared as to be paralysed. She remembered the fear she first felt when seeing a wild wolf in the Mishkash; a fear that she had learned to overcome.

A few years earlier, she and Khuch were walking in the Mishkash together and spotted the wolf not far away. In hindsight, it knew they were there and could have attacked if it wanted. But it still frightened Aisling so much that her legs froze and she could only watch as the wolf went about its business. Khuch held her hand then and she felt a magic warmth flowing into her through him. He was so calm, and his calmness was magically toxic. She felt the warmth spreading through her whole body and regained the will to move. Khuch as a child was already capable of magic that most of the adult Khun were not, and as they grew up together as children, then as teenagers, she felt that she could never grow tired of his company.

"Witch," the man watching her finally spoke, his voice soft but confident, and much deeper than expected from looking at his small frame. She broke from her thoughts back into the present, staring at the man, and feeling the memory of Khuch's calm influence. "What is your name?" He spoke with excessive care, as if he couldn't expect her to understand his language.

She did not answer. The man sat down, still looking at her. He was clearly not sure how to act. Fortunately, he thought, the trip would not take long, maybe another hour, before they reached the Capital. He continued to stare at Aisling, partly from a desire to witness the supposed magic he'd been told to expect, and partly because he knew from experience that looking out the windows of a speeding Noicraft made him dizzy. They moved unreasonably fast, and their smoothness and silence through the air was disorienting. He found that talking helped with the nausea.

"What's your name?" he asked again, still sitting. There was an honesty to his behaviour that disarmed Aisling. She wanted to answer but decided that silence was a better option. "Where are you from? Are you from Blue Island? You don't look like you are." The man started rapidly asking questions. "How long you been living there? You know why you here now? How many of you living down there? How many witches?"

"I'm not a witch," Aisling finally spoke up when the number of questions frustrated her, surprising herself. All the men in the craft looked at her.

"Of course you are, witch," The man continued in his unbelievably deep voice. He leaned forward with his hands on his knees. "Why else we been sent to find you?"

"I'm not a witch," She repeated, more defiantly than before.

"Don't talk to the witch." A different man came into the room, the man who had searched her backpack. He was holding her journal. The man with the deep voice nodded and leaned back, still staring at Aisling. The man with the journal, who seemed to be in a position to give others orders, stood in front of her case. He wore a grey, padded uniform like them. His face was clean-shaven and he had a very big nose.

"We were sent to capture a witch," he explained, his weight shifting from one leg to the other, as if he didn't like to stand still. "A witch was seen creating water from nothing and disappearing into the forest. You are that witch."

Aisling tried her hardest not to show any sign that she knew about the water.

"As you know, this government has decided to crack down on witches."

"But there's no such thing!" she protested. The case was barely wide enough to move her arms, so she kept them awkwardly by her sides. The men in the room laughed at her pathetic stubbornness.

"You hear that, boys? No such thing as witches! You can all go home then," the man leading the others continued. "It's been all over the news? You listen to the news? No, of course you don't. This country's full of witches. You know something about that? You know where we can find more?"

Aisling remained silent. The man was not bothered by her silence.

"Doesn't matter if you do or don't. We're gonna find you all. You know what this is?" he asked, tapping on the case. "Can't cast any spells in there. Keeps us safe from you. Anyway, they're gonna love this book of yours, back at the office." Aisling cursed herself for ever keeping a journal as the man flicked through a few pages, stopping at the one where she had drawn a glowing glob of floating light above a hand. Her only consolation was that she didn't write any explanations. "They are really gonna love this. I'll save the hard questions for later, witch. For now, I'll just say this: we know you weren't alone in the forest. We will find the others who lived there with you."

Then he left the room, and Aisling tried to find a comfortable way to sit on the metal floor. A voice came over a loudspeaker. Aisling and Khuch used to play with the speaker and radio taken from Peter's Noicar.

"Landing in two minutes." The man with the deep voice looked relieved to hear that announcement. The two men playing cards had not been interested in the whole conversation. They collected their cards lugubriously and packed them away, almost disappointed to be arriving.

The only indication that they had stopped moving was a tiny bump felt when a refuelling hose attached to the craft. It was a really remarkable piece of technology. This was the first time Aisling had ever seen a Noicraft. Peter had seen them occasionally back when they still lived in the city, but even so, he had never flown in one. As an engineer he had tried to gain contracts with the big manufacturers, just before their businesses were made bankrupt and were bought out by the government. It was bad timing, but he refused to work for a government that engaged in such unethical business practices. He owned a small Noicar garage in Nelasive, tweaking engines, and for the right customer installing illegal modifications such as the Wind Engine. His own invention, it improved the efficiency of the existing government-issue engines by nearly forty percent, and reduced noise by at least half. His patent application was accepted but days later was declared illegal as it was deemed 'unsafe'. Peter was furious at that news and his colleagues started to create conspiracy theories about the government and Noi. He believed them all.

The men in the craft exited through a door that led to a small flat area, leaving Aisling alone in the case. She tried to see what was outside, but the night time and the Noi meant she could only see blue. A figure approached the door and stepped inside. It stopped walking, still a few metres from Aisling, and silhouetted against the blue background.

When the figure came fully into the craft and Aisling could make out his face, she was struck with déjà vu. The man also appeared surprised and confused, like he was trying to recognise her from a distant memory.

"My name is Jack," He declared, not looking at her properly, and more speaking to the room than to her directly. "You have been arrested for witchcraft. What is your name?"

"Uncle?" He looked at her closely.

"Aisling? You've grown up." He sat next to her. "I hope you can excuse the case. I'm sure my team has already explained the danger you pose us."

"I'm no danger," she protested. "I'm the one being kidnapped!"

"No, I'm sure you're right," Jack laughed, crossing his legs tightly and draping his arms over whatever he could reach. For a second, Aisling believed he might help her, but she quickly felt like a fool. "Just as Peter was never a danger either."

Aisling felt his words grow distant, and her eyes droopy. The case was filling with some sort of gas, and she tried holding her breath, but there was nothing she could do to prevent passing out.

When she came to, Aisling blinked rapidly and regained her senses. It took her a minute to remember what happened. Where was Jack now? She was in a room with transparent walls. A small area had been sectioned off around a toilet, with shoulder-high frosted walls. At least that was somewhat dignified. The walls were made of the same thick clear material as the case on the craft, which she was told was anti-magic, but there was no way she was going to risk trying magic now. Not with the guards constantly watching.

Uncle Jack. He knew her. Hopefully he could help and get her out. He would tell them it was all a misunderstanding. She couldn't tell how much time had passed from when she was talking to him.

Her cell was in the centre of a larger room with one ordinary-looking office door on the side opposite a small cot, and a window in the wall behind the toilet. It was day time, she noticed. The room beyond her cell was carpeted with an inoffensive grey, like you might find in a corporate office block, and fluorescent lights ran in two rows across the panelled ceiling. They were filtered to remove some of the harshness of Noi. A small panel with buttons and switches was built into the wall of the cell near the door to the room, but there didn't appear to be any way in or out of the cell. It was a very boring room. A guard sat in a chair by the door, and every few minutes got up to walk a lap around the cell. He was clearly very bored.

The door opened and another guard entered.

"Finally!" the bored guard said. "I thought this shift would never end."

"Anything interesting?" the second guard asked uncaringly.

"Nothing. She just woke up."

"Wish I could sleep in until ten in the morning."

"See you tonight." The first guard left the room, and the second took over his seat.

"So, you're the witch? You don't look so scary."

"Can I talk to Jack?"

"Sure, you can." The guard didn't seem surprised. "He'll

be here soon to question you."

"Question me?"

"Of course. What did you think? Jack would just let you go?"

Aisling thought better of telling too much detail. She guessed it could be a bad idea to let people know Jack was her uncle. Despite having grown up in a tiny community, some of her dad's distrustful nature had rubbed off on her.

"When is he coming?"

"Before lunch."

"Can I have some breakfast?"

The guard grunted something into the wall panel, and a minute later a shabby young woman with dark skin entered the room with a tray full of hot food.

"It's a challenge for us to feed you, you know? How are we supposed to get this delicious plate in there without breaking the anti-magic case?" He took a piece of bacon from the tray and bit half of it off. "But Janice knows how. She's a witch too. But for all her powers, she can barely even speak our language." The woman then brought the tray near the panel in the wall of the cell, which opened for her, and she passed the tray inside to another platform for Aisling to take, not looking Aisling in the eye. When Janice withdrew her hand, the panel closed. Then Aisling was struck by recognition.

"Thank you," she said in Khun. Janice looked up at Aisling full of confusion.

"You're welcome," she whispered back automatically. She stood there looking at Aisling, trying to recognise her, because she had none of the strong features of the Khun and her face was a different shape altogether. It confused Janice that Aisling could speak her native language.

"Hey!" the guard interrupted, getting up threateningly.

"None of that witch language in here!" He looked at Janice and pointed at the door. She nodded and left. Looking at Aisling, he warned her, "That was a dumb thing to do, witch. Not going to earn you any trust. Now eat your breakfast and be grateful."

She did as she was told. Sitting on the floor, she first tried the coffee. It was excellent and perfectly hot, but she didn't question why she was being treated to such good quality food. Maybe that's what prison is like, she thought naively.

The guard wasn't very interested in talking like the one on the craft had been. He liked to look out the window and fiddle with a handheld game that he smuggled in. It must be a very boring job, Aisling thought. She was used to having the freedom to go outside and explore the forest, not sitting inside all day. She was curious about Janice, and tried asking the guard about her.

"How do you know Janice is a witch?" He ignored her. "Have you seen magic?"

The guard didn't engage and instead got up to do a lap of the room, just like the guard he replaced. He looked out the small window and sighed. He could see quite a few blocks away, but there was nothing particularly interesting to look at. It was not a very inspiring view: mostly concrete buildings and only a few small trees and plants. The window had no ledge. It didn't even open. *Things look more interesting in the day*, he thought, *at night it's all just blue. Even this view is better in the day.*

"Listen," he started, "I have to be in here for twelve hours, and I'm not interested in getting to know you. My orders are to keep you in there and raise an alarm if you escape."

"Escape?"

"So, no talking. We can treat you worse. Consider

yourself lucky."

Aisling thought about it. There was something weird about her situation, being kept captive, but not unpleasantly. They must really be scared of witches, she thought. But why? Only the Khun know about magic and they keep their secret very closely guarded. Outsiders weren't supposed to know magic was real.

"Have you ever seen magic?" she asked him.

"No talking," he tiredly snapped.

"Me neither."

"Shut up."

"Ooga booga boo!" She sprung to the edge of the case; the guard flinched almost imperceptibly, but she saw it.

"Stop that."

"Abracadabra!" She was laughing now.

"I said stop it!"

"Hocus pocus!" She waved her arms around.

"Enough!" The guard clicked a button on his radio and a second later the dim blue that lit the room turned red. Aisling knew she'd provoked him but didn't care. She had been thinking about escape since he put the word in her head. If she could just get out of the case and hide for two minutes, she could cast a Light magic spell and be invisible. Then she would simply walk right out the door and back to her dad.

The door opened and Jack entered with another woman in a suit trailing him. She wore glasses and had an unpleasant expression on her face like she had smelt something disgusting.

"I'll take it from here," he said to the guard, the one Aisling had taunted. The guard left, and the woman clicked a button on the wall panel that turned the lights back to their original pale filtered blue. Jack closed the door after the guard, locking the three of them in the room.

Jack took a step towards the case and stared at Aisling. She didn't look much like Peter, but she met his gaze with the same defiant look he knew well. Jack barely blinked, and it was off-putting. Aisling was first to look away, towards the woman, who had sat on the only chair in the room.

"Uncle Jack, what am I doing here?" she asked him. The woman seemed not to care that Aisling had called him uncle.

"You were seen using magic. We are authorised to treat any magic user as government property."

"I don't know what you mean," she lied, unconvincingly, sensing that perhaps things weren't as simple as she wished.

"Water magic." Jack was still staring at her, expressionless.

"What's that?" She kept up her lie as long as possible, thinking maybe he would give up and send her home.

"Miss Morris?" he addressed the woman on the chair without turning around. His suit was perfectly fitted and uncreased. Aisling thought any movement would ruin it.

The woman took a small bottle from her bag, and opened it. Aisling thought she might be thirsty, but then Miss Morris raised an outstretched finger to the rim of the bottle and called forth a few drops of water. They crashed into the bottle as Aisling stumbled on the spot, losing her balance. Miss Morris put the bottle away and resumed her impassive position, observing Aisling's reaction.

"You see, Aisling," Jack spoke forcefully, his hands clasped behind his back, "magic is most certainly real. When we received a report that a young lady was inexplicably flooding the street in a mining town, we couldn't ignore it."

"How can you prove I did anything?"

"The evidence is against you. We have a witness, and we have also conducted a thorough study of your magic journal.

Would you rather be tried for harbouring illegal immigrants? I'm sure the public would call for you to be hanged. There is such ugly negativity in the discussion about them at the moment. The Leader himself is calling for stronger punishments. It would be wise of you to listen to my proposal," he paused before adding with a smirk, "my niece."

"What then?" Aisling asked, shoulders hanging low, defeated. The journal. She was practically handing them all the Khun's secrets on a silver platter.

"You will help us with our research."

"What research?"

Miss Morris burst out laughing and finally spoke.

"Dear girl, do you live in a cave? The Ministry has been researching alternative energy sources since before you were born."

"Oh yeah… I heard about that…" she sheepishly said, trying to think back to what she heard on the radio. All she could remember was Peter saying it was all lies. She wished that just once he'd said something other than 'don't trust the government'. She quickly reasoned that if she were tried, she would never be alone to perform a Light magic spell of invisibility, but if she agreed to help them, she had better chances of eventually being alone and escaping. "What do I have to do?"

"How agreeable of you." Jack smiled like a hyena. "We will get to the specifics later when we write a contract for you. It will take us a few days to finalise the procedure. Until then, do you accept my offer?"

"I guess so."

"Terrific. We will see each other again soon."

Miss Morris stood up and unlocked the door. The bored guard came back in. Jack and Miss Morris exited and the guard looked at Aisling standing weakly, leaning on the wall of her case. He shrugged and sat back down, eager to return to his game. A pigeon slammed into the window, looking for somewhere to land, but unable to find footing it flapped away again and Aisling's thoughts turned to Khuch and the simple message he gave her.

Aisling's days in the cell were extremely boring. The guards refused to talk to her to pass the time, and it must have been just as boring for them, she thought. They worked in twelve-hour shifts, although what they expected to happen, she didn't know. She had nothing in the cell to keep entertained, not even a radio to hear the news. She figured the guards were paranoid that she could cast some sort of spell through the radio, despite the anti-magic case. She could only see a small glimpse of the outside world through the window, which didn't offer much and couldn't be opened. She found herself sleeping just to pass the time.

Two days passed since Jack's last visit before he finally appeared again, unannounced. He strode into the room carrying a leather briefcase, his suit perfectly pressed and face perfectly shaved. He had the same small face as her dad, but somehow looked meaner, especially when he smiled. His eyebrows were thinner, and his ears didn't stick out the way her dad's did.

"Can you give us some privacy?" he said quietly to the guard, framing an order as a question. The guard stood up lazily and left the room. Jack opened the briefcase and took out a contract for Aisling to read and sign. He fiddled with the controls in the wall panel and then to Aisling's amazement, her case disappeared completely, leaving her sitting on a bed awkwardly positioned in the centre of the room. Jack took a step towards her.

"As you can see, the government has done extensive

research into magic these recent years," he began, and handed her the pages. She flicked through them while he spoke, landing on the final page that bore the Leader's signature. "You know me as your uncle Jack, but my title here is Executive Director of Magical Research. Publicly, my department doesn't exist. Neither do I for that matter. The contract you have in your hands will outline your responsibilities as an employee of the Department. I apologise for the delay in creating it, but since you have been living secretly with your father and other, presumably illegal persons, it has been hard to confirm your identity through official channels."

"Hard to confirm my identity? We're related!"

"Procedure requires documentation," Jack answered flatly. "In any case, we are here now. I will give you a minute to read the contract and sign it – you can read, can't you? Remember, the alternative is to be tried for harbouring illegal immigrants, which the Leader is particularly sore about. When we find your father we will offer him the same deal, assuming he has also learned magic by some black market means as you have."

"Black market?"

"Aisling, you have to understand. Officially, magic doesn't exist. The only sanctioned magic is performed by my Department, which also officially doesn't exist. Anything else is a crime against this country, and a crime against nature."

"Crime against nature?" Aisling could feel her temper rising. She tried to imagine how Chuluun would react to this situation. It somehow calmed her.

"Indeed. Now if you wouldn't mind focusing on the contract."

Aisling read a few of the clauses and felt overwhelmed by

the complicated legal language. She tried reading it closer but got confused. Staring at the page, none of the information was being absorbed.

"I don't know what any of this means," she complained, giving up.

"Essentially, you agree to participate in our research – *all* of our research – and agree that your results and personal data can be shared with other departments and ministries. You understand that speaking about this contract is an offence punishable by life imprisonment or death. We have an obligation to ensure you are clothed, fed, paid, and remain healthy within the limits of our research. You understand that there is an element of danger involved in scientific research," Jack summarized mechanically, as if reading from notes.

"So, if I don't sign, I'll probably die or at least go to gaol… but if I do sign, I could *still* die or go to gaol."

"Yes."

"Then why should I sign it? Can't you just let me go home?"

Jack laughed and ignored her second question.

"By accepting my offer, your chance of death reduces greatly," he said without expression, but still with his disarming stare. His voice was extremely resonant even in the carpeted room, not like the congested voice she remembered him once having. Aisling's voice on the other hand was full of anxiety and refused to echo. "You will also be a legitimate citizen for once, since your dad foolishly moved away from civilisation and never bothered to get you a birth certificate. You will be a government employee entitled to all the benefits that come with the position outlined in section two of the contract. You will be paid well, and above all, you will be contributing to the success of your country and its future."

"You said there was danger in the research…"

"I understand your concern." He smiled with his mouth, but his gaze remained predatory. "Should you walk willingly into danger? You have a choice, although the alternative is certainly worse."

"Then I don't really have a choice, do I?"

"Not really, no."

"Okay… I'll sign it."

"Excellent choice," Jack celebrated with a hint of irony and handed her a pen engraved with his name. She signed in several places that were marked with little stickers and gave the pen back. "And the contract. I will give you a copy. Welcome to the world, Aisling," he said and drew out a plastic card from his inner coat pocket. "This is your first official form of identification in your life, I suppose. You can use it to move around the building, from your living area to the laboratory. It will not allow you to exit the building. We cannot allow witches to move freely through the city."

Jack clicked a button on the panel and spoke into a small microphone, and a minute later Miss Morris entered the room.

"Congratulations Aisling, you've made the right choice today," she said warmly, reaching out to shake her hand. Aisling saw that her fingers looked like they had been broken several times. She felt like the choice had been made for her. "Please come with me, I will take you to your new home."

Holding her new card tightly, Aisling followed Miss Morris through a series of corridors, trying to remember their route. After a few turns it became too hard to remember because everything looked the same. The building must have been enormous, she realised. They reached an elevator, and Miss Morris gestured for Aisling to enter before she followed and pressed the button for the twenty-fifth floor.

The doors opened, and Aisling was greeted by a much more inviting environment. It looked like someone's home, or a hotel, or something in between. At least there were paintings on the walls, and a plastered ceiling, and a carpet more interesting than the boring office fabric she was used to. It was a little overstimulating, in fact, and she tried not to focus on the details. There were some pieces of furniture that held trinkets and other small decorations. A Noiclock told her it was past eleven at night- the first Noiclock she had seen since she was taken.

Miss Morris led the way to the third door on the left, and asked Aisling to swipe her card next to an electronic scanner positioned to the left of the handle.

"Only your pass and the cleaners' and security's will open this door," Miss Morris explained. "This area is yours; it is to be your home while you work here."

Feeling apprehensive, Aisling kept thinking it was better than being hanged. And she might be able to finally try out her Light spell inside. She swiped the pass and heard a faint electronic bing, followed by an unlocking of the door. Miss Morris turned the brass knob on the big wooden door, and ushered Aisling inside. Aisling's jaw dropped.

It was huge. One side of the room was designed to be a cosy living room complete with a soft-looking sofa facing a fake fireplace. There was a small desk and chair in the corner. The other side was a small tiled area with a basic, but functional kitchen, already stocked with some staple foods. A door led into a bedroom, which had the biggest bed Aisling had ever seen, covered in luxurious pillows. There was an ensuite which had a shower as big as her entire bathroom back at home. In both the main area and the bedroom, Aisling's attention was drawn to a large window overlooking the city. Blue lights radiated from all the buildings below her as far as she could see. It was like floating above the ocean.

"I hope you will be comfortable here," Miss Morris said warmly. "Get some rest tonight, because tomorrow we start work. There is an information pack on the desk there for you to read. I will be back here tomorrow at nine to collect you. I know it's late now, so there's no problem if you haven't read everything, you have time over the next week. What's important now is that you are well-rested and relaxed for tomorrow."

"This is all for me?" Aisling couldn't believe it. The apartment was bigger than her old home. Miss Morris chuckled and smiled.

"You'll get used to it. Goodnight."

"Goodnight," Aisling replied distractedly, not paying much attention as Miss Morris closed the door behind her.

It was all so overwhelming that Aisling's plans to make herself invisible with Light magic were forgotten while she explored the apartment. She was drawn to the window and stood there looking out at the sprawling city beneath her. She had never seen so many buildings before. It was scary to think how big the Capital was, how many people lived there, how many of them were unaware that there was real magic just out of their reach, that the Leader was keeping secret the best thing in the world – for what? For Noi? – that these thousands of people might never know the freedom that magic had given her and her dad.

She turned and saw the booklet on the desk. She opened the first page and saw tiny print and complicated diagrams and tables and knew she was too tired to concentrate on it.

She tried the couch and found that it was exactly the right softness and size. She could easily fall asleep on it, but forced herself to get up. She went to the small kitchen and opened all the cupboards and the fridge. She was pleased to find her favourite tea and thought she might make a cup before nestling into the huge bed.

She placed the teabag in a cup and prepared her mind to create hot water. But nothing came. Confused, she tried again to conjure water like she had done a million times before, but again nothing came. Worried that somehow, they had taken her magic away and she would be useless in the experiments, she filled the cup with cold water from the tap and began to cast a heating spell. It was a cruder way to make tea, but that was how she had done it before learning a spell for hot water.

But as hard as she could concentrate on the cup, she could not heat the water. She had never made tea any other way and had no idea how to make hot water with Noi technology. The concept of it seemed so weird to her, using a toxic substance to make her water heat up. Trying not to cry from frustration and confusion, she tipped out the cold water and thought maybe she could try again tomorrow.

She went to the bed and it was so comfortable compared to the room she had been in before; she was asleep in seconds.

But her sleep was not restful and was instead heavy with dreams. Once again, she dreamt of Iwizadi and the round room, but this time a woman was there too. Or so she thought. Because whenever she tried to see the woman, she had the chilling sensation that the woman was behind her. Iwizadi's book was open this time and she saw the words "anti-magic" written in an elegant script.

She jolted awake. The whole apartment was inside an

anti-magic case. This time she did cry. It was a tremendously satisfying cry in which she unleashed her days of frustration, loneliness, and despair. She saw through the window an owl in flight somewhere far below and wished she had never run back inside her home for Khuch's page.

She thought of her dad, Khuch, Chuluun, and all the others, and said in a tiny voice, "I will learn Bird magic."

Chapter 4

The light from the early morning filtered through the thick
canopy, a beam striking where Peter had camped the night
before. He was already up, boiling water to make sure it was
safe to drink. Small particles and spores drifted through the
beam of light, creating a dizzying visual effect. Peter stared
at it for a moment while holding his hands near his small
pot of water. After a moment, there were signs that the
water was heating up, though there was no fire underneath,
and less than a minute later it was boiling vigorously. Still
not moving, Peter then cooled the water with another spell.
The whole process was over very fast, and Peter was grateful
that Chuluun had taught him such a simple combination of
spells.

Aisling had the tea in her bag. No matter, Peter thought,
he could get by with just water. In his haste that night, he
had packed a disorganised assortment of things: one change
of clothing, a toothbrush, some flour and biscuits, one pot,
one mug, a sleeping bag, and whatever was already in his
backpack from when he didn't unpack it after their last time
camping. Luckily there was a knife in there too.

It had been nearly a week since Aisling was taken, and he
had not seen anyone on his journey. He had been in the
forest, attempting a difficult passage south-west towards the

Capital, taking a long route around his former hometown.

It truly was a great forest, covering a huge area of land across nearly half the country. No wonder the Leader hadn't made much headway here; the Mishkash was impenetrable in some places. It was perfect for someone who wanted to hide. He figured he would go as far as possible before eventually leaving its security and having to navigate the equally dangerous inhabited areas. They were definitely government men who took her, and after some time spent in panicked despair, he resolved that he would visit two people he knew in the capital: his brother Jack, and his brother-in-law Tom. Neither would be happy to see him.

He was no stranger to survival. Hunting in the forest was a regular activity he engaged in, and he had no trouble on the first day alone finding and trapping a deer. But since living with the Khun, camping had been changed forever. No longer did he need to search for materials to make a fire, or even a suitable campsite to make one in. It was no longer necessary to find dry ground, or build a shelter from bugs and flying insects. All the basic elements of survival were taken care of by magic. And he felt confident that he would not see anybody so deep in the forest.

He sometimes saw crows, and felt strangely comforted by their presence, though he could not explain why he felt that way. How was he to know of the rift among them, where only some could overcome their species' ancient grudge towards humans? Sometimes it felt like they were guiding him around obstacles and other times it felt like they were placing them in his way.

He tried a few times to talk to them, but they did not reply.

Magic really was incredible, he thought. How was it that such a miraculous power had been kept hidden for so long?

Of course, he knew. He knew it would be abused in the wrong hands. If he could use magic to cook the flesh of a deer from a distance of nearly five metres (he had experimented), he could certainly use it to harm a human, to cook them from a distance too. There was no doubt that the Khun were justified in keeping it a secret. In the wrong hands, even the most basic magic would be disastrous.

He also wondered whether anyone was capable of learning magic. The Khun were somewhat surprised when he and Aisling had been able to perform their first spells, as if they expected them to fail. It puzzled him how magic worked at all, and his best theory was that it was something inherited.

For the first time in a long time, Peter thought of Iwizadi. Alone in the forest for days already, his brain had dug up a surprising range of forgotten memories. It knew he didn't want to be alone. He cursed himself for not standing up and taking on the captors and it made him so angry: angry at himself and angry at the world. He was angry at Aisling too. Why did she run back? What could have been so important? He could have taken them on. He should have cooked them from the inside when they took her. He should have cast a blinding light and broken their necks. His daughter.

She loved the Iwizadi story. Since hearing the Khun version of it, she often asked about him. Why was their version so different? Which version was right? Was Iwizadi good or evil? It was all second-hand news, all fairy tales. Who really cared at the end of the day?

He dried the pot using a weak Fire magic spell, evaporating the droplets that remained. When everything was packed up, he tightened his backpack and started walking. He was confident with Fire magic: he thought it was probably his strongest magic, and the most useful out on this extended camping trip. Every time he used it to cook a piece of meat or boil water, he remembered Chuluun first teaching him all those years earlier. Peter's Fire magic came out so strong that in a flash, the water Chuluun prepared for practice was boiling and sputtering dangerously, and Peter was so absorbed in creating the magic and consumed with a desire to burn that he couldn't shut it off. He wanted to burn the water; to punish it. He hoped that he could burn the world. For Maria. They should suffer like he did.

Chuluun slapped him on the face and the spell was broken.

Peter was dazed for a moment, but then he broke too. Chuluun put a massive arm around his friend, who was now crying like a lost child.

"They killed her, Chuluun. I was there. I saw it." Silence and stillness passed before a comforting rough voice cut through the room.

"Now you see the danger of Fire magic. It wants to burn the user." Peter regrouped and nodded at Chuluun, who offered him a cup of wine. He sipped at it. "Fire eats everything. It is hard to control, we must be strong when we use it. We will try again tomorrow."

"I never felt so angry in my life. Will that happen every time?"

"No." Chuluun was firm in his answer, like he always was when he spoke. "The first time is the hardest. You will learn to control it. And you will learn to control yourself too." Peter felt reassured by this, though still a cocktail of negative emotions swirled through his body and he was afraid that the next time he tried Fire magic it would be worse.

"Thanks, Tsenkher."

Now Peter was able to perform complex and nuanced Fire magic, having mastered its destructive desire and learned to protect himself from it. He could combine Fire and Light magic to conjure one of the Khun's floating heat lamps as effectively as any of them could, earning him much praise. He was even credited with creating a new Fire spell that could keep a user warm through any weather, though Chuluun hesitated to ever use it. Peter's spell had been of great use on his third day alone in the forest, when a heavy rain prevented him from making any progress. Crouching under an overhanging rock ledge, he visualised a gas flame: one that he could twist a knob to change its intensity, from a matchstick flame on one end to a world-ending inferno on the other. He mentally dialled it to a weak strength and meditated over its little orange pulse for a few seconds. Starting with his head, a warmth radiated all the way down and through his body. It spread to his clothes, and passed out of his skin. The rain on his skin evaporated off him and he steamed, feeling warm and dry.

He opened his eyes and was totally dry and cosy. It was bizarre, but he felt like he was in a warm bubble, immune to the soaking rain. He sat comfortably underneath the rock waiting for the rain to end. When it did end several hours later, he reached into his mind and again visualised the little gas burner. This time he simply switched it off. The spell was over and he immediately felt the cold of the water dripping onto him from the rock. It felt like losing a friend. Already dusk, Peter decided to stay under the rock for the night.

The ground was cold and wet when Peter awoke at dawn. Memories of his dream lingered in his mind's eye and he could picture a faceless man in a round room, blocking a doorway. A woman was there too, but he could only see her when he wasn't looking, out of the corner of his eye. She looked just like Maria but it was impossible to see clearly.

He wanted her to look like Maria. Peter caught his reflection in a mirror and was horrified to see that his face was blurry too. All the faces were like a painting of a memory viewed underwater. He shivered at the thought and was pleased to know that soon the dream would be forgotten. Except Maria could never be forgotten. She was the reason he did anything. As Aisling grew older, she looked more and more like her, which was hard for Peter at first. Over time he got used to seeing her face again. It helped him remember.

Fire Magic had proven to be the best therapy. The more he learned to control the flame, the surer he was not to be burnt by it. But he was also sure that he would have fire in him for the rest of his life. Chuluun taught him how to harness for good the thing that for nearly sixteen years had been consuming him. The gratitude he felt towards Chuluun helped him control it even further.

After packing up his belongings he set to walking, with each step squelching through the soggy underbrush and leaf litter. Determined to find and save his daughter, he pushed onward. There was no path, as nobody had been determined enough to carve out a settlement in this part of the country. He knew from geography class in school as a boy that he should be approaching the hilliest part of the forest, and that he could expect several days' worth of difficult, dangerous hiking before finally emerging from the forest near Darvozasi, a satellite city to the Capital. From there he should be able to easily get to the government offices in the Capital and talk to Jack, and seek out Tom if he was still living there. He had been thinking for days about what to do after that, and eventually decided not to plan anything beyond just talking to Jack and Tom and seeing if they could help.

Around noon he came across a shallow, flowing stream

with some natural pools and decided it was a good place for a rest. He drank from the stream and splashed around in it, trying to clean out the film of dirt that had accumulated in his ears. The stream was more exposed than he was used to, without much tree cover, and the sun felt good on his face after days of darkness and rain. He hoped that Aisling was warm and dry, wherever she was.

A hummingbird hovered in front of his face for a second before flitting upwards to a high branch. Peter tried to follow its zippy movements but quickly lost track, and while his attention was turned skyward, he saw what must have been an eagle, very high above; higher than even Noicraft could fly. Tesver crossed his mind, the creepy old bastard. He was probably keeping track of Peter's journey somehow. The thought of it was more disturbing than comforting, even though he himself would have used such a power to do exactly the same thing.

After a quick bite to eat, he got up again and continued. He wondered if the Khun might have some magic that made trekking easier. Probably. They could do a lot, but as Peter had criticised one night with Chuluun and a bottle of wine, they were unimaginative. Surely, they had the power to make some sort of transport spell, but they wouldn't because they couldn't imagine it. They never wanted to try new things.

He noticed the ground sloping upwards a tiny amount and knew he had reached the start of the hills. From this point everything was going to get harder. But he thought of Aisling. She was capable, she was brave, she was powerful as a ... *witch*... it felt dirty to use that word. He had faith that she was going to be fine. He wanted to give her the best life he could. He saw the crest of the hill rising ahead of him and the flame of determination burned within him as he charged ahead.

With no company to keep his mind distracted, Peter found his thoughts turning inward dangerously often. He pushed forward over the hills, slowly closing the distance between himself and the Capital, unsure but hopeful that he would find Aisling there, or Tom, or at least Jack. He was already sick of the forest. He knew some people never would tire of it, people like Tesver, but he was sick of its unending density. He was sick of how every step felt like the forest was working against him, throwing one obstacle after another to prevent him from moving forward. Without a path, he was forced to tackle his way through branches and bushes, hoping that his route would not end up at the edge of a cliff and force him to backtrack and try again.

More and more frequently, he could feel his flame surging when powerful memories fought their way to the front of his mind. When he thought of that night, all those years ago, his flame roared so violently he wanted to burn the whole forest to the ground, and it took him a good deal of willpower to refocus on the current situation. Still, the final image of her face kept intruding in his thoughts just when he was sure he had buried her again.

Peter was only a small man, but wiry and deceptively strong. A lifetime of labour and inexhaustible energy gave him a thin, muscly body. He looked weak, but before Aisling was born, he had been a fighter, a boxer. Now he was still fighting, but it was different. He was too old for the types of things he used to do. Forty years old. *When did that happen?* He wondered.

The Capital was a rough city thirty years ago. After Peter and Jack's parents moved there for their dad's job, they were faced with a whole new world. A world full of all sorts of people, and all sorts of opportunities good and bad. Jack, the younger sibling by four years looked up to Peter and followed him everywhere. It didn't take long for them to make friends in their age group at school. It didn't take them long to make enemies either. As the older boy, Peter was more often the target of the local boys, but they weren't afraid to use Jack to taunt Peter, to invoke his protective nature so they could ridicule and embarrass him.

In the present, Peter struggled forward through a thick tangle of vines, cutting some here and there, calling on Fire magic to make a kind of knife out of fire and wind. He was unfocused and tired and frustrated. His magic was sloppy.

Their father, Peter Senior, worked for the government as an engineer, and taught Peter the things he needed to know to start working in that field. After accepting a lucrative position in the Capital as a consultant about the government's latest push for new Noi mines, they saw less and less of him. Their mother, Monique, wasn't around much longer after the move. After a few months she disappeared back to some small village on the remote west coast where she grew up. Halasat, it was named. Later in life, Peter would understand why she left, the same way he did when he abandoned the Capital for their small hometown. The same way he left Jack with their father. They never saw her again.

Leaves and thorns whipped around Peter's legs as he fought his way down yet another hill, and waded through an ankle-deep creek bed. The next hill loomed higher than the previous one.

Fourteen. Younger than Aisling. But old enough to raise his brother. He wondered if he should ever have told Aisling the details of his childhood. She seemed to sense that it was not a good thing to ask about, and he tried not to say anything that would make her want to ask. She did ask about her mother sometimes.

Her face appeared in his mind again.

School for Peter in the Capital didn't go well. Forever bullied by the other gangs of kids, he quickly learned that he couldn't get by as the calm little boy from the small town. He threw the first punch, connecting poorly with Luke Brown's sniggering face. All six of them beat him to a pulp while Jack ran home and hid. Peter returned home, limping through the smoggy concrete streets, dripping blood from nose, mouth, ears. Construction crews nearby working on building the latest skyscrapers either averted their eyes or gave him a weary thumbs up, one worker asking if he needed help, good on you for getting up and keeping on.

He was fine, he said.

And he was. He knew he would be. It was during that walk that Peter the skinny nobody from the countryside decided he had to be Peter the fierce fighter and this could never happen again. He cleaned up, made spaghetti for himself and Jack, still scared and not saying much, and expected Peter Senior to give him a stern word when he came home late as he always did.

But in the morning, he still had not arrived. Peter made sure Jack was ready for school and together they left the house in the morning. His right eye was turning a dark shade of purple and his left cheek was swollen. His hands hurt when he gripped anything and his left knee was sore when he put weight on it. But he was tough Peter now. He could show no weakness.

They didn't speak all the way to school. Jack was always quiet and weak, but being younger he would grow up in the Capital and fit in, for better or worse. When they reached the school, Jack went to his classroom, and Peter went on a mission. He asked if anyone had seen Luke Brown, and tracked him down. He cornered Luke in the bathroom, said hello, and while Luke was starting to sneer at Peter's broken face, he saw Peter's look of menace and determination and his smile disappeared when it slammed into the mirror, then the steel basin where some of his teeth found the drain, then he was on his back and couldn't see past his tears and blood and through his shock he felt Peter's boots cracking his ribs and pummelling his kidneys, and he tried to roll onto his front and crawl away but he felt himself dragged painfully by the hair across the room and propped up against the wall, and saw Peter line up a punch and blacked out.

This hill was steeper than the others so far, and he slogged upwards, hoping that when he crested this one, he would see the edge of the forest and the distant buildings of Darvozasi.

He wiped Luke's blood on his jeans and walked from the bathroom into the school corridor. The whole thing had only taken about a minute. How long would it be before someone found Luke? Not wanting to risk anything, he went home, packed a bag and rode his bike to the city centre. Through the deafening sounds of construction and faint smell of concrete dust and sweat, he went to the main bus terminal, still under construction. Blue strips of Noi lit the way to the open cashier, and a timetable on the wall showed that no buses were leaving the capital today due to road closures. He was stuck.

From the top of the hill, it was hard to get a clear view west due to the setting sun, but there was the unmistakable edge of the forest only a few kilometres away, and beyond it the city of Darvozasi started its nightly blue glow.

Defeated, he rode back home and arrived before midday. To his surprise, Peter Senior was home. He looked at his son with curiosity.

"Why did you do it?" he asked. What could Peter say. He

was bullied for so long and stood up for himself. Did he go too far? Luke deserved it. "The principal came to my work to tell me. You're not going back there."

"Fine."

"I'll get you an apprenticeship. You can work on machines." In that moment, Peter loved his absent father.

"Thanks."

"Did he do that to your face?"

"Yes."

"Prick deserved it."

Peter set up his camp on the hill where he could see Darvozasi in the distance. It was a warm night, no rain for once, no wind. Luke deserved it. But *they* got away with it. Maria. *This time they'll get what they deserve, taking my daughter. What I should have done earlier.*

He was fifteen when he started working at Jameson's Automotive. He had learned some things about engines from Peter Senior and it was a happy time. Allan Jameson was a fat, rosy-cheeked man who seemed to know everything about Noicars. It was his obsession since he was a child and saw the first model released to the public. What an amazing time to grow up. Allan had been trying for years to have his patent for a new type of Noi-powered bike to be accepted, but it kept being rejected for various reasons, or he was never happy with the finished product.

Peter learned a lot from Allan and they worked together for four years. But as with school, it was violence that ended everything. When Luke and the gang discovered where Peter had disappeared to, he was hassled relentlessly, often getting into fights. Some he won, some he lost, but Luke never forgave Peter for that savage beating he had been given in the school bathroom.

He took up boxing as a way to release some of his rage,

and trained hard until he was able to fend off several of the gang members at once. He was a terrific boxer, winning tournament after tournament. His favourite sparring partner was Tom, who had a sister his age, Maria. She used to come watch sometimes and Peter thought she was the most beautiful girl in the city.

But in those years that Jack was alone at school, he found himself part of another gang of local kids. Jack went with them committing petty crimes and being nuisances. They weren't as violent as Luke, but it was something Peter hated seeing in his younger brother. He missed his hometown where this wasn't a problem.

Excitement and regret kept Peter awake that night on the hilltop.

He was nineteen when he had enough. Peter Senior worked late nights, Jack was at school, and Peter worked early mornings and trained at the ring at night. Allan and his gym buddies kept him company through the day and night, substituting for a family. He hated his mother for leaving, even though it was something he thought about doing too. When he saw in a newspaper that his old hometown was proposed as a site for a huge Noi mine, he was excited. He saw opportunity: it was a chance to move home and start a business. When he saw another newspaper advertising jobs for builders in the area, that was all the convincing he needed. He told Allan he was leaving the city and thanked him for teaching him everything. He went home and packed a bag, like he had done those years before, he rode to the central depot, already unrecognisable compared to the last time he did so, and bought a one-way ticket back home. He left a message at the gym before he left: I'm going home, goodbye. He thought of school, Jack, his dad, and didn't regret a thing. He thought of Tom and already missed his friend. He thought of Maria, and somehow, he knew he would see her again.

Chapter 5

An old crow landed on Tesver's head and made a melodious gargle. There were a lot of birds in the forest, and it was hard to get any accurate information, let alone hear anything. The crow visited Tesver often and liked the strange old man, despite not getting any treats from him since she was a young bird. She liked to hear what Tesver had to say, the things that were happening in the human world, and she felt important whenever she was asked to deliver news. The last week she had been nearly constantly asked to fly here or there and find this person or that person. She enjoyed it and always came straight back to Tesver with a reply, rarely stopping to feed or rest. Tesver often preened her with his long and weirdly talon-like nails. Sometimes he had other birds near him, but he liked her the most. He could trust her.

The past week, the messages were all a bit harder to understand, but she did as she was told. He seemed to be magnetic and she had a sense of where he was at all times. Maybe he knew where she was too. She thought maybe he was a bird born in a human body and felt sorry for him, not having wings. Sometimes she tried to talk to other humans but they couldn't understand her, and she was confused by this.

"Kraka, my dear."

"Yes?"

"Can you find Orn?"

"What should I tell him? I'm afraid he does not like to receive visitors."

"This time he will have to, I have tried every other option."

"I know his nest, on the cliff face, he sees everything."

"You must enlist his help finding where the others are being kept. We have tried long enough and have run out of options. They must be found. If they are alive, he will find them. Agree to anything he demands."

"I will try."

"I believe Aisling will be in the Capital. She must be found if there is to be any hope of peace between the Khun and the people of this country. She is proof that we can live together."

Kraka pushed off from Tesver's matted hair and flew towards the west. It would be a long flight to Orn's territory, and an even more difficult task to find him and convince him to help. But Kraka was the smartest and most trusted of all the allies Tesver had made amongst the birds. She had been his first friend on the new continent, and been his faithful friend and servant for nearly twelve years. She had been the one to convince the pigeons, those forgetful buffoons, to help with spreading news. She recruited the ibises, the ducks – bless them – the pelicans, the owls, the seagulls, and most recently the other crows, though some remained unwilling and untrusting. Now, Tesver wanted her help enlisting the eagles, starting with Orn. She would try. She would find him, and if he didn't break her neck, she would talk to him.

In twelve years, there had barely been a whisper of any

other humans making contact with the birds. That was the whole point of Tesver's recruiting. He was both ambitious and desperate, having received nothing useful from the other birds. He turned to the eagles as a last resort. If there was any bird that could find the other magical Khun, it was the eagles, but they were proud and dangerous, and in spite of all her instincts telling her not to fly directly to Orn's mountain, Kraka flew directly there out of loyalty to Tesver.

Once, some years earlier, a common pigeon had flown from the capital in the south-west all the way to the forest to find Kraka and tell her that she had made contact with a magical person there. But by the time it reached her, it had already forgotten the person's name or how to find them. Kraka was angry, but Tesver calmed her, saying it was always like this with pigeons, they couldn't be relied upon for anything. But spurious as it was, that was the source of Tesver's suspicion and hope that the Khun were held in the Capital.

As Kraka sped off to the west, to the mountains so far distant that they were not visible, Tesver spoke to a tree.

"Are you there, Bu?" A well-camouflaged owl twisted its head and became visible. She flew down to rest on Tesver's outstretched arm. "Any news about the girl?"

"I have lost track."

"Since she was taken?"

"Yes."

"What can I tell the people?"

"Be patient."

"She is very important to us all."

"I have eyes everywhere. It won't take long."

"It's been almost a week. I fear she is lost."

"Be patient. With Orn's help we will find her. We know where she is not."

"Alive or dead."

"Yes."

Bu then pushed off Tesver's arm and hid on another nearby tree. In the time since they had run from the government, Tesver had learned that they were not the target of the search. Several birds had seen Aisling captured and taken aboard a craft, presumably headed to the Capital. But since then, there had been no sighting of her, meaning they must be keeping her indoors somewhere. The birds had also told him how Peter was separated from her and now travelling through the forest alone, fearing capture.

Tesver went alone into the forest and found a nice clearing in which to make camp. He could happily live there with nature for the rest of his life, but they had all promised to seek out the other Khun who had travelled to this land hoping for a new life. It was his duty to look out for his fellow countrymen. Chuluun regretted they had been too comfortable for too long, and it was their duty to find the others. Begrudgingly, Tesver agreed, and despite having not heard of their whereabouts for over fifteen years, decided to put his advanced Bird magic to good use.

"We would have heard something by now," he warned.

"Khun do not disappear without a trace," Chuluun answered. "We will find them, dead or alive."

"And what then?"

"It is unclear."

"Maybe it is best not to find out," Tesver ventured.

"There should be hundreds!" Chuluun erupted. "Why can't the birds find them?"

"There are some places birds do not go."

"Then we must go."

"Orn will give answers. The eagle knows all, he sees all."

"Can we trust him?"

"If Kraka can trust him, so do I."

It was three days since Kraka flew west on her mission to find Orn. She wasn't the fastest bird, but she had stamina and she could cover huge amounts of territory without tiring, and she was smart enough to know how to avoid danger. That's why Tesver had chosen her for the task of recruiting other birds. He trusted that she could at the very least find Orn, and probably talk to him. It might take a few more days, but when she made contact, a network of faster birds was set up to rapidly deliver the answer to Tesver-faster than it would take Kraka alone to return.

Tesver with the other Khun had since regrouped and established a camp deep in the forest. A week since their departure they unanimously agreed that nobody was following them and it would be sensible to establish some sort of meeting point in the forest. Tesver talked to birds seemingly all day and all night, hardly sleeping. Meanwhile, Khuch hoped that Aisling had understood the message he gave her. He was worried, but he knew that if he could hear just one message from her, everything would be alright.

In typical Khun style, nights were occupied with drinking wine around a central fire globe. Since completing his rite of passage, Khuch had been allowed to participate in these nights. There were a few younger children in the group, but the few years that separated them from Khuch suddenly felt like generations after he was finally initiated as an adult. They treated him more distantly since he was initiated and it was a lonely time for him without Aisling there. Despite his official status, he did not yet feel like an adult. He didn't enjoy the taste of wine or its stinging sensation, and had little to contribute to their stories of nostalgia. In truth it had been a very lonely week since leaving their settlement – his hometown he thought of it – and it was only after many nights that he realised he didn't miss the land as much as he missed Aisling.

In the beginning, he knew there were differences in the way that his people behaved to how Peter and Aisling did. The Khun were like small islands. They moved steadily at all times, and rarely showed any physical affection, short of the occasional pat on the shoulder. Their men and women were publicly individuals regardless of how they acted when alone. The Khun never spoke much but spoke with assuredness and gravitas. But Peter and Aisling, they were openly affectionate with each other, and with Chuluun, with whom they felt most relaxed out of everyone. They talked all the time; just an endless stream of words narrating their activities. He liked that dynamic with Aisling, and out of everyone he knew, he talked most with her. Khuch sometimes wished his people would just tell each other how they felt instead of dressing their thoughts in riddles and stories. It seemed the only time they expressed any emotion was at these night-time sessions, talking sadly about what they remembered from Gazar and Khot: places he didn't even know. After some wine, he felt angry that all his family and friends could be that way, unable or unwilling to say and do the things on their mind.

"Gazar is who you are," Chuluun had told him repeatedly while growing up. "Don't forget your home". Home, he thought. *I don't know what that is. I was born somewhere far away, now everyone I know is moving there together. Almost everyone.*

But when he was with Aisling, Khuch felt like he could be fully himself. He saw the way she and her dad hugged, and heard the way they talked openly about their doubts and hopes, and he longed to join in. Even though he was older, he had a growth spurt later than Aisling so for a few months she was taller than him and took great pleasure at pointing it out, resting her arm on his shoulder. But he grew taller eventually, and fitter and stronger. By anyone's standards he was quite handsome, and he sometimes hoped Aisling thought so.

There was one time he tried to show affection, in the forest when they saw a bear, but he felt so out of character he wasn't sure what to do. How did Khun adults ever make friends and get married? Their whole culture felt so cold to him.

"In Khot, my ancestors had a great house and land." One of his neighbours was reminiscing. She was a woman his dad's age named Sanakh. She seemed to be one of only a few Khun who had actually lived permanently in Khot. The others were sitting still as they always did, staring into the fire globe, nodding very slowly. Most nights one Khun alone would tell stories from their past and the others would listen without interrupting. Khuch could never tell how much was exaggerated and which parts were true. There seemed to be no distinction between their own memories and those of their forebears. "We had land for horses, chickens. We kept everything clean with magic. There was no shame and no secrets. We all used magic. But we could see greed for Noi growing in the distance. North of the farm was the hill with the palace, and every year it grew bluer, while the land itself felt less and less blue.

"Later when I grew up and was married, my husband used to tell me 'Sanakh, I am worried. They are hurting the land', but I said he was a fool. Poor Unen. He was proud to fight the invaders like our families had been doing for generations. He went to war and didn't come home. We saw the blue drained from the land into the palace and its mountain. Before all the greed the land was blue. Flowers glowed in spring. And it was a nicer blue, not like Noi. Noi blue is too harsh; the colour is like pain. The blue of Gazar was like comfort.

"Do you remember the great river Gol that flowed through Khot from the palace mountain to the sea?" There was easy nodding from everyone as they stared at the fire globe. "It was clear and had excellent taste, and one drink could heal any sickness. I heard the palace and city was built there to keep Gol private. But travellers were always welcome to visit, to try to drink from the magic Gol. It was all magic: all of life and all of the land, and we Khun were the keepers of magic. And the travellers promised to keep our magic secret. Not like now, how we hide and live in secrecy. How we must use disgusting Noi when outsiders come. How Gol has turned to poison.

"My grandmother remembered the time before Noi, told to her by her grandmother, who was only a young girl at the time. My grandmother's family and my grandfather's family came to our land in spring and they rode their horses along Gol, in fields of glowflowers. I rode there with Unen too, but it was different to how my grandparents described it. They were so young but they knew they were going to get married. Night came and the flowers opened, showing their inner light, the beautiful blue of Gazar, always releasing bright spores to the air that floated like misty rain.

"Unen died fighting to save Gazar and magic. I remember when he said 'Sanakh, Noi is destroying Gazar' and I knew he was right, but I was scared. He rode up the river on a horse, the same way we rode when we were younger. But this time the glowflowers did not glow. The magic was stolen from the land and Gazar was corrupted completely. The palace glowed, like a beacon to guide Unen. I watched him ride next to Gol while the sun set, until he became too small to see. And he was gone.

"Like all of life before Noi, he was gone. And he can't come back. This is life now. Magic is all secret. No Gazar, no Khot, no more glowflowers. No more home."

"We will return home," Chuluun broke in, recognising the end of the story. "Gazar is waiting for us."

"Gazar is destroyed," Sanakh argued. "Gazar is not the same."

"Then we will make a new Gazar. We will heal Gazar." Many Khun nodded and grunted.

"It is beyond healing." The other Khun agreed with Sanakh.

Recognising their stalemate, Chuluun and Sanakh nodded solemnly to each other and resumed a position of stillness and silence. It was not part of Khun culture to argue points like this with no definite solution. Only Khuch was silent throughout this exchange. The children had gone to bed, leaving Khuch the only one present who had no memory of Gazar. It was not his home. How could it be? It was all just fairy tales to him, and always such sad ones it made him want to shake sense into his family and friends, to make them look towards the future and live in the present instead of pining hopelessly for a forgotten memory.

When the night was over, and Khuch lay down protected from the wet weather by a magic barrier covering the whole campsite, memories of Peter and Aisling flickered through his mind. *Where is my home?* He fell asleep and dreamt of riding through the fields of glowflowers by the river Gol. Aisling was there and he was happy.

"We are not doing anything," Khuch told his father. Chuluun listened patiently to his son's concerns, "We have been camping here for a week already and you have no plan. How are we going to rescue Aisling? Where are we going to live? Do you intend to live here in this clearing now?" Light filtered through the thick vegetation and Khuch had become used to seeing things semi-illuminated. He missed his old home with unimpeded views of the stars.

"We all must be patient," Chuluun answered when he saw that Khuch was not looking for a fight, only to get his frustrations off his chest; he was often frustrated recently. Khuch sat down on a rock not far from their tent. "We are waiting for Kraka to complete her mission before we know what to do. It is not our way to act without information."

"Except when you sailed to this country." A centipede was approaching Khuch and he watched it crawl onto a large leaf. He picked up the leaf and moved it away from him.

"That was an exception. You know the war changed things. We were desperate then. Waiting for information then could have cost our lives." Sometimes Khuch felt a flare of anger when Chuluun spoke because it seemed like he had an answer for everything and could not be proven wrong.

"Well, we need Kraka to return before we find Aisling, but what about us?"

"We have not been able to agree on anything," Chuluun relayed. "Some of us want to stay here, some want to find and rescue the others who sailed here and disappeared." He paused for a moment before speaking the next line, and Khuch noticed the centipede crawling back his way, determined. How did it always know where to go? "And others think it is time to return to Gazar."

"Who thinks that?" If Khuch was surprised, he did not show any sign of it. He had been expecting to hear that suggestion eventually, the way the older Khun talked about their homeland. All their stories were filled with nostalgia, overladen with a sickening saudade. Sometimes it drove

Khuch mad. Why couldn't they ever tell happy stories? Even Iwizadi was filled with sadness in their version and Khuch had been pleasantly surprised by the way Peter retold it. He grew up hearing nothing but tales of loss, and despair, until Peter and Aisling came to live with them, and he heard, for the first time, stories of hope and love.

"It is only Tesver and I who think that." Chuluun's great stony face, wide with wrinkles, betrayed nothing. "He has heard from the seabirds that there is fresh change across the water. I do not know how far we can trust such rumours – second-hand, third-hand, or more – or how reliable the messengers, but I do have hope. I have always hoped that one day we can return to Gazar, and restore it to its former glory, and *improve* it. Tesver thinks I am a fool, but he trusts the birds. His ability to use Bird magic is strong, like Iwizadi and the other masters from history."

"You really believe it could be time now? What about Aisling? What about Peter? What if we choose not to go?" Khuch knew his culture's laws. He knew it was his duty to follow his father should he choose to travel back to Gazar. He knew that when Chuluun said it was time, he would have to go across the sea to a homeland he did not know, and he would have to leave behind any thoughts of Aisling. And he knew that in the future it would be his stories full of nostalgia for a lost home and a lost love. The penalty for staying behind would be banishment from Khun culture and Gazar for all his life.

"I will not decide this quickly. We will know when the time is right. It might not be soon, but we will know." Maybe Chuluun could tell why his announcement had upset his son, but he said nothing to address his concern. He worried for his friends too, of course. Peter was like a brother and Aisling a daughter, but his immediate concern was those who came from Gazar. Peter and Aisling had no duty to Gazar, no obligation to follow, although he was sure they would if they were there when he made the decision.

A sparrow landed on a rotting log near Chuluun and spoke to him.

"Tesver has news, he is in the usual place," the sparrow chirped. Chuluun thanked the sparrow, and slowly turned his great bulk to go to Tesver. Khuch followed. Their conversation was over.

The usual place was a dense area of bushes about two hundred metres from the main camp up a hill. From there they had a view down into a valley, untouched by humans. Full of life. Like everything else in the area, it was soggy from the recent heavy rain. Tesver's meeting place was darker and greener than anywhere else nearby, and smelt faintly of animal waste mixed in with the strong freshness of vegetation. It seemed as though he had chosen the area of densest life in the whole forest, as if the Mishkash itself had drawn him by some magic to that very spot. It was rumoured that magic was strongest where life was strongest.

They heard him before they saw him. Tesver was standing amongst some old, wet trees, his long hair falling matted around his shoulders, his clothes ragged and covered in twigs and leaves and bird droppings. He camouflaged so well into the forest that they would not have noticed him had he not spoken. His skin had taken on a quality of tree bark as his spirit moved deeper towards Bird magic with time and practice. As he stood there, birds flitted all about him, some landing on his head, shoulders, hands. He stood in the middle of a strong beam of morning light that made its way obliquely through the canopy. He looked ethereal standing there, silhouetted in the beam over the backdrop of the lush green valley, as birds moved peacefully this way and that, and spores drifted upwards on a breeze, visible only in the beam.

"I have good news from the swallows," he announced as they approached. "Kraka has made contact with Orn, who has agreed to assist. He will extend his range to cover the skies over the Capital, and search for Aisling and our lost Khun." Chuluun and Khuch came to a stop opposite him, a few arms' lengths away. Khun felt uncomfortable with anything much closer.

"This is excellent news, Tesver," Chuluun replied. Khuch shuffled a little on the spot, knowing it was not his place to lead this conversation. He could only listen during important meetings at which Chuluun was present. The eldest family member was the voice of all that family.

"Yes. But there is a condition." Tesver rotated his head to the left so that it was slanted down with his ear over his shoulder. His eyes were bright yellow like an owl in that moment. "There is danger over the Capital and he is reluctant to fly there. In return for help he has asked for all birds to pledge allegiance to him, which Kraka accepted. This will disrupt our communication network and create spies and distrust."

"I think we had no choice," Chuluun admitted, with a hint of disappointment.

"Perhaps not."

"He is our only hope now."

"No, there is more hope from the sea." Tesver stroked the feathers on a sparrow that landed on his finger. "I have news from a gull named Mafur, who has spoken to a Gazari sea eagle named Haforn. Haforn says the soldiers are sailing east from Gazar. They are leaving, more boats every day."

"And you trust this rumour?" Chuluun was still like a rock and could have camouflaged himself as a piece of the hill.

Only Khuch looked out of place as he fidgeted with a piece of loose fabric in his pocket.

"It is no rumour. The time approaches."

"Perhaps."

"We have lived without hope for sixteen years. It is time to trust in good news."

"Do not let your impatience create false hope."

"Impatience! Have we not been patient enough these sixteen years? And my hope is built on trust. I trust the birds more than I trust some Khun! It is you Chuluun, who has lost hope!"

"I have hope."

"Then believe that what Haforn reports is true. Trust the birds. We should be going east back to the shores, not waiting here for the pride of an eagle to betray us!"

"Do not let your hope make you gullible. Do you not trust Orn?"

"He cares for Orn only. I place more trust in the gulls."

"Perhaps. But we are desperate. I do hope. I never stopped hoping. Sixteen years later we are still looking for the lost Khun. Sixteen years later we are still listening for news of Gazar. It is the other Khun I worry for. They talk of Gazar, but they have no hope of returning."

"We will return."

"Yes. When the time is right."

"When the time is right."

"Keep listening for news from Mafur. If he is reliable, we will take his word as truth."

"I trust him to report accurately." This seemed to satisfy Chuluun and he nodded solemnly.

"Then what of Haforn? Can he be a spy? Can his news be true?"

"All we have is hope."

"That is why we need more sources. We need to hear about Gazar from more birds. I will believe the rumours when we have news from more birds. Not sooner."

"It is true that messages can be miscommunicated or forgotten by even the best messenger."

"Or lies can be spread," Chuluun warned.

"Lies can be spread." Tesver had a habit of repeating sentences mysteriously, a bit like a talking parrot.

"But other than Gazari sea eagles, what birds can travel such long distances? How can the news reach us if not for them?" Khuch interjected, knowingly breaking convention. Chuluun made no movement, and the conversation continued.

"You are right," Tesver nodded. "There is a flaw in the network. All news from Gazar must pass through the sea eagles. And all news *to* Gazar, for that matter."

"Have you sent news to Gazar?" Chuluun asked with a rare betrayal of his concern evident in his voice.

"No. I speak in theory."

"Good. You know it could lead to them finding us." His voice returned to its usual rumbling quality. His voice commanded respect, despite its slow pace and low volume.

"I am aware of the situation." But Khuch was worried. He had not given any thought to that idea and worried now that any careless Khun could accidentally betray them. Including if one of Tesver's messengers made a mistake.

"Is there other news?"

"Not yet. Kraka begins her flight home, I will give her rest for some days when she arrives. We now must wait for news from Orn."

"And Mafur, or some other bird."

"Some other bird…"

"What should we do about the tension among the other

Khun?" Chuluun asked, hoping that Tesver would have some useful suggestions. In sixteen years Chuluun had not had to face so much dissent and indecision.

"You mean between the ones who will wait endlessly to be led and the ones who will search aimlessly in the wrong direction? I am the only one who is acting now to do anything." Tesver spoke with a sudden venom.

"You know they are not adept at Bird magic like you. You cannot be so harsh in your speech."

"They do nothing but argue."

"These are your family and friends and neighbours."

"My family is lost somewhere on this continent."

"And mine is dead, except my son."

"I can spend more than sixteen years searching. I will spend six hundred if that's how long it takes."

"What is more important to you? To find them or return to Gazar? What if the news from home reaches us before they are found?"

"I refuse to give up hope." Tesver replied enigmatically, trying to avoid answering the question. Chuluun saw through his ruse and pressed him.

"But what will you choose, if the opportunity to return means abandoning our search?" The tension was so strong, Khuch could feel his muscles clenching, his jaw tight. He thought of Aisling and was desperate to hear Tesver say he would wait for his family. If Tesver said he would wait, maybe Chuluun would listen and wait with him, and maybe Khuch would have time to find Aisling. Tesver did not speak for a long while, trying to think of the best thing to say. A colourful little parrot landed on his outstretched arm, and cooing, he spoke to it instead of to Chuluun directly, as if it were easier for him to speak to birds than people.

"What if they have forgotten me? Look at me. I am old.

I am half bird, half tree now. I am no Khun. They will not recognise me."

"You are Khun. You are from Gazar. Clean yourself, and they will remember you." The intensity of Chuluun's gaze never faltered.

"I will lose the trust of the birds. They are fickle. Bird is who I am now. You know there is no turning back on the path to mastery." He raised his arm and the parrot flew into the endless forest.

"You are bird and Khun."

"I would choose Gazar," Tesver suddenly declared. "But I fear the choice is not mine to make." The words stung Khuch, as he saw Chuluun put a giant hand on Tesver's shoulder, ignoring the wetness of his rags covered in bird droppings. They held eye contact for a long time.

"We will go together, when the time is right."

"When the time is right."

Khuch knew that it was not part of Khun culture to hesitate when it was time for action. If Tesver said it was time to go, there would be no argument. He had to hope that they found Aisling first.

"Will the others follow us?" Khuch asked, as the conversation seemed to end, but already knowing the answer.

"Follow us." Tesver said simply, in his parrot-like way.

"Follow us." Chuluun agreed, with surety. Chuluun almost looked to be smiling peacefully, hopefully, but it was hard to tell with his big solid face. A knot grew in Khuch's stomach, troubled with anxiety and the thought that at any moment his personal quest to find Aisling would be called to an end. It wasn't fair, but that's how it always was with Khun. That's how it was with Chuluun especially: he was their leader by general consent, and if he said it was time, it was time.

Every day was spent waiting anxiously for news from the birds, as the Khun grew more and more restless. Chuluun was having a hard time keeping the group calm while they waited for information. They were surprised by how used to living in their settlement their had become and were eager to find a new place to live. Khuch hoped that news of Aisling would come before news of Gazar, but he felt deep inside that waiting was the wrong thing to do. He had to act, or risk losing her.

"I can't keep waiting like this." He decided to confront Chuluun.

"You will wait. We are strong together." As usual, Chuluun was firm in his speech. No matter how old Khuch grew, he would always feel childish around Chuluun.

"I need to find Aisling. She is Khun too." Taking matters into his own hands would mean either the Khun reject him from returning, or punish him severely. He needed Chuluun's approval before leaving to find her.

"The birds will find her."

"There are places birds can't search."

"I have also thought this." Chuluun rose from where he was sitting and moved his great bulk towards the central fire pit, staring at its empty centre.

"Then let me go."

"I cannot."

"Why not?"

"Other Khun rely on our solidarity." He continued staring at the pit. "If you go, they will also want to separate. Maybe never see us again. Maybe never return to Gazar together."

"You want to return to Gazar together?" Khuch was suddenly angry. "What about Peter? What about Aisling?

Are they not Khun too?"

"I have also thought this."

"And?"

"They are Khun. But they are also from this land."

"So?"

"They do not belong on Gazar," Chuluun spoke softly with shame in his voice.

"Do they not belong with us?" Khuch was yelling now. He had never yelled at his father. He had never even shown anger of any degree. It was confronting for both of them but it was too late to stop.

"We wait! Together!" Chuluun was yelling back.

"We can't go without them!" Khuch growled. Chuluun was aware that some other Khun were pretending not to listen and with an effort lowered his voice. The last thing he wanted was for others to believe he was planning to leave in secret with Khuch.

"We wait."

"It's been long enough." Khuch also lowered his voice to a near-whisper. "The birds are failing. I will find Aisling myself."

"No. We must wait for news first."

"And what then?"

"Depends on the news."

"What if the birds find her?"

"Depends."

"On what?"

"If it is time to go to Gazar."

"So, you will choose the blind hope of returning to Gazar over the reality of finding those who belong with us? What if Gazar is still at war? What if you are wrong?"

"Khuch Chaddhal," Chuluun sat on a log and stared at Khuch, his black eyes tiny in his enormous head, yet somehow fierce, "sixteen years we have thought only of our return."

"And my whole life I grew up with those two."

"Peter is a true friend. He is a true Khun…"

"And Aisling?"

"She is also Khun…"

"But you still say they don't belong on Gazar." Khuch stared at a leaf on the ground in front of him. It looked crunchy but he knew it would be soft from the rain. "And neither do I."

"You were born on Gazar, Gazar is your home."

"My home is here with them."

"Not possible."

At that moment a squawk announced Kraka's arrival and they all saw her fly towards Tesver's grove.

"We must hear this." Chuluun stood up and started walking, Khuch following. "Her news will determine our action. Kraka will end this discussion."

They climbed the hill and as usual saw Tesver's ethereal form silhouetted against the valley behind him. He held Kraka on an outstretched arm in front of him and the sight gave Khuch a chill. Tesver's power of Bird magic went beyond anything the Khun had known from any storytelling night. There were no stories of Bird masters.

"Kraka tells me she has met with many birds," Tesver began to translate. Even though Chuluun and Khuch could both talk to birds, they found it hard to keep up with Kraka's speed and natural speech patterns. "She has met with Orn and he helps us, though not without complaint."

"This we know."

"Quiet. She has met with many birds on the way, and detoured to the edge of the forest. There is report that Peter has reached the edge of the forest near Darvozasi."

"Darvozasi?" Chuluun wondered. "He must be going to the Capital."

"Probably. There is no other reason to go there. He seeks his daughter," Tesver assumed, and Khuch looked hopeful. This was the best news they had received in days. He looked to Chuluun for confirmation of his hope, but his dad continued to stare at Tesver. "Orn has enlisted pigeons in the Capital."

"Pigeons!" Chuluun baulked. "They are unreliable! We are better going ourselves!"

"Yes, even Kraka laughed when she heard. But friends are limited in the city."

"I suppose so."

"And Orn has famously good judgement."

"That is true."

"Kraka has also heard from some gulls in the north. They know of the gull named Mafur and say he can be trusted. They do not know Haforn the sea eagle, their lives have not crossed before."

"So, we can trust Mafur. That means-"

"Yes."

"The soldiers are really leaving Gazar."

"So it would seem."

"This means the next news from Mafur is our signal to go."

"No!" Khuch cried. Chuluun and Tesver looked at him, and he realised he had spoken out of turn.

"I already told you, you cannot go alone," Chuluun said in his usual way.

"Young Khuch Chaddhal," Tesver addressed Khuch directly, taking Khuch off guard, and staring into Tesver's beady, birdlike eyes, Khuch felt completely disarmed, yet awestruck as if witnessing the confluence of all life and magic itself. Tesver really had become half bird, and his gaze revealed the fierce intelligence of a bird of prey. "You wish to save the girl Aisling."

"Yes."

"Why?" The question was heavy, but asked without judgement.

"She belongs with us. She is as much Khun as I am."

"Belongs with you, you mean." Khuch was embarrassed but held captive by Tesver's penetrating, inquisitive gaze. "Many years ago, when Bird magic chose me, I didn't know how little I knew. About Bird magic, about nature, the world, Khun, everything. The birds have changed my perspective on everything." Chuluun and Khuch listened intently, feeling as though they were about to hear something important. Tesver broke his stare with Khuch and turned to face Chuluun. "Let the boy search for her."

"Tesver! He cannot!" Chuluun was furious at the suggestion. Tesver however, was unflinching.

"Birds have taught me about many things, and I continue to learn from them," he said cryptically. "Many migrate, even Kraka. Many mate for life, like Orn." Khuch was embarrassed again at that suggestion, so factually stated.

"Migrate…" Chuluun pondered.

"Khuch Chaddhal will have two homes."

"How you can say that? Gazar is the only home for Khun!" Chuluun bellowed. "Khun are not Birds!"

"I didn't know how little I knew," Tesver repeated mysteriously in a voice that floated out over the cliff edge, and strangely Chuluun's temper subsided, as if carried away by the wind.

The three men stood in silence for a long time, each looking at nothing in particular. Tesver and Kraka cooed at each other as if in love. She preened herself, still resting on his arm, still held out from his body this whole time, solid like a tree branch.

"Okay," Chuluun eventually said, breaking the silence. "Khuch Chaddhal will go. He will be as a migratory Bird from now." He put a hand on Khuch's shoulder and spoke softly. "You will find the girl Aisling and the father Peter, who are both friends and Khun. We still stay here to wait for news from Mafur, and when the time is right, we will sail. We will not wait for you. Make sure you are back in time."

"How will I know the way?"

"Let the birds guide you," Tesver chimed in.

"Thank you both. All," Khuch corrected himself, addressing Kraka. She stared at him, not showing any sign of acknowledgement.

"The Capital is far from here. You must not use magic outside the forest. You are illegal in this country and they will arrest you. May Gazar protect you on your hopeless journey, and may you realise that Gazar is your only home." Chuluun farewelled Khuch and walked back towards his tent, shaking his head.

"The journey will be hard for you," Tesver said with his unblinking predatory stare. "Kraka will go with you to the forest edge. The fastest way to the Capital is with the police."

"Thank you." Khuch began running south, aiming to reach the nearest road within the next day, ignoring Tesver's veiled suggestion that he get himself arrested.

"It is not wise," Kraka said to Tesver when they were alone again.

"Nothing is." And he shook her off into the air to follow Khuch.

Chapter 6

Since agreeing to Kraka's request, Orn had been bombarded with smaller birds trying to visit him and pledge allegiance. But he didn't need their assurances, he was by birth the sky king. And now he was starting to regret the condition he imposed upon Kraka. It would have been better to just agree to help the search and go back to his normal life when it was over. Instead, his solitude was constantly being interrupted and he could only blame himself for needing to show off his pride to Kraka. A fool he had been. But... there was something about Tesver that reminded him of his own royalty among birds.

Maybe when it was over, he would find that damned Tesver and deliver the news personally. Either he wouldn't find the girl, and spend the rest of his life fending off well-wishers and longing for peace and quiet, or he would find the girl and things could go back to normal. And who knows if she would be dead or alive? Better to just get on with it. The sooner this was over the better.

He launched from his remote clifftop and soared above the country. He had lived a long time already, nearly two hundred years, and had seen the gradual degradation of nature radiating from that disgusting blue and grey lump in the south. The Capital they called it. That's where Kraka wanted him to go. *But why him?* He had asked. Because sire, you are the fastest, strongest and wisest in the skies, you can see where we cannot.

He shouldn't have agreed. It was a fool's quest to search for a girl hidden in the immense sprawl of man-made concrete mountains amidst that blinding blue. But he felt generous that day and just wanted her to go away. Now he regretted even waking up that day.

Why not send the pigeons to do it? They love the human people and feed from their cities. He questioned her. Because sire, the pigeons cannot be trusted to remember any details. That was true, he agreed. The pigeons are famously forgetful.

After launching into the sky, he played for a while by touching the clouds then bursting through them into the Upper Sky. The view was always surreal from there, and he knew not many of the lesser birds could reach him. It was a peaceful place. But he needed the Lower Sky to see the world. He was always fascinated by how he could land at his nest at night in the Lower Sky, but by morning the clouds had moved it to the Upper Sky. Most mornings he awoke to see the sea of clouds rolling beneath his great mountain. It was nearly too high for Kraka, but she managed to reach him, out of breath. He assumed she was lost, or just begging for protection against some other bird who was getting too aggressive. Birds rarely visited him before Kraka, and now he couldn't get rid of them fast enough. *This is a human problem. Why did I agree?*

He flew down through a gap in the clouds, preferring to go around them than through them because the moisture felt bad on his feathers, weighing him down. He oriented towards the distant Capital on the horizon and settled into a relaxed glide, just beneath the ceiling of clouds. He could probably cover that distance in an hour or two if he didn't stop.

Solitude was the secret to the eagles' long reign, something other lesser birds didn't, or couldn't understand. Always pestering him. That was the reason his ancestors moved higher and higher up the cliff until other birds had trouble reaching him. No lowly pigeon could ever find a way up there by accident. *And if it did, it wouldn't remember the way down*! He laughed to himself.

And the humans. His father told him all about them, and he witnessed it himself as they built and built. Many centuries ago, they started arriving. At first, they constructed little wooden huts, they blended in with nature. Then one of them stumbled upon a hole in the ground and climbed out with armfuls of raw blue earthblood. Noi, they called it. They all went mad, and quickly their construction became larger, until it no longer resembled nature at all. *The earthblood pulses from all their hideous things. They should never have taken it out. Tesver at least knows this much.* Orn thought about this for a long time, but could not work out why Tesver lived in hiding if he was the only human who understood the world the right way. *Do humans not value wisdom?* Maybe that's why he agreed to help; he knew Tesver was not like all the others. He was one of the Earth People. Humans, he dismissed. Why don't they just leave the earthblood in the ground? Huge tall buildings in the Capital, bleeding blue into the air. *It is sickening.*

Orn's father had seen the Capital rise from a loose collection of huts to a small village. Orn had seen it grow into a concrete forest. He had also seen the great holes appear in the land. The places where they were opening the earth's skin to harvest its earthblood. *Sickening.* Too quickly, he witnessed as the Capital expanded through the wild territory, turning trees to dust and dirt to concrete as more and more people lived there. Now it was many thousands, or tens of thousands, maybe more.

But smiling to himself he felt satisfied in knowing there would always be just one sky king.

Even those great floating houses, emanating the blue of earthblood couldn't compete with his speed, his effortless grace, his agility through the air, his hunting prowess. They couldn't fly as high as he could, and they could never reach his nest at the boundary where the Lower Sky and Upper Sky meet to perform their daily dance.

The Capital loomed closer and Orn was surprised to see it spread further into the horizon than he expected. He avoided this part of the sky because of the humans, and it had been many years since he had visited. It was built in a flat plain with no good mountains for nesting. He remembered how his father taught him not to trust them at any cost. So why now was he helping the wizard? He was rescuing humans from other humans. *What madness!* The blue from the Capital glowed around the clock, and Orn found it distorted his vision unpleasantly. *Better to just go and get this over with.*

Still flying at the upper limits of the Lower Sky, he was able to see far enough to make out the people far below. Yet the sprawling city and its swarming mass of humans troubled him more and more with each second that passed. The task of finding one girl hidden in this city – possibly hidden, for they didn't know for certain – seemed impossible. What's more, the only place to hide was in the Upper Sky, and that depended on there being enough clouds. It was dangerous. But he was the sky king.

I will know if she is here. I can almost feel her already. Strange, it feels like the place I am destined to go. He remembered his dreams in which a faceless wizard talked to him about the future. *Is this part of Tesver's plan? Is this a trick?*

Orn directed his flight towards the tallest building in the city, which happened to be the Leader's residence and also housed the government offices where Aisling was hidden from the world. He knew he could not glide forever and he would need to rest eventually. The highest place should be the safest. From there he could direct other birds to spread out and report back. Pigeons most likely, a crow if he was lucky. The roof of the building was flat and held one of the great floating houses and a radio tower. It was not ideal, and he could easily be seen if someone came out from the little door, but it would have to do. He intended for this to be a quick mission.

In broad daylight, he descended from the cloud ceiling and quickly spotted a semi-hidden little nook in which to nest for a few days. He let out a cry on the way down, loud enough that any bird in the city could hear:

"Greetings all birds of the Capital! I am Orn, the sky king, come to seek out a person hidden here. I request your help at its highest point."

And landing on the tower, he waited, preening his feathers some, and enjoying the comfort of rest after such a long flight. Surveying the polluted landscape, he plotted how to go about the search. Pigeons were loyal and trustworthy, but forgetful and moronic.

A handful of pigeons landed on the rooftop and started milling about, pecking at the floor. Orn flew down from the tower to greet them.

"Thank you for coming."

"Hail! Sky king!" one bleated.

"We pledge allegiance!" another hooted.

"Yes, thank you all," Orn tried to be patient. "I am looking for a girl. A young woman. She is named Aisling.

She is captive in this city. She is one of the Earth People."

"Hail!" a third pigeon joined in amidst the cooing of the others.

"Will you help me find her?" Orn asked directly to the slowly growing group of pigeons.

"Find who?"

"Go! Find the magic girl Aisling! Find the Earth People!" He lost his patience and shooed them all off the edge. As they flew off the building, down to get lost in the various streets, alleys, windowsills of the great city beneath them, he could still hear shouts of "Hail! Sky king!" growing fainter and fainter.

I fear this is a lost cause, he thought. *The wizard Tesver will be disappointed. Those idiots have probably already forgotten the task. They will show up here tomorrow with no idea what I'm talking about. Why am I even doing this?*

It is for the Earth People. We assumed they were all lost. Orn had heard rumours of Tesver living somewhere in the north-east near the uncrossable sea, with a small group of other Earth People, but had not investigated. He knew that Tesver had been sending messages with various birds and was aware that he, Orn, was the sky king. Orn never felt the need to see with his own eyes. The rumours were enough for him to know that there were still Earth People living in the world, and that was enough.

His father had met an Earth Person once in a small town in the far west that smelt strongly of magic, in the time before the humans dug their great pits in the ground, hundreds of years before. He told Orn about the man, whose name is forgotten, and their magical relationship. They had been very close friends and the wizard had taught Orn's father much magic. But Orn had not heard of any others until only about fifteen years earlier, when some birds began chirping about the old wizard Tesver in the north-east, in the far reaches of the Mishkash, a short flight from the great sea. It was a good thing, he thought. Best to leave the Earth People alone. Still, the questions remained to Orn: where had they been for all those years? Why did they reappear now?

Chapter 7

"Magic research isn't as glamorous as you might imagine," Miss Morris explained as they walked through the lab and into a small glass-walled office at the opposite end of the room to where they had come in. She shut the door behind them and offered Aisling a seat. "There was a time when the media thought they were getting exclusive stories from the various ministries, and tried to publish sensational stories about the whole thing, trying to generate some kind of public outrage but- Coffee? Tea?" She was standing by a Noi-powered kettle behind her desk.

"Tea please."

"-but since nobody could prove that The Department exists within the government, the media outlets refused to publish anything. So they didn't look crazy, you understand? Milk? Sugar?"

"Yes please."

"But naturally a few papers didn't care for their reputation as much as they did for a story and tried to make us look like mad scientists in here, performing dangerous human experiments. Creating monsters like Doctor Frankenstein, creating magical super soldiers." She sipped on an espresso loudly, choosing to pause on that image. "Needless to say, those media outlets were either silenced or are now looked at as nothing more than loudspeakers for conspiracy theories. One of them is actually doing quite well now as a fictional tabloid, very popular among the crackpots in the city. Voice, I think it was called."

Looking out through the glass walls at the lab, Aisling could see nothing that looked dangerous. Some scientists were sleepily working at desks surrounded by mountains of papers with coffees and crosswords holding their attention. One woman sat in a cubicle with huge headphones on and her eyes closed, moving her mouth constantly. There was no decoration to suggest magical research, no whiteboards, not even anything to indicate the names or positions of the people working there. It was a very boring room, filled with desks, papers, folders, filing cabinets, a few fake plants. The walls and floor and ceiling were the same boring material she remembered from the cell. The only interesting thing she could see was another glass-walled room adjacent to Miss Morris' office, which had a microphone in it and on the lab side of the glass, some desks positioned such that they could be sat at while looking into the room.

"Since it's your first day, we will need to go through some routine tasks together. You have your welcome booklet there? Good. Now towards the back there are some forms for you to read and sign. The first one is for your banking details so that we can pay you."

"I don't have a bank account." Aisling looked ashamed.

"Dear child, you really came from nowhere, didn't you? Never mind with that one for now then, we will set you up with State bank today. The next form there is for you to agree that we will pay you a standard government pension unless you nominate another fund… which I don't suppose you will."

Aisling was confused by all this and let Miss Morris talk.

She flicked through the pages in front of her absently and waiting for the research to begin. She was nervous about it, but whereas forms and cities confused her, magic felt natural. On the other hand, magic was what got her into this situation to begin with, and she was nervous to perform anything for others to see.

"This last form is consent to undergo a medical check before we begin, and you agree that the results will be shared only by relevant people. It is a requirement of the job to have a baseline medical check, and a routine check every year. You can read the full terms here on this page."

"When do you want me to do magic?"

"Very soon, when all the paperwork is completed. Then I will introduce you to our research team and they can explain what they are doing and what they are looking for."

Aisling was a bit more excited about that. The forms she was looking at meant nothing to her. In her home with the Khun there was no need for money. They grew an abundance of food thanks to magic, and any other material goods could be built or repaired using local materials and magic. Her dad kept some money from his old life, and she remembered he needed to use some in the city to buy water. Whenever someone was sick, either Chuluun or another lady called Eryyl would just use a Healing magic spell. Eryyl could heal anything. Such a foreign concept... money was a strange thing. Banks, contracts, medical check-ups, pensions... it was like another language... she wanted to start participating in the research so she could use magic again and feel herself.

After signing everything and understanding little of it, Aisling was led across the lab to where a middle-aged scientist was sitting behind a tower of folders with papers strewn all around him. He looked very athletic, and like he spent a lot of time outdoors. He greeted Miss Morris warmly. "Daphne!" he called with a big grin that showed off his perfect teeth. If it weren't for his tiny sunken eyes surrounded by enormous dark circles, he would have been very handsome. Aisling found herself unsure of whether she wanted to stare at his creepy eyes or his dashing smile. It was confusing to look at him.

"In this office, it's Miss Morris, thank you Doctor Young."

"Of course, Ma'am."

"I'd like you to meet Miss Hargreaves, our newest employee."

"Pleasure."

"She has just joined as a Participant."

"Oh terrific!" The Doctor's voice lit up, almost enough to brighten his dark circles. "How exciting for you. And for us, naturally. We don't often get Participants. What's your name?"

"Aisling."

"I'm Kurt. What's your speciality?"

"Huh?"

"How did they find you?"

"Oh uh, a man saw me making water by acci-"

"Water magic! How delightful!" Turning back to Miss Morris, he asked, "I'll be taking her for a medical, then?"

"Indeed"

"Alrighty then. Easy peasy. Aisling, if you'll just follow me to the consultation room. I'm sure we should be letting Miss Morris get back to her work now."

"Thank you, Doctor Young."

Aisling followed the enthusiastic man out of the lab and into the first room across the windowless corridor. The elevator beckoned her freedom as they passed by, but she recalled Miss Morris explaining that her card could not be used to exit. As they walked, the Doctor babbled away, more to himself than to her.

"Water magic you say? That's very interesting magic, very hard to contain. We had a participant some time ago who was quite adept at it and it was a pleasure to watch. She could make all kinds of delightful shapes in the air, make bubbles, make it rain for just one person. She could send tiny storm clouds out to follow anyone she wanted to piss off. It was quite funny actually. So, what can you do with it? Do you know any other magics?"

"Uh-"

"Oh, we'll get to it, be patient Kurt, we'll see soon when we start work, pick up where she left. Water magic... incredible stuff. Aisling, I should explain that every room in the building is wrapped in an anti-magic field except for the labs, where we need magic, obviously. Go ahead, try something now. Go on! See? You can't use it here. That was a puzzle to set up, believe me! Anyway, here's the consultation room. Go ahead and stand just there against that chart, I'm going to take some measurements. Height?"

"I don't-"

"One sixty. Weight?"

"I-"

"Only fifty-two. Age?"

"Sixteen."

"Thank you. I have to take your blood pressure too, just going to wrap this around your arm now, that's it. Anti-magic is quite amazing too don't you think? That's the other side of the coin. I find it so amazing. No no, it's supposed to feel tight, don't worry. Anti-magic can only prevent specific magics, so if a new magic is discovered we have to develop an anti-magic just for it and then go and update all the fields. Tiring work but so rewarding. What other magics do you know?"

"Um-"

"I know a few Water spells and a few Light spells but nothing like what you Participants can do. The things I've seen in this lab! You wouldn't believe some of the spells! Beyond your wildest dreams! I need a blood sample for analysis. This can be uncomfortable but it's over quick. Okay count back with me: three, two-"

"Ah!"

"And hold it there, that's it, nice and easy. I'll send this for testing and I think we're all good to go. Any illness in your past?"

"No."

"Participants are always so healthy. How often do you exercise?"

"Exercise?"

"Of course, no you are fit. Physical lifestyle. You know, I'm not supposed to say this but I think it's the Noi makes us unhealthy. You all have ways to avoid illness. Amazing. It's really Healing magic is the most interesting to me. But it could make my whole job irrelevant, you know?"

"Um-"

"Imagine it! I spent years and years studying and training to be a doctor, only to be able to look after someone worse than the Participants can do with a little Healing magic. Makes me think it was a wasted effort. Do you know any Healing magic?"

"A little."

"Oh really? You have to show me! Wait not here, you can't, the field. When we get back to the lab, we'll learn all about your abilities. Healing magic… amazing. Any illness in your family?"

"I don't think so."

"Good, good. Any other magic users?"

"Um, no." Aisling swallowed saliva and hoped the doctor couldn't tell she was lying. If he did, he didn't pause to dwell on it.

"Ever get hurt while using magic?"

"No."

"How often do you use magic?"

"Um, a lot."

"A lot. Yeah, most Participants say that. Last lady said she didn't know how to operate a Noi-powered kettle! Can you believe that? Just imagine! Something so basic, it's a whole other world. I admit I'm a bit jealous of you though, living without Noi. It's pretty expensive now you know?"

"No."

"No, of course you don't know. Why should you? Lucky you. Anyway, that's about it in here, we should get going. Eleven o'clock, right on time. I bet you're dying to use magic again, aren't you? Not to worry, won't be long. Let's go. Back to Miss Morris now, I'll have the results of your blood test back this afternoon, but of course you'll be perfectly healthy. Participants always are. Amazing."

"Thank you."

Kurt and Aisling entered Miss Morris' office, Kurt saying "knock knock" as he paused at the door for a second.

"All looking good Daph- Miss Morris. We can get into the good stuff now."

"Thank you, Doctor Young." Turning to Aisling, she stood up, picked up a folder of papers and gestured towards the door. "Let's go."

Kurt led Aisling through a door that was in the wall between Miss Morris' office and the weird glass-walled booth. Inside was a small room with clothing hanging up, and another door leading into the booth.

"Let's get to work. Go ahead and change into that white lab suit there, and when you're done make your way into the 'magic room'. I'll be outside with Miss Morris, keeping an eye on things and giving you directions."

Aisling did as she was told, and a minute later she was dressed in a body suit made from thick, stiff fabric. She opened the door into the booth and her eyes took a moment to adjust to the brightness. From the inside, the walls were reflective and she could not see out into the lab. Kurt's voice came through a speaker.

"Just go and stand in front of that microphone there in the centre." She took a few nervous steps, not sure where to look. Everything was polished white and sterile. There were some drainage grates at the edge of the room and she assumed they must be for Water magic. A small table hosted some glasses and an empty jug. "The whole room is cutting-edge technology. There are sensitive devices all over it that measure everything: your body heat, your brain waves, blood flow, atmospheric changes, everything. The room is incredible technology. Cost a fortune. Anyway, the microphone is there for you to contact us because the walls are totally soundproof. Just give it a test would you, make sure it's all working."

"Test," Aisling spoke quietly.

"All good, I heard you just fine. Miss Morris is going to take over now and we'll run through some basic tests to see what level of magic you're capable of."

"Hello Miss Hargreaves." Her voice seemed so cold and grey after having listened to Kurt babbling away for the last half an hour. "We are going to start you off with Water magic, since that was what we first learned about you, and happens to be our current focus."

"What am I supposed to do?"

"The first thing we want to see is you fill one of the glasses over there with water. Like what the witness saw in Nelasive. Take your time."

Aisling went over to the glass, and hovering her hand over it for a second, it rapidly filled with water and spilled over the edge. She had some trouble stopping the spell, but brought it under control. Outside, Kurt and Miss Morris looked at each other impressed with her ease. Speaking to each other with the microphone off, Miss Morris said:

"She is much stronger than the last Participant. She might be the one we've been looking for. Don't hold back. I have to speak to the Minister for Defence."

"Yes ma'am."

At first, Aisling found it weird to perform magic on command, and she found that in the confined environment of the observation room her spells were not as powerful as normal, and were harder to do. That didn't seem to bother Kurt, who was perpetually amazed after every test. On her first day she was asked to perform a simple Water spell dozens, maybe hundreds of times, filling various containers. She didn't understand why, but Kurt assured her that repetition was an important part of science. It also got easier the more she did it, so she didn't mind the repetition too much. Meanwhile, the sensitive instruments in the room measured everything about Aisling: her blood pressure, the room temperature, humidity, and all sorts of things she asked about but couldn't remember. Kurt said it was also important for science that they know all these things. Aisling was learning that the experiments were less about magic and more about collecting huge amounts of information. Not at all what she expected. On that first day she only performed one Water spell, over and over again. *At this rate it will take my whole life to get through all my spells*, she thought. The slow pace and the emphasis on learning before acting did not resonate with her personality, but she saw the benefit over time and it was almost enjoyable.

When the working day was over, Miss Morris showed Aisling the way back up to her living area. During the day, the kitchen had been fully stocked with food and drink: the sorts of things they liked in the Capital were not what she was used to. Almost all the food, even the vegetables and fruit, came wrapped in plastic and looked so uniform. There were three apples that looked exactly the same. Back in her home, the vegetables the Khun grew all looked different. They were tastier too; these ones in her new kitchen tasted bland.

She took an apple and stood by the huge window, eating it while looking out. After the excitement of the morning and the confusion about what all the people were doing and the fancy equipment, it had been an uneventful, and very repetitive day. She wondered if she would have an opportunity to freestyle spells like she normally did or if every day would be so… restricted. Endlessly chewing on the tasteless apple, she felt trapped.

There was an unusual movement of pigeons near the building opposite her, which she had a good view of from her high vantage point. There was a small flock of them that seemed to be fighting over each other to look into every window of the building. *How bizarre.* She watched them make their way past every window before moving to the next building and had a strange feeling that this was something she should remember.

Bird magic.

Someone or something was compelling the pigeons to move like that, she was sure of it. They would never do that on their own. But what were they doing? Were they looking for something? She thought of her home and all the people she had been taken from. She remembered Khuch's instruction to learn Bird magic and felt so angry and sad and frustrated at the same time.

"How am I supposed to learn Bird magic in here?!" she threw the apple core across the room roughly at the kitchen. "How can I continue to live here with no magic?" And she sank down to the floor in the corner against the window, watching the erratic movements of the distant pigeons making their way to the next building along. She wanted to cry but couldn't.

That night she had the same dream as always, but this time, the man spoke to her. He had Kurt's voice.

"Every room in the building is wrapped in an anti-magic field," he said, Kurt's words from that morning echoing around the room a few times.

"I know."

"So, you have two options." The man's voice was not Kurt's any more. It was the same mellifluous voice she had come to associate with him. This voice did not echo, but cut through the dream space and demanded her attention. "You can leave the field, or you can use a magic that has not been prevented."

"Like in the story."

"Exactly. When they locked me up, they did not know about Stone magic."

Aisling woke with a start. In all the years she had seen the man in her dreams, she had never had a clearer sign that he was Iwizadi. It was undeniable now. She was convinced that Iwizadi had talked to her and that he was real and still alive. He must be alive! The most powerful wizard in history! He must have found a way to create Dream magic, like how he made Stone magic. She wanted to cheer for his success, the way she would for an old friend.

It was the middle of the night, and rather than feel alone, or creeped out by the knowledge that Iwizadi was visiting or controlling her dreams, Aisling was heartened. She was formulating an escape plan and he wanted her to succeed. Maybe she could find a way to practice Light magic in private after all. What was it he said? Leave the anti-magic field, or use a magic that has not been prevented.

She did not stop to question why Iwizadi was helping her.

If every room is wrapped in an anti-magic field, she reasoned, then I just have to leave the rooms. She looked out the window. It could not open, and it had no balcony or ledge outside. Besides, it was terrifyingly high up. No, that couldn't be an option. It was not possible to leave via the window. There didn't seem to be any other openings in the walls or ceiling that she could explore and she put her frantic excitement aside for the night, thinking she would watch their route to the lab tomorrow carefully for any opportunity.

The other option was also a good idea. But how could she know which magics were blocked by the field? She knew Water magic was blocked, because it was the first magic she tried to use. Same with Fire magic because she couldn't heat her water with it. Light magic too, she knew, from when she learned to use the Noilamp beside the bed.

She looked at the Noiclock by the bed. It was after three in the morning. She should have been sleeping, but she was too excited and hopeful. Time. Time magic. She smiled uncontrollably for a moment before telling herself to be calm.

"Okay, let's try this."

Time magic was difficult, that was for sure. And

dangerous. The easiest Time spell she could think of performing was still incredibly difficult to perform. She went to the window and tried to see the pigeons flocking around the buildings in their weird way, but it was too late at night for them and too dark for her to see. She could see no birds or bats or anything to try the spell on. There was very little in the Capital to remind her of nature.

"Shit shit where are you all?"

It would have to wait until the morning.

But morning felt so far away and Aisling wasn't at all tired any more. There was always Stone magic that could make the morning come faster for her, but she hadn't ever learned to use it. In fact, most Khun thought it was just a fiction from the Iwizadi stories. None of them could do it. Same with Dream magic, since Chuluun had been unsuccessful in his attempts. Now Aisling was certain that it was real. It meant she was starting to learn Chuluun's limits.

Dream magic! That was the answer! It had worked within the anti-magic field so it must not be prevented! Well, maybe. She had received a Dream magic spell. Did the anti-magic field work to prevent magic in *both* directions in and out?

But she didn't know how to use Dream magic. Nobody did. Nobody except Iwizadi, and she could only see him when he cast a spell on her dreams. She began to lose heart, realising that her best opportunity to use unrestricted magic was completely out of her control.

Okay what else is there?

There was Matter magic: spells that could make objects appear, grow, disappear, or shrink. She sat on the bed and tried to calm her anxious mind, but with so many random thoughts flying in every direction it was impossible to reach the right sort of calmness needed to perform difficult spells.

She breathed in deeply, the way Chuluun had instructed when she and Peter first started learning from him. She held the breath in her lungs for a few seconds before slowly releasing it. While she held her breath her mind felt stiller, but as soon as she exhaled it started up again and she couldn't keep her thoughts quiet. *I have to relax.* She tried again. Breathing deeper this time and letting her arms drop to her sides on the bed, her feet flat on the floor in front of her. She stared at a blank patch of wall ahead of her.

This time when she slowly exhaled, her mind hesitated before trying to whip its thoughts into a flurry again. She continued breathing this way for several more breaths and the image of Chuluun entered her mind: his giant figure sitting perfectly still and balanced on his tiny stool at home. His face carved from stone. *How old was Chuluun?*

Thinking about his statue-like posture calmed her even more, and after another minute she finally felt ready to try a spell. It was silly, she hadn't needed to do this deliberate calming exercise for years, but being away from her home, a prisoner, away from Peter and Khuch was so stressful. She wished Khuch was with her to hold her hand again. She imagined the warm feeling of liquid calmness spreading all through her and she was ready to cast. It was that feeling that had got her through the first day of testing. She promised to tell him that if she ever saw him again.

She stood up and walked to the kitchen as if in a trance. She positioned an apple on the counter and stared at it expressionless with one hand over it, the way Chuluun always did. In a second, a smoky tendril extended from her palm and engulfed the apple. The smoke dissipated, leaving behind a much smaller apple, and the joy at having performed a Matter spell was strong enough to lift Aisling from her trance, flooding her mind with racing thoughts once again.

"So, they don't know about Matter magic."

And feeling like she finally had some ammunition to use against her captors, she crawled back into bed. Despite her excitement and swirling, anxious thoughts, she was asleep in a minute, although she did not dream of Iwizadi again that night.

At sunrise, natural light streamed into her bedroom. Aisling woke up feeling energised. 7:02 her Noiclock said. She went straight to the window, hoping to see some birds and try out a Time spell before Miss Morris came to take her to the lab. Unfortunately, there were no birds she could see, even with her wide window looking down on the whole city. It felt void of life, more ghostly than her dad's hometown.

Her room was always a comfortable temperature and she hated it. It felt so unnatural to have everything so comfortable all the time. She hated the building, but admitted to herself that the room was good, much better than the cell she first stayed in. But it lacked a certain warmth that had nothing to do with temperature. Even though she didn't have many things at home, her old room was decorated with things she had collected or built or been given. Toys and Noi-powered devices that Peter had shown her how to take apart, shown her how they work. Next to her bed on a table she used to keep a gift from Khuch: a perfectly smooth stone about the size of her palm. He had cast a spell on it so that if she held it, it glowed her favourite colour – always the colour she wanted to see. It was an incredible piece of artistic Light magic that went beyond the purely pragmatic ways that the other Khun used magic. He was different to them somehow: he cast spells just to play with them and make beautiful things.

She remembered when they were little kids and first started to make Light magic. They used to wait excitedly for the nightfall so that they could make all kinds of shapes and colours together. He was first to master the floating blobs of Light and she was so jealous at the time. She smiled now thinking about how silly she was. But he was jealous when she was first to infuse their clothes with Light magic so that they glowed.

And finally, it was him who created the gift stone. Her favourite thing. She still didn't know how he did it. She tried to get him to share his secret on the night he gave it to her, while the adults were having one of their traditional storytelling sessions around a Fire Light and the younger children were in bed. She pestered him and he was laughing the whole time.

"Come on! Tell me!"

"No! It's a secret!"

"Why? I love it! Just tell me pleeease." They were sitting very close the way they had always done, but had started to feel different to when they were little.

"Okay."

"Really?"

"Yes. Give me your hands." She did as she was told. The warm feeling of calm she knew him for immediately spread into her hands, up her arms, through her whole body.

"I will show you." He leaned forward and she leaned forward and he kissed her and she kissed him back. She wondered if he cast a Time spell then because the kiss seemed to last forever. "That's the secret."

Aisling didn't understand it in the moment, thinking he was just trying – and succeeding – to get her to stop asking. But later she did understand. It was the same power that she felt whenever she remembered his warmth. That was the secret: that feeling she got from him, the feeling that she was exactly where she needed to be, and that everything was alright. He had managed to put that feeling into a Light spell and into a rock. The colours it radiated were always the colours she felt thinking about him.

At nine o'clock she still hadn't seen any pigeons, but felt confident that the day would be better than the previous one, with the secret knowledge that she could at least use Matter magic. A knock on the door meant Miss Morris had arrived to take her down to the lab, and she grabbed her ID card and information book on the way outside.

"Good morning, Miss Hargreaves," Miss Morris greeted her with a suspiciously insincere warmth. She seemed so familiar compared to other times when she was frosty. She was all or nothing, and Aisling couldn't predict it. "Are you ready to go?"

"Yes."

"How did you sleep?"

"Fine," she lied.

They walked toward the elevator together, through the ornate passageway, Aisling forgetting that she had left the tiny apple sitting on her kitchen counter.

Chapter 8

It was interesting how most world cultures had heard of Iwizadi and had their own version of his story. In the Capital, children grew up hearing about Iwizadi the criminal, who was drunk and violent, but amazingly powerful. It was his brother Umwahu who was given much more importance. The people from the Capital grew up hearing about the great reformist leader Umwahu, who overcame a terrible upbringing in a household of crime to become the finest leader the world had ever known. Umwahu found it necessary to abolish magic to put an end to the organised crime that was consuming the great old city, and that meant putting his own brother Iwizadi in prison.

Naturally, with all the official rhetoric stating that magic didn't exist, children in the Capital who heard their bedtime stories about Iwizadi and Umwahu in the distant past never felt the need to question anything. For them, magic wasn't real, it was just a thing of stories. Peter was the same. He grew up with the same version of the story he told Aisling as a little girl, which is why it was such a shock for him to first learn that magic was, in fact, very real.

The Capital version had somehow become heavily politicised over many retellings, and introduced all kinds of complex themes that might have been irrelevant to a child anywhere else. But in the Capital, politics was everywhere. You could see it in the streets: posters of politicians promising the best for the people. Graffiti criticising the leadership. Signs outside every construction site – of which there were many – advertising the Ministry of Whatever had grand plans. You could hear it on the news: interviews with politicians were common, all spun to make Abe Brown's leadership look infallible and benevolent.

Umwahu grew up in a family of thieves, the story went. He saw the injustice in the city, and the widespread corruption creating conditions that bred crime: inequality, discrimination, nepotism, neglect... When he grew up, he knew that things had to change or the cycle that afflicted his family would never recover. They operated a sophisticated organised crime venture, making use of their unusually strong magic abilities. To stay ahead of the competition, Iwizadi used to stay up late in his study devising new types of magic that could be used in their operations. Umwahu decided enough was enough when he was eighteen years old and left the family home. He began a long political career, gaining support primarily from the lowest classes in the city. Over years of tireless efforts, fighting off attempts to derail his career and even assassination attempts, he gained a strong following as a leader for the people, promising to end the cycle of inequality.

Years later, when Umwahu was sworn in as leader of the city, he could finally work towards promoting a free and fair country: a country of opportunity for everyone. It started with imposing a complete ban on illegal magic, excepting for energy purposes or in the creation of anti-magic fields. Penalties were harsh, and people were encouraged to report each other for any sightings of magic.

In his first year, fines for illegal magic were so frequent

that they paid for all major city works and repairs. Nearly one in fifty people were imprisoned, and violent crime and theft were reduced by nearly ninety percent. The majority of the population was thrilled with the result and Umwahu started to gain a cult of personality among the happy residents.

Some more careful magic users survived the purge, including Iwizadi and the rest of their criminal family. Whenever they were reported for using magic, they could offer a suitable defence and managed to escape all fines and imprisonment while continuing to profit at the expense of others. Umwahu knew it was due to Iwizadi's impressive creativity with magic, and made him the police's top target.

After two years of avoiding arrest and a long investigation had captured enough evidence against him, Iwizadi was eventually caught. He was sentenced to life in prison, and the creation of his anti-magic cell was one of the most complicated feats of magic anyone had ever known. His cell had to be prepared before he was arrested, so a basic cell was prepared to prevent any sort of dangerous magic from within reaching outwards. It also prevented Iwizadi from simply disappearing and reappearing somewhere else.

But that was the extent of the official knowledge of magic. Often, Iwizadi would reveal another new type of magic that the field wasn't equipped to prevent, resulting in a flurry of activity as the prison guards rushed to find an appropriate anti-magic and contain him. He seemed to have so much unique magic and it was fun for him to tease his captors and make them panic.

Eventually, after more than three years, Umwahu and his team were satisfied that Iwizadi was contained safely to the best of their ability. They only knew about one magic he could perform in his cell, and it was deemed not a risk to anyone outside: Stone magic. Iwizadi was smugly satisfied knowing that the combined efforts of the government could not combat all of his magics, and turned himself to stone. He figured he could simply wait out his life sentence and start again when Umwahu and all the government had died of old age. But Umwahu saw things a different way: the longer Iwizadi lived, the longer he could spend in prison. He was not getting out for any reason, as long as any government still ruled the country.

The next part of the story is the same in the Capital and in Peter's hometown: Umwahu was succeeded by a capable young party member named Isiko, who released Iwizadi. Isiko was naïve, and held great faith in the goodness of people. He had not lived through the dangerous times that marked Umwahu's upbringing. He looked at the city and the people in it, and wondered how could anything be as bad as people told him? Magic could be the ultimate force for good, he thought. And he declared that magic was not to be illegal any more.

By that time however, only a few people remembered how to use magic, and just like in the other version of the story, Isiko implored Iwizadi to help teach the people. Naturally, Iwizadi accepted, hiding his true agenda. Iwizadi laughed when he was released, feeling like barely any time had passed in the cell. He went to his study in the old family home, which had been unoccupied since they were all arrested, and recovered his magic journal, in which was written all his experimental notes.

It was said that Iwizadi betrayed Isiko by gathering all the remaining magic users in the land and fleeing with them to found their own society, threatening to return to take over the city when they were strong enough. Isiko, on hearing this news felt betrayed by Iwizadi and ashamed that he had not believed him. He ruled well until he died, but was in constant fear of the day that Iwizadi returned to invade.

Many variations on the story existed, but they all agreed that a long time ago there was a very powerful wizard named Iwizadi who spent time in prison, and later disappeared with his book. Where the stories couldn't agree was on his motivations, his intentions, his character. They couldn't agree on anything his brother Umwahu did either. Curiously, all the stories ended at the same place: with Iwizadi disappearing. It must have been a sensible place to end the story rather than to make things up. That's why some people believed he must have been a real person, otherwise nobody would have a problem with making up the next part of his life. Even more curiously, there were only rare local stories of Iwizadi's return, whereas you might expect dozens of stories about the return of such a historical folk figure.

One such story came from a remote fishing village, Halasat, on the far south-western tip of the country. The people there told a version of the story that involved a great tragedy befalling the city of Libalele while Iwizadi was in prison. The city was victim to earthquakes, fires, floods and plagues, and its people attributed their cause to Iwizadi from within his cell. The city fell into ruin, and Iwizadi simply waited until people from another land found him and released him.

His gratitude to the new people was short-lived, but he taught them magic in return for freeing him. They were a simple people, with a harsh language and abrupt manner, but took to magic well and built their society around respect for its frightening power and respect for the natural world from which all magic ultimately came. Upon seeing that the people were thriving in harmony with nature and magic, Iwizadi was convinced Libalele could be remade with people who were less corrupt. But without a clear leader, he was said to have taken his belongings and left to wander the earth, searching for someone who could properly take charge of the city and lead Libalele back to its position of renown. They said he had been wandering through every land on the planet for centuries, perhaps longer.

The people of Halasat were unique for having a common story about what happened to Iwizadi after leaving, and they were receptive to any reported sightings. About the time that Orn was born, a fisherman claimed to have had a vision of Iwizadi during a storm at sea, and by praying to him the storm had subsided and he had safely steered his boat back to shore. More recently, some children reportedly saw him entering the village inn, and when they went to investigate found it to be empty. And from time to time, people in the village used to complain of seeing him in their sleep.

For the Halasetters, Iwizadi was more than just a story. He was a real man who was going to come back when he had found the person who would lead Libalele and its new inhabitants to glory. Due to Halasat's remoteness, they had little interaction with the rest of the country, and any visitors were likely to dismiss them as superstitious, backwards people who had somehow twisted a children's story into a prophetic vision of a religious saviour. Indeed, the Halasetters when asked could not have pointed to Libalele on any map or explained why their version of the story was so different to any other.

Upon learning that some people were practically worshipping Iwizadi with a religious zeal, the First Leader sixty years ago was forced to decide whether it posed a threat or not. Fortunately for the Halasetters, he decided that it was not worth the effort to label old superstition as treason, and allowed the remote community to continue its strange beliefs. There was however, bound to be tension between the Halasat version and the Capital version, where one welcomed the return of the wizard and the other feared it, and this led to the Leader devoting resources to research magic. Just in case.

And so magic research had been underway at the Capital for decades, even longer than Jack and Daphne knew. Only the current Leader knew the full history of it. There were spies planted long ago, who relayed information whenever the Halasetters reported a new sighting. Reports were fairly frequent in the beginning, where every few months someone would report having the same dream about a circular room. But sixteen years ago, the reports stopped coming, which led the government to doubt the value of its spies, and the wisdom of paying attention to Halasat at all.

One thing the Halasetters did not know was what Iwizadi wrote in his book. They knew it was significant, otherwise he would not have taken it when he left Libalele to search for the next chosen Leader, but they couldn't guess what was in it. Some parents made things up when telling their children the story: the book contained the whole history of the universe; the book contained his heart or soul and he needed it to live; the book was only a metaphor for all the superhuman knowledge he had gained.

But for all their religious belief in Iwizadi, the Halasetters mostly had no command of magic, except for the rare accidental use of some rudimentary spell, which they preferred to keep quiet about. It was for this reason that the Leader believed they were not a serious threat, and that they should not influence any policy. They were brushed aside and forgotten as a strange village on the outskirts of society and left to do their own thing because their land had no natural Noi deposits. It was not of value to the Capital and the Leader had other problems to keep him occupied.

One of his problems was the sudden influx of refugees from Blue Island in the north-east, and the reports that some of them had been seen using actual magic; magic that was potentially very dangerous, but very valuable. Magic that could see his armies conquering the great states in the east across the sea. He needed an excuse to persecute the refugees so he made a lot of noise about their legality and it wasn't long before everyone was talking about illegal immigrants and how to get rid of them. It was almost too easy.

Abe gained power as his ageing father died quietly, and shortly before the refugees started arriving in great numbers. Almost right away he was faced with the magic issue, and within a month it was confirmed that magic was real. His work from then on focused more on keeping magic a state secret than on actual statecraft and leadership. The Department of Magic Research – the Department as it was known – was established as a subdivision of the research and development branch of the military, and was originally tasked with documenting magic for the purpose of simply gathering intelligence. Halasat was practically forgotten at that point in time and receded into obscurity at the far edge of the country.

The Department was well-funded, and relied on the refugees, or Participants as they were also called. Refugees were sighted and disappeared, and by that time, Abe's relabelling of them as criminals had taken hold. There was something happening to them, and whether they were alive or not was unknown. The media was kept quiet, and the people didn't want to know.

Jack liked the story of Iwizadi too: the Capital version. He liked to think about how his work related to it. He was trying to prepare the Capital for the inevitable. He wanted to do the best thing for the greatest number of people possible. It was off to a good start, he thought, tying a belt around his bicep, raising the vein to the surface and sliding the needle into his arm. Her journal was full of good stuff. Things about magic they had never considered. It was a gold mine. He pushed gently on the syringe end and watched the clear liquid enter his body. He felt the effect almost instantly as his blood pumped the solution to his brain and spinal cord. He inhaled deeply and closed his eyes, enjoying the feeling, before removing the needle and holding a wad of cotton wool to the point where it had exited his arm. He exhaled forcefully and grunted.

After only two days they had produced enough data for a new batch of Substance M. Impressive. She was by far the most powerful Participant that had ever entered the Department. She would be very valuable indeed. The boys in the Ministry of Defence were already studying her journal to train the soldiers. With a little injection they'd be just as potent a user as her. Maybe stronger if they got the recipe right.

On the second afternoon he had gone to visit the lab and see her in action. It was spectacular, beyond his expectations, and he had to force himself to hide his excitement in front of his employees. That insufferable doctor and that bitch Daphne. She insisted on stuffy formalities, calling everyone Miss this and Doctor that. Bitch. If she hadn't been an early Participant herself, she'd be Retired by now, certainly. She was too useful and knew too much to be Retired.

He clenched his fist involuntarily, feeling the effects of substance M taking control of his cells, rewriting his DNA. It was an incredible feeling, letting it take over. Shame it was so hard to produce. Even one dose took an ordinary Participant over a day of study. *But this girl, my niece*, Aisling... she was powerful off the charts. And that meant more substance M. That's what the Department was ordered to create. It was Jack's purpose. Instead of relying on others like he did growing up, since assisting in forming the Department there were people relying on him. It felt good to be powerful. It was a much better job than his previous position in the Ministry of Energy, but he owed his career to that, and regretted nothing about it.

Jack disposed of the needle in a special container and walked to the kitchen, feeling like he was floating with each step. He was like a man possessed. He pulled a glass from the cupboard and held his hand over it. Water appeared to fill the glass in a second. Jack twisted his wrist and the water just as quickly emptied into nothingness. He played with the water level for a minute: up, down, up, down, then put the glass down. Yes! In ecstasy he threw the glass against the wall and watched it shatter into a million pieces. He laughed giddily and his face contorted. This was a truly powerful new formula for Substance M. Aisling had indeed been the one they were waiting for. It would keep Abe happy.

He held both arms out in front of him and started producing a few drops from his fingertips in mid-air, pretending to play the keys of an invisible piano. The drops hung there floating where he conjured them and he grinned until his face hurt from the effort. Yes, this was a very potent batch of Substance M. He waved his right arm slowly through the air and left a trail of water droplets hanging in front of him. With his left arm, he traced the same path and the water vanished. With the powerful drug in his body, he wrote words in the air and erased them, with no evidence that there had been liquid hanging there at all. He danced to music nobody could hear; the music of magic.

He reached for another glass and considered it for a moment, before raising a hand over its rim and filling it with fog. He put it down and turned back to the room, looking around at all its walls and corners before raising both hands above his head.

He laughed euphorically as the whole room filled with fog. He was going to get that damned Book of Iwizadi, the one he saw in his dream, he just had to wait for the right opportunity. No, better, he was making the opportunity. He hadn't come so far in life by waiting for opportunity.

Two hours later, he blacked out and pissed himself, the drug leaving his body through the easiest route. But he didn't mind. The residual effects of Substance M remained in the body to a small degree, and he was permanently made magic. Permanently more powerful.

The crow's nest on his window was occupied as it always had been, and an inquisitive pair of eyes watched the whole scene, remembering every detail.

Chapter 9

I know she is okay.

Peter started his final trek to Darvozasi at sunrise, aiming to reach the city in the early afternoon. The road got easier and easier as he went, but a practical issue bothered him.

He had very little money and didn't know how he would survive outside the forest. He had stocked up on dried deer meat and edible plants and carried a good supply with him, but not more than two- or three-days' worth of food. And as for water, that was another story. Like most of his plan, he relegated the specifics to his future self, having faith that he could improvise when he needed to. He had been homeless in the city before. He could manage.

And so can she.

Peter remembered a time some years earlier, when Aisling had gone into the forest with Khuch looking for mushrooms and other edible things they couldn't easily grow in the vegetable garden. Ever since they arrived, Aisling had invited Khuch everywhere and he always accepted. Except since his initiation. They were inseparable, and his status as an adult Khun must have been hard for them both. He was expected to take life stoically like Chuluun, but it was clear that he had more in common with Peter: he liked to act; he liked to question why; he liked to take things apart and rebuild them. On the other hand, Khuch had more in common with Chuluun than he might admit: he would patiently watch while Peter taught him how his Noiclock worked and they took it apart and put it back together. Even as a child, he used to mull things over in silence for a while then suddenly take decisive action. He took things maybe too literally at times, whereas Aisling was a formidable lateral thinker.

They complemented each other's shortcomings and were an excellent team. And everybody could see the way they looked at each other. Everybody saw when one night at the traditional storytelling around the magical fire they shared a quick kiss. They thought nobody could see. Peter didn't bring it up.

That time they went to the forest they must have been about twelve or thirteen years old; it was hard to remember, but when they came back Aisling didn't mention they had seen a wolf up close. She didn't seem to be bothered by it at all. She seemed to be distracted by thoughts of something else, and kept looking at Khuch. Instead, it was Khuch who told Peter about how they saw it skulking not far from where they were walking, and how Aisling froze. She blushed when he told her dad that he held her hand and cast a spell to make the wolf think it was intruding on another wolf's territory. She was embarrassed that she thought the warmth she felt from him was anything else.

That wasn't typical Aisling, he thought. She usually wanted to act on impulse without bothering to know what she was doing. Lucky Khuch was with her to use Animal magic to send the wolf somewhere else. Lucky he knew what he was doing.

She will be fine.

Wherever she was at that moment when Peter emerged

from the deepest reaches of the forest and saw a road not far away, he hoped that she had learned something from Khuch about making good decisions. He knew that with enough time to consider a situation, she would do the right thing. But what if she had no time?

What if he had taken too long? What if she had no time because of him?

He walked faster after leaving the forest, partly because the ground was easier to walk on, and partly from a desire to get out of the open.

And what of Jack? After everything that happened between them, why would he help? And Tom?

If it weren't for the days of physical exertion, Peter would not have slept since Aisling's capture. His mind was filled with worry for her safety, worry for Chuluun and the others. Bad memories of Maria, of childhood, of the Capital, of Jack all haunted him. Worry that when he found Jack, he would not be helpful. Worry that he wouldn't make it to the Capital at all. Fear that he wouldn't find Aisling. Fear that his effort was now in vain. Worry that he would be arrested for harbouring illegal immigrants and tortured for using magic.

But in spite of all his thoughts, he pushed on.

I will find her.

He began walking along a defined road that linked Darvozasi to some of the outlying farms in the region. He would look much less suspicious entering the city via the road, he reasoned, than if he simply emerged from the wilderness. A Noitruck hummed along the road behind him and pulled over a short distance after passing him. A fat farmer with a friendly face leaned out the door and called to him,

"Need a lift to the city?"

"Thanks." Peter jogged ahead to greet the farmer,

immediately adapting to the unexpected, like he always did. He felt a speck of memory float through his mind, when he left his family home after Jack was arrested as a teenager.

"Where ya comin' from?" the farmer asked as Peter climbed into the cab.

"Got lost in the forest. Been walking in circles for days." Peter lied. It was better if the farmer didn't know the truth.

"Bloody hell. And you're alive and all that?" He was genuinely impressed.

"Yeah, I'm pretty tough," Peter joked.

"I'll say. So, where ya headed? Alright if I drop you in town here? I'm driving all the way to the Capital today."

"That's actually where I'm going. I'm staying with my brother over there." This made the farmer a little suspicious.

"How the hell'd ya end up all the way out here if you're staying in the Capital?" he asked.

"Well, I came this way to hike on some of the mountains. Done it a few times before but that storm last week must have turned me around."

"Orright, keen mountains guy, eh? Bet you won't be back soon after today!"

"Prolly not."

"How long ya been out there anyway? Y'look pretty tired. Have a snooze if y'want, I'll wake ya up."

"Nah I'm all good, I'll stay up. I think it's been about ten days." Then remembering his lie added, "Was supposed to be only five!"

"Bloody hell! Well, I'm happy I found ya, saved ya another day!"

"Yeah, it's lucky."

"Spose y'lost some stuff out there? Ya don't have much gear."

"It was a wolf."

"Bloody hell man! I dunno how ya survived out there. I know I wouldn'a if it'd been me! But ya look orright, barely a scratch on ya."

"Not my first time in the forest. I know the wild pretty well."

"Say, ya got a bit of an accent. Where ya from anyway?" The farmer must have heard the influence the Khun had on Peter's speech. He had lived with them so long that his speech was now accented and he had to force himself back into the same patterns of speech that most others from his city had.

"That's interesting, nobody ever mentioned it before." Peter replied, deliberately switching into his native Nelasive accent and shedding any trace of Khun.

"Sounds north-eastern." The farmer didn't give up. Accents were his hobby and practising them was how he kept his mind active on long drives.

"I'm from Nelasive originally."

"I knew it!" He was pleased with himself. "I could hear it, the way ya say 'wild' gave it away."

"You're very good."

"I spent a bit o' time there meself. Had relatives there. Y'know the Fidelis?"

"Never heard of them," Peter lied.

"Too bad, great people they were."

Were. Peter thought about dropping in on the Fidelis when he visited Nelasive with Aisling, but decided it was best not to draw any attention, good or bad. This was the first he'd heard of them since leaving all those years earlier. They were dead. He wished he'd gone to visit them even once since he moved away.

They passed a sign indicating the route to the Capital and the truck turned. A minute later Peter saw Darvozasi from the window. They were passing around it instead of through it. This bypass hadn't existed when Peter last travelled to the Capital. The old road through Darvozasi was still there, but with drivers enjoying the high-speed bypass, the city centre wasn't getting as much business from tourists as it used to. Peter remembered stopping there when he took the bus out of the Capital all those years ago. A wave of nostalgia washed over him as he watched the distinctive yellow facades rushing by in the distance. He would have enjoyed stopping there. It was one of the few cities he knew with no Noi mine nearby, and it seemed cleaner and friendlier. At least it did in his memory.

"What are you transporting anyway?" he asked the farmer, realising he hadn't asked yet.

"Milk. Just crates and crates of milk. Capital is our biggest customer. These'll go straight to the warehouse up there for Mooney's, ya know the supermarket, then get moved out tonight to the individual shops. Fresh milked this morning. Man, it's a fast business. Milk business wasn't always like this. But tastes changed and everybody wants milk now."

Peter let the farmer talk about milk for most of the trip and spent a lot of the time looking out the window. He wasn't used to talking to people and found it tiring. They passed a couple of turnoffs for Noi mines. Peter wondered how strong a Fire magic spell he would need to destroy a mine. What would happen if raw Noi was set on fire?

She will be okay.

He didn't remember falling asleep, but when he woke up, he was confronted by the blue light and concrete of the Capital. It was night already.

"Oh yerawake!" the farmer said tiredly. "We're just about there. I can drop ya off somewhere near the warehouse if ya want? What part of the city does ya brother live in?"

"Uh, are you going past Central Depot? Or anywhere close to that?"

"Yeah sure. Easy. Lucky ya said so, that's only a few blocks from 'ere. Y'can jump out at the traffic lights when we get there. Just two minutes."

"Thanks so much."

"All good mate. Ya brother'll be happy to see ya alive! Betcha'll be happy to have a shower and a hot dinner!"

"Sounds great to me."

"Oh here, this one up ahead's going red. Just go left up that street a couple blocks and there's Central."

"Thanks again."

"Any time mate, be careful out there in the woods next time, eh?"

The truck came to a stop at the traffic lights and Peter jumped out, waving the farmer goodbye from the pavement as he continued on his way. He recognised where he was: corner of King and Victory. The buildings looked a bit different to how they were twenty years earlier, but the streets were the same, and he knew them well. He started up Victory towards Central, noting the curious mix of old and new: crumbly buildings covered in graffiti and political slogans interspersed between new high-rises. 'Abe Brown' was smeared in huge letters, with the 'A' stylised in the symbol for anarchy; 'No Water No Life' was a frequent slogan, just like in his hometown. He looked up to see how high the buildings were now, and the sky was covered with the same depressing glow he remembered well. Stars were only visible in the countryside.

This was his old neighbourhood, the area his family lived. His school was only a few blocks away, and in the other direction was the boxing gym. Their old home was around the next corner. Allan's garage was a bit further, but with a bike it took only fifteen minutes or so. But back then there weren't so many Noicars or construction zones. It might take longer now. 'Progress'. 'Making lives easier'. He scoffed. So much of his life had taken place in this small radius.

Instead of continuing up Victory towards Central, Peter turned right onto Brown and started towards the gym. He needed a friendly face, a shower, a place to stay the night. He needed Tom.

He hoped that Tom would not blame him for what happened to Maria.

But he knew that Tom would, because it was his fault.

The gym was exactly as Peter remembered. It still had the same harsh Noi lighting it did all those years before. It had the same posters on the walls and the same old equipment, lovingly maintained. The ring was empty when Peter walked in, still in the same position occupying a lot of the floor space in the centre of the room. A couple of guys were lifting free weights on the far side underneath the large yellow-tinted window. They looked up when he entered, maybe expecting a friend to join them, but saw that it was a stranger and ignored him. He stood in the entrance looking around for a second too long, and a man opened a door to an office on the side of the room.

"Peter?" he called out, confused. His voice was nasal and unpleasant. He started walking towards Peter, his movements staccato as if suffering tendonitis or arthritis somewhere.

"Hello Tom." Peter was nervous, he hadn't boxed in years, he was out of practice and out of shape. He felt his body tensing up and preparing for a fight.

"I told you if I ever saw you, I'd kill you." Tom walked right up to Peter and stood just an inch from his face.

"I remember."

"But I was young and angry." He hugged Peter tightly for a second then released him and struck him twice: a quick left jab to the face and a right hook that landed in Peter's mid-section. Peter took the blows in stride, certainly not the hardest he'd been hit before. "What are you doing here?"

"I need your help." He rubbed him jaw. They walked into the dingy little office and sat down. "Just a shower and a place to sleep tonight."

"You're a brave man coming back here. Must be something big happening."

"They kidnapped my daughter. Your niece."

"Seriously? Aisling? What for?"

"Mistake," Peter lied. "They think she's a refugee."

"And the news says all refugees are witches."

"I haven't heard the news in a decade."

"Shit this is bad." Tom absent-mindedly squeezed a small device to flex his forearms. "That's a serious problem. You know they've started executing them?"

"What?"

"You really haven't listened to the news, have you Pete?"

"Tell me."

"First one was just a few months ago. Refugee was hanged. Said there was proof he was a witch. All we've heard about every day for years is witches. Whole city's gone crazy, thinking witches are real."

"They might be."

"Huh? Doesn't matter... so you came back here to get your daughter."

Peter was aware that Tom hadn't mentioned Maria yet, and he was scared to bring it up.

"My brother works for the government. I'm going to track him down tomorrow and sort this out."

"Jack? Good luck, if he's anything like I remember." Tom threw down his forearm device and laced his fingers behind his head.

"Worse."

"Let me know how I can help." Tom stood up and paced the room twice, unable to stay still for more than a few seconds at a time. "You know it's his fault what happened right?"

"Jack?" Peter was confused. He was sure it was his fault, not Jack's. What was Tom talking about?

"You probably don't remember it, they knocked you pretty hard and you blacked out for a bit."

"I remember enough."

"Believe me, it was Jack, not you." Tom sat back down and slumped forward onto his hands. "You were right to leave. I wanted to go too, but I had this business, you know? I was established here."

"I thought you hated me."

"I did. But you did me and my family a big favour by getting Maria out of here. Best thing that happened to us in a long time."

"I thought you hated me for taking her to the place she got killed."

"You really think that? Maybe we went too hard in sparring practice. No, of course I hated you for disappearing with her, but it was for the best, there's no future here in this city. I wished I could go too. You want a beer?"

"I don't drink," he lied. He had drunk plenty of wine with Chuluun over the years.

"Power Pete doesn't drink? Man, it has been a long time."

"Not since I left this place." They sat in silence for a few seconds, Tom nodding approvingly, remembering how it was when they were much younger.

"Tell me one thing," Tom looked at Peter seriously, "Was she happy there?"

"Very." And suddenly Peter couldn't keep it together. He had lost all his friends, walked for two weeks to rescue his kidnapped daughter from a place he promised never to return to, and heard that his old friend never hated him like he thought. It was finally enough to break him and he wiped his eyes and nose.

"Shit man." Tom's eyes threatened to leak too. "I've got the toughest fighter in the city crying in the toughest gym. It's ridiculous." They laughed through the tears.

"It's so good to see you."

"Good to see you too. Stay here as long as you need. I'll help you find Jack tomorrow."

"Thanks."

"I've thought about bashing his face in, every day since it happened."

"He would have you killed."

"He's always been protected. It was those kids in the gang first, now it's the government. I don't know which is worse. Or if there's even a difference."

"Can you tell me more about the witches? Any news from overseas?" Peter asked, curious, thinking of Gazar.

"Abroad? Are you serious? You know we never get news of anything outside the country, and hardly ever anything even outside the city. It's all government propaganda."

"So, nothing's changed."

"If anything, man it's gotten worse."

"I remember why I left this place."

"Have you been in your old hometown this whole time?"

"Not exactly," Peter hesitated, thinking immediately he should have just said yes. "But what news do they report?"

"It's all propaganda. They say we're being invaded by

those refugees, that they're witches. Some people reckon they're the long-lost followers of Iwizadi coming back to take the city. The government made them all illegal."

"That's fucking insane."

"Of course it is! But once that fear is in the public mind, you can't get it out."

"How many people believe it? Iwizadi is just a fairy tale." But Peter knew otherwise. Since learning that magic was real, he believed Iwizadi must have been real too.

"Tons of people believe it. It's all they ever talk about on the radio because we have no news about overseas: nobody knows why the refugees are here, so they make guesses. Then someone brought up Iwizadi one day and suddenly everyone believed it. Even the government's spreading the story sometimes. We reckon it's just so they can start executions. Easiest way for them to deal with the situation. Don't have to feed and house dead people, you know?"

"Have you ever seen a refugee?" Peter was feeling like he couldn't keep his secrets hidden much longer and fought hard against the impulse to tell Tom, to show Tom everything.

"Once in the city I saw one near the big government office buildings. She was wearing a uniform and she didn't look dangerous. Obviously a refugee from her face. She had the officials with her. A man and a woman. She had dark skin and a different sort of face to us. Obviously a refugee."

"Yeah, I get it."

"But they say you can never tell. I mean look at you Pete: nobody would guess you're a champion fighter."

"Not for a long time. You think that woman was dangerous? Or just trying to survive?"

"Doesn't matter what I think, government killed her anyway. After a few months. They talked about the execution on the news."

"But wait a minute. They were talking about refugees invading us decades ago when I used to listen to the news. How is it only recently they've started executing them? How is it only recently we have proof they're here at all?" Neither man trusted the government or the information they were being fed. Tom shrugged, unable to answer. A flapping sound at the window of the office made them jump, and they saw an uncountable flock of pigeons frantically trying to look inside. Tom shooed them off.

"I don't know what's happened to these birds lately, they've just started doing this weird thing a few days ago. They do it at my home too, it's really freaking me out." Peter was heartened to know this. The Khun are involved, he thought, there is hope.

"Yeah, it looks pretty weird," he commented to avoid suspicion. "I've never seen them do that before."

"Maybe something magnetic," Tom thought out loud. "They say pigeons have magnets in their heads or something like that."

"Could be. Or maybe they've been poisoned. Poison in the water maybe."

"Could be. Noi poisoning. Either that or it's got something to do with witches. Iwizadi could talk to animals in the story I think."

"It's just a fairy tale Tom. Geez it really got to you, huh?"

"I think it's fun to think about, but of course you know I don't actually believe any of it."

"Then the refugee woman executed on the news?"

"She was a political prisoner, not a witch. There's no such thing as witches. They called her an illegal immigrant and they make the rules. The public mind filled in the rest."

"And what if there were witches?" Peter tested the waters.

"Well, we could probably learn something from them," Tom admitted, the blue Noi lights flickered off and on a few times before resuming their usual potency. "Like maybe they know how to fix these damn lights."

"You wouldn't be scared?"

"Probably a little, but I reckon there's always more to the story."

"Probably," Peter agreed. He looked out the window, weighing up his options. He came to the Capital to find Aisling and bring her home, back to the Khun. Then what? *I guess we'll go with them wherever they go.* Gazar? Why not? And to find her he needed to convince Jack to release her. Not likely! Jack would never help him in a million years! But Tom was an old friend and already helping. They had history. They could talk openly. Tom could be trusted. Rather than simply ask Jack nicely to release Aisling, Peter thought it might be a better plan to enlist Tom's help and break her out.

"Tom, there's something else," Peter began. "You asked if I'd been at my hometown, but I moved away from there not long after Maria died."

"Where've you been then?"

"In a refugee camp."

"Are you serious? What was it like? Are they dangerous like the news says? Like the government says? How'd you even find them? Tell me everything."

"Nothing like that at all."

"And witches?"

Peter took a calculated risk, and at the time was not able to tell if it was wise or foolish. He sat perfectly still for a moment, concentrating on his breath, visualising that with each inhale he was breathing in all the light and goodness of the world and with each exhale he was expelling the toxic parts of his spirit. "Pete?" Tom pushed, thinking his friend was having a medical episode. Peter dreamily lifted his left hand, palm up, then pointed his finger at the flickering blue Noi light. The tip of his finger began to glow white, then a small glob of light shot out and found its mark in the light. His hand stopped glowing and the light was now strongly producing a light that was not quite white, nor the usual blue of Noi.

"The fuck was that?" Tom edged backwards. "What'd you do to my lights?"

"Tom, I have been living with *refugees*." The way he emphasised the word 'refugees' was to hide the alternative label: 'witches'. Tom came closer, scrutinising his old friend. He looked much older and sadder. His hair was thinner, but he looked healthier too.

"They taught you that?"

"They taught me a lot."

"That's why they took Aisling isn't it?"

"Yes."

"She's a witch."

"…yes."

"Unbelievable."

"Will you help me find her? I don't trust that Jack will help."

"Not if you show him that! You'll disappear and be forced into human experiments. Of course I'll help. Aisling is my blood too. Let's do it for Maria."

After their agreement, Peter was sure that Tom would be his ally. That was not the case. He was convinced by Tom's performance that he had been forgiven for what happened to Maria. But he was wrong about that too. Tom had feinted, waiting for the right time to strike, to knock Peter out. It was always a boxing match.

The police arrived at the gym before Peter woke up, and he was arrested before he had a chance to see Tom. He was taken to the central government offices and pushed roughly into a cell identical to the one that held Aisling not long before. Peter was silent the whole time, cursing himself for trusting his old friend, for revealing his true motives. It was a foolish thing to do, and now he was stuck. On the bright side, he might be able to see Aisling sooner.

Waiting was not easy for him. He was a man of action and being stuck in a small room, unable to search was torture. Already the night before, he was feeling the claustrophobic crushing sensation of being surrounded by concrete and tall buildings, and missed the freedom of being alone in nature.

The door to the room opened, and Jack entered pompously, theatrically feigning surprise.

"Well, well, well."

"Nice to see you too."

"To what do I owe the pleasure?" Jack stood at the wall of the cell and looked right at his brother, seemingly oblivious to the tension between them.

"I shouldn't be here," Peter began.

"Then why are you in there?" Jack tilted his head to the side, curious.

"I was looking for you."

"For me?" Jack pretended to be shocked. "Whatever for?"

"Can't I visit you, brother?" Peter used Jack's own words from the last time they had spoken. Jack laughed but said nothing, waiting for an explanation. "I need your help," Peter said softly to the floor.

"What was that?" Jack's arrogance knew no bounds.

"I need your help," he repeated louder. "Aisling was taken."

"I'm sorry brother, for wasting your time. The girl is fine."

"What do you mean?"

"She's right here, working for me." Jack examined a loose thread on his jacket.

"Why is she working here? She belongs in the country, with her family." Peter knew he'd made a mistake in saying that.

"You forget: she *is* with family," Jack sneered. "And if you want to talk about family-"

"No, I didn't mean-"

"Why don't we talk about how you abandoned yours?"

"Jack..."

"How you saved yourself and your girlfriend and left our dad here to slowly die? How you left me to care for him and raise myself? I was a child."

"You're still angry."

"Of course I am." Then, regaining composure, "But I suppose it's all in the past now, isn't it? None of that matters now? Because you're in there, and I'm out here, and now I have your daughter. You're held captive by family and this time you can't run away."

"Stop it, Jack."

"There's nowhere left for you to go."

"Stop it."

"Fine." Jack took a few steps around the cell. "Why don't we talk about why you've been arrested? You were seen using magic."

"And that's so serious a crime now?"

"It is an act of terrorism. We take it seriously."

"Terrorism?"

"Do you have a radio in that hovel you call home? If you did, you would know that any user of magic was declared a terrorist nearly a decade ago by the Leader himself."

Peter was silent, fuming.

"And on that topic, why don't we mention your neighbours?"

"What about them?"

"They're illegal immigrants are they not?"

"So what if they are?"

"They are also magic users, correct?"

"Fuck you."

"You are aware that hiding illegal immigrants is also taken seriously?"

"You have no proof."

Jack laughed menacingly and Peter felt disarmed by it, the suddenness of such a thing in the middle of a heated discussion. Jack had proof, there was no doubt.

"Can I continue?" Jack asked with fake politesse. "You have been arrested after a witness saw you using magic and tipped off the police, warning them that you were seeking to threaten a government employee – me – and attempting to kidnap another female employee."

"That's not-"

"These are serious charges. You are also under arrest for harbouring illegal immigrants to this country, which itself is a serious symbolic crime."

"Symbolic?"

"There is very strong anti-refugee sentiment among the public at the moment, which is headed by the Leader himself calling for stronger border controls." Jack paused before delivering his ultimatum. "I'm going to offer you the same deal I offered Aisling: You can choose to work with my department's research division, and we can make this whole situation disappear. Or, you can choose to go to trial, where you will likely be publicly executed."

"Execution," Peter stated confidently without hesitation.

"Peter, think it over," Jack implored. "If you are indeed a magic user – and I have every reason to believe you are – then you would be a great asset to our research."

"Fuck your research and the Leader. Execution."

"Think about Aisling," Jack baited Peter. Peter fumed, because there was little else he had thought of for the last two weeks. "Would she want to see her dear father tried and hung?"

"What happened to you? Let me go."

"I can't let you go." Jack blinked a few times, as the words spoken out loud held layers of meaning and he caught himself off guard.

"Yes, you can," Peter pushed. "You can let me go. Say I'm not a magic user. Say I don't know about refugees."

"I'm afraid I don't have a choice." Jack twisted the dialogue. "But you do. Will you help our research? Will you contribute to this country's success? Will you see your daughter again and live a useful life? Or will you throw away your life? For what? For pride? Imagine the look on your daughter's face when she realises she is about to witness her father's execution. Don't be a martyr, Peter, there is no cause."

"You're sick," Peter spat. "How can you play with my life like this? And Aisling. We are your family."

"Ha! Family?" Jack laughed coldly. "My family was a sick father who needed to be fed and changed like a baby. It was a brother who abandoned me when I was only little. It was a gang of friends who shoplifted for fun and fought constantly. Don't talk to me about family." Peter winced at the mention of the gang, remembering the last time he saw them.

"Brother…"

"By name only."

In the silence, Peter raged. He forgot momentarily about the anti-magic field, reaching inside himself, seeing the gas burner of Fire magic swell and grow with intensity. The emotions of the last twenty-four hours bubbling up from where he had stashed them. Tom pretending to forgive him, pretending to be his friend. Knowing that Maria's death was all his fault, and that Tom knew it. He saw the flame grow bigger, engulfing the space, blinding his inner vision. The flame grew and grew, stronger and stronger, like when he first used Fire magic and felt overcome with anger. Now, he didn't care. He wasn't going to stop it. He wanted to burn. He wanted the Fire to spread and consume everything. The burner spilt over and the background of his inner vision began to burn.

Jack saw the walls of the cell flicker and understood that Peter was attempting to use magic.

"It's no use Peter It is not possible to use magic in the cell."

His voice brought Peter back to reality for a moment who realised the futility of his effort. He struggled to bring his flame back under control, to douse the burning of his mind. Fear that he was too late prevented him from stopping quickly, and his imagination continued to burn strongly. His skin was hot and he couldn't concentrate. His sight was blurry and he couldn't hear Jack's words.

It took a minute, but Peter brought his Fire magic back to its latent state where the flame burnt quietly and controlled. He snapped back to reality.

Jack was watching from next to the door, secretly worried. He had never seen magic so strong. He could not admit it to Peter, but Peter's Fire magic had nearly overcome the anti-magic field. Any stronger and he would have escaped. How did he learn to do that? There were no reports of anyone ever breaking a field, but in theory it was possible.

Jack saw that Peter's eyes had turned red. He stared in wonder at his brother, at his eyes that mesmerised him like a campfire at night, and cleared his throat, "I will give you some time to consider the offer."

Peter grunted something and a faint amount of smoke was expelled through his nose.

"I will come back tomorrow, to see if you change your mind. Magic of your quality would be a tremendous asset to your country." The country. Jack was thinking only of himself; of how he could distil Peter's Fire into a usable dose of Substance M. Imagine such power. He shivered.

"My country is Gazar," Peter mumbled.

"What's that?" Jack didn't hear Peter clearly. After witnessing him nearly break the anti-magic field, Jack had a greater respect for Peter. He needed his participation in the research. Needed it. Such power could not be wasted. But he needed Peter to believe he had no alternative.

"I said, 'fuck you'." Peter felt his burner flare briefly but quickly contained it.

"Well fuck you too," Jack joined in. "And for that matter fuck your gym, your boxing, fuck your car shop, fuck Maria."

"You can't talk about her." Peter resisted the flame's powerful urge to swallow the world. "It was your fault."

"You know that's a lie."

"No. All this time it was you."

"This might be a good time for me to leave. You need time to calm down." He opened the door to leave. "See you tomorrow."

The door snapped shut and Peter was alone in silence. He was aware that the anti-magic field prevented him from exploding, from setting the building alight, and he was grateful that nothing happened. But he was also aware from the inner workings of magic that the field was weak, perhaps weaker than him. He knew that by concentrating on the flame's intensity he could burst out. The sensation of the field was there in his mind when he visualised the candle, like being in a small box. But he knew that if he made his flame big enough it would spill out of all sides, the corners and the seams, until the field itself was consumed in his anger. This field was pathetic. But such a spell was a danger to himself.

It didn't make sense to Peter. Jack was so angry, had he been angry like this the whole time? Twenty years? And what did he mean it was a lie that it was his fault? It was definitely Jack's fault. Peter remembered the Noicar, Jack's gang, the robbery, Tom was there, the inept police standing around lazily, left Peter alone with Aisling. It was Jack's fault she didn't have a mother. And now Jack offered him death. He would take a father from Aisling too.

Join or die.

In the heat of the moment, Peter chose death. There was integrity in death but there was hope in life, no matter how compromised. He would need more information, to know if Aisling was here, that Jack was telling the truth. There was no point agreeing to anything without proof. What would Chuluun do? There was a reason he was the Khun's leader.

Peter was aware that he was betrayed twice in one day: by his friend and by his brother, and he did not know which was worse. His drive to rescue Aisling had brought him this far, and it was the same motivation that would lead him to choose to help. So long as he had proof she was alive.

Giving up now would be a waste of life.

He thought he should just break the field and do it his

way. *Fuck Jack.* But there was too much unknown: what would happen to him if he cast a Fire spell that strong? Waiting might do him good, he decided; he had been moving for so long, with so much on his mind. Rest would help.

Sitting on the bed, the full weight of the situation fell on his shoulders. He slumped forwards and let the stillness and silence catch up to him. Maybe he needed Aisling more than she needed him. At her age, he was already fully independent. The negativity gripped him and forced him downward.

She doesn't need me.

These were the thoughts that it was hard to get up from.

I'm finding Aisling and together we will go to Gazar, away from this madness, he vowed.

A pigeon slammed into the tiny window in the corner of the room and looked at Peter with surprise. He was never alone, even if sometimes he felt it.

Chapter 10

Aisling entered the testing booth again, expecting the same as the last few days. It was quite boring, and she was asked to perform the same magic over and over again. On the first day she had spent hours filling and emptying a glass, and just when there was a pause from the loudspeaker and she thought perhaps they were moving onto something else, Kurt's voice came through and asked her to fill the glass again. The initial excitement of being asked to demonstrate the thing that made her unique was fading into the dull weariness of routine.

She had completely forgotten about leaving the tiny apple carelessly on the kitchen bench. It had been removed by the cleaner while she was in the lab that day, and so far, there had been no consequence: no scolding from Miss Morris, or extra interrogation about all the types of magic she could perform; nor had the anti-magic field been updated to prevent her using Matter magic at night. It was one of the few ways she could keep entertained and keep her skills sharp- the experiments she was assisting with were uninspiring. It seemed like the people were only interested in studying magic in tiny pieces, which for her was weird. For Aisling and for the Khun, magic wasn't performed in discrete chunks like that; it was a holistic thing, an event, a way of being. It made no sense to break it down into pieces when all the pieces added together to create something more than just their sum. Magic was like breathing, like language.

The one positive she could think of was that she was getting very good at demanding water to appear and disappear in various forms and shapes. If she'd practised this thoroughly a month earlier, she would not have lost control outside the supermarket and been arrested. Also, back then she had been limited to producing water connected to her body, but after the repetitive experiments she was capable of calling water from the air in any place. It was a great improvement in that regard. She wondered if Kurt or Miss Morris noticed her skills improving.

"Today we want to test your ability to generate ice." Kurt's voice came over the speaker. "Let's start by filling the glass like before, then I want you to freeze it."

"So, we're finished with Water magic?" Aisling said while picking up the glass. There was a pause and she thought maybe he didn't hear her.

"I don't follow."

"Ice is, I guess it's water, but I need to use Heat magic to create it."

"Together?"

"Yeah, Water and Heat magic together." She effortlessly filled the glass with water.

"Um."

"Lots of things I need two different magics together. I thought you would know that."

"I did not. That makes things... more complicated for our data." he trailed off. "Just hold on a minute, I'll be back."

Aisling stood in the room waiting patiently for instructions to come, but it seemed to take a very long time.

She sat down cross-legged in the centre of the room and sipped at the water. It was always exactly body temperature. Eventually Kurt's voice came back.

"Change of plan. We're sending someone in. Still doing just Water today."

"Okay." Aisling stood up and anxiously waited for a minute until she saw the side door open and a familiar woman enter. Aisling recognised her as Janice, the Khun woman who had been there when she was held captive in the cell. She wore a navy-blue polo shirt, clearly some kind of uniform.

"Aisling, this is Janice. She used to be another Participant, now works as a cleaner here."

"Nice to meet you." Aisling smiled at Janice, who stared in the way Khun often did, and Aisling felt both relaxed and on edge.

"Janice never got far with the research. We would like to see what two Participants together can achieve with Water magic. We are interested in finding out if the magic is specific to one person, or if multiple people can control the same spell at the same time. Aisling, why don't you show Janice the fog?" Aisling dutifully set about filling the booth with cloud, seeing a worried expression creep over Janice's face before she lost sight of her in the cloud. "Janice, can you remove the fog please?"

There was no change immediately, although Aisling felt a grip on her hand through the fog. Janice came close to her, hidden from observers, and whispered in her ear in Khun, "Do not show them. None of us show them. Only enough to stay alive. They are dishonourable. I found your tiny apple and hid it. They don't know about Matter magic. Be more careful."

Janice stepped back to her original position and slowly

lifted the cloud. Aisling tried to keep her face neutral, but couldn't remember how much she normally frowned or smiled.

"This is great!" Kurt announced. "Can we do it the other way now? Janice, you create a fog and Aisling, you remove it."

On and on the experiments went, always so simple and boring. Aisling knew she would not get another chance for a private conversation with Janice and thought about her words the whole day. She had been careless with the apple. What if someone else found it? Could she trust Janice? What did she mean 'dishonourable'? And how many Participants were there?

At the end of the day as she was leaving the lab, she found Kurt looking at some complicated numbers and charts and asked him, "Kurt?"

"Yes Aisling?" He was like an eager puppy, always so curious about the most mundane things. Aisling was starting to tire of him. She needed a rest and enjoyed being alone at night, safe in her room.

"How many Participants do you have? Why aren't you doing the same experiments with Janice?"

"It's kind of a long story. You know the agency goes back a long time. Unofficially of course, because as you know, we don't exist out there in the real world." *The real world,* she thought, *whatever that is.* "We've had a number of Participants join us and leave us from the beginning until now. We've only ever had one at a time because it's so rare to find anyone. Janice is one of our older Participants, she joined over a year ago."

"Leave us to go where?" He pretended not to hear her. "Why isn't she doing experiments now? Why is she cleaning?"

"Ah well, we did a lot of experiments together, like we do with all the Participants who come here, but we never get any really promising results. They all had only a little magic ability, so we hadn't been making much progress. That is, until we found you!" Kurt, it seemed, really had only scientific intentions and was unable to connect the human lives to their data. He seemed to have no idea that Aisling was blackmailed into coming, her alternative being almost certain death. He was so invested in science he couldn't see the ethical problems. Maybe he really didn't know who the Participants were or where they went after the experiments. Aisling worried that by eagerly showing off her powers she had somehow compromised the collective efforts of the Khun to keep their secret hidden. 'Dishonourable', Janice had said.

"What happened to the other Participants? Why have I only seen Janice and no one else?"

"Oh, most of them leave quickly. They get offered other positions and move to a different Ministry, or they simply resign and end their contracts." She thought this was suspicious.

"But Janice works here in a different job?"

"Yes, after her experiments provided very little promise, she asked if she could do something else rather than move agency." Aisling thought Janice was probably avoiding death by hanging. She must be a very practical woman. She must have seen a lot.

"Thanks Kurt."

"Any time. Get some rest. Tomorrow we might be ready to try some of that Heat magic you mentioned. I just have to set up the experiments to collect the right data."

"Goodnight."

That night as Aisling looked out at the city from her

window, she could see pigeons continuing to act strangely the way they had been doing for a few days. She wished they would come up to see her, even though she did not know Bird magic to talk to them. She just wanted them to know she was there. Maybe that was all it would take. She knew that Time magic wouldn't work: the night before, she tried to cast a slow-motion spell on the stupid birds, but was unsuccessful.

While she watched the pigeons flocking random windows on random buildings down below, she devised a plan for finding a way to talk to Janice again. This was something Chuluun taught her from a young age: not to act without information. She knew his words, but she had found herself acting thoughtlessly more and more often over the previous year. Sometimes it had caused trouble, like when she tried to use a Time spell on herself to run faster, not knowing the dangers of magic loops. It still seemed too complicated to understand. Now, more than ever, she knew she had to keep her thinking slow and act in a way that Chuluun would approve of. Information first. But how? How could she talk to Janice in private?

Janice cleaned the room during the day, so what if Aisling left her some code, or clue? It seemed like the only way, but it was a risk. What if Janice wasn't the one who found it?

And to make things worse, it looked like only Matter magic and Dream magic weren't blocked. How was that supposed to help her? She waited at the window for the flock of pigeons to see her, wondering how long before they tried every window in the city. Distantly in the sky she saw the shadow of a tremendous eagle move across the moon and out of view. "Come here, please," she mouthed.

Dishonourable. The word had been in her mind all day since Janice delivered her warning. It was somewhat frightening, but Aisling reasoned: *what are they doing here that's honourable?* What was even the point of this research? None of it made sense without the big picture.

Down on the streets far below, she could see traffic going in and out of a tunnel.

What if I shrank the tunnel? She thought, understanding the dangers that magic could create if misused. *What if I shrank it so that the Noicars all crashed into each other while I just stood up here watching? I could.*

Revelation smeared a lopsided smile across her pale face. *What if I shrank myself?*

It was such a strange idea, one that she had never played with before. In her memory it sometimes seemed like Khuch was larger than other times, when he was strong, when he was brave. She felt small sometimes. But that was just her mood playing tricks on her. She had never seen any of the Khun use Matter magic on each other. But it should be possible. What consequences would there be for her magic power? Would that shrink with her?

Information first. It was acting without thinking that caused this mess, she owed it to everybody to know what she was about to do before doing it.

The pigeons were finishing their evening rounds and soon they would be gone until the morning. She trained her focus on one of them. Even though it was far away, her magic amplified her focus and she could feel the presence of that one pigeon as it flapped ridiculously amongst its family. She visualised a great ball of loose grass cuttings in her hands and squashed it gently. The bird was suddenly too small to see and Aisling felt like cheering.

Now, can I make him normal again?

Having not lost her focus on that bird, she reached across space, following the tether she had mentally constructed, joining her to it. She visualised releasing her grip on the grass ball and it regained its shape, filling out to its natural size and density. She could see the pigeon again carrying on as though nothing had happened.

So, it was possible. But she needed more practice. The repetitive experiments in the lab had taught Aisling the value of slow and deliberate practice, and she thought about how she could use the same principles to become powerful at Matter magic. She would need to be immensely powerful to shrink herself and not lose her footing in the world. There was so much risk, but so much possibility. It was a dangerously promising future that had begun to unfold, with endless roads leading to the same goal: freedom.

She thought of her dad, wondering where he was, who he was with, what he was doing. Would he try to find her? She had never been so alone.

From his nest hidden in the steel arms of the radio tower, Orn witnessed one of his servants inexplicably shrink to a fraction of its size, only to re-grow to its ordinary size seconds later.

The girl is here. She signals.

Regally, he stretched his wings and preened his front feathers. There were many places where the girl could reach the pigeon with her magic, especially if she were a strong wizard, but the search could be narrowed. He screeched into the night air, calling all pigeons back to the rooftop. Being outside their ordinary work hours, a great number quickly gathered.

"We have received a signal from the girl. She is somewhere close to the window that you will see yonder, where there is now a woman and baby. We will narrow the search to this area alone. Half of you will retire- it will raise suspicion to see all of you together. Tomorrow we search this street in more detail, and I hope that will be the end of it."

"Hail sky king!" one of the pigeons at the back called out amongst much cooing.

"Yes, yes," he answered, distracted from his thoughts. "I want eyes on these buildings at all times, including this building you stand on now."

"Hail!"

"Why do I bother?" He turned away.

Orn sighed heavily, tired of dealing with the pigeons. He shooed them away with his great wing and resumed nesting. Hopefully tomorrow would be the end of it, and he could go home to be alone again. That wizard Tesver had caused more trouble than he was worth, even if he was an Earth Person. Orn thought he should have declined to help.

A few days earlier, Orn had noticed a crow's nest on the east side of the building he was on, quite high up and only seldom used. He wondered if he would get to meet the crow who lived there before he finished the job and went home. They were much more his style of bird: loyal, intelligent, and hardy. This whole thing would have been finished much faster if he had a team of crows working for him instead of bloody pigeons.

He stretched again, embracing the silence that often coincides with full moons, and settled in for a night of rest.

After only one night of focused search, the pigeons found the girl. Orn was satisfied with their work and dismissed them all.

He flew over to a rooftop where he could see her window and waited for her to appear. He had to confirm it was her before delivering the news to the old wizard.

In the early evening he saw her there, and he saw her changing the size of various objects. It was curious. She seemed to be doing it purposefully, but having fun at the same time. Sometimes, Orn had trouble understanding humans. She also didn't look like one of the Earth People, which came as a surprise to him.

A Noicraft approached the city from the north-east, and Orn watched until it came to land on the roof high above the girl, almost within reach of his nesting place. He decided to fly higher and see who was in it. He saw a group of soldiers leave the craft with a muscly young man. The prisoner's face was different to those around him; he looked more like one of the Earth People. They disappeared inside the building. Humans hunting humans.

The wizard will want to know this, and about the girl.

The easier part of Orn's mission was to make contact with the girl. He waited until she was looking out the window and flew towards her, slowing as he approached. He hovered in front of her for a second before taking off into the sky and back towards his mountain. She was still looking out the window after him as he disappeared into the night, his voice loud and clear over the city:

"I have found her! Tell the Wizard Tesver that I, Orn, have found the girl! Kraka!"

And to her great surprise, through the soundproof walls and glass that made up the building and through the anti-magic field, Aisling was able to understand his words. She could understand all of it and she knew that something good was happening finally. She did not hear his full message, however. The one he told his messenger when he arrived back home at his mountain. She could not have known that Orn recognised her from a dream; a dream in which he saw her kneeling over a dead man.

Aisling took a step back from the window and smiled broadly at seeing the proof that the Khun were looking for her and the hope that she might be freed. She would have been horrified to learn that another person was arrested like her and to know that it was Khuch.

Orn, after resting at his mountain only a few minutes, sensed that his work was not finished and begrudgingly turned back to his temporary nest and waited. He felt like he must wait for the girl, but he couldn't explain why. A power bigger than himself was compelling him to act.

Chapter 11

The news of Khuch's arrest reached Tesver quickly. If the swallows were to be trusted, he exited the forest after just one day of travel and attempted to blend into a group of people on the road south. The swallows repeated what they heard from Kraka, that Khuch accidentally wandered into a political meeting at a small town, hoping that he could disappear in their crowd and be ignored until he found a ride to the Capital. Unfortunately, the man leading the meeting, a local politician named Dirk Spratt, instantly recognised Khuch's dark features as foreign and turned the crowd against him. Rather than wait to be lynched, he ran and was arrested a short time later.

Tesver found the news bittersweet. They would likely take him to where Aisling was held, where he would need to think quickly. Thinking quickly, however, was not Khuch's strong point. Acting quickly was. It would have been preferable for him not to be arrested, but it was by far the fastest and most direct route to the girl. And they all wanted Khuch to make it back in time for their departure to Gazar.

Tesver sighed, knowing that he would have to tell the others, imagining their reactions.

At that moment, a chirp announced the arrival of a sparrow. This particular sparrow was named Vereb, and was

Tesver's messenger from Mafur the seagull. This news was what the whole group had been waiting for.

"What news, Vereb?" Tesver chirped back at the sparrow.

"News from Mafur. I have been tasked to deliver a message."

"I am listening."

"The sea eagle Haforn proposes the autumn equinox as the date you shall travel to Gazar; he will ensure the seas are safe. The soldiers there are reduced in numbers to one tenth of their maximum, and many operations have ceased. Haforn knows not the reason for their cessation. Eastern soldiers are returning home and Gazar is in the hands of Khun again. Some eastern peoples remain with families and grow foods."

"The autumn equinox… is there more to the message?"

"That is all."

"Thank you Vereb. Please thank Mafur for me." Tesver tied a sprig of thyme to Vereb's leg, and opened his palm to reveal a handful of seeds, flowers, and insects. Vereb hopped down Tesver's arm from his shoulder to his hand and began pecking at the feast.

It was a crisp autumn morning, and the sun was filtering through the thick canopy. Tesver's hand was positioned in a beam of sunlight, and Vereb appeared to enjoy the warmth of it. The underbrush was damp; each day damper than the last as more and more leaves fell scattered, giving homes to worms and centipedes. A moist odour rose from it all. The forest was Tesver's home more than anything, and he was faced with a choice: to faithfully relay Vereb's message to the group, or to ignore it and remain in the forest – his forest.

But he shook the idea from his mind. Sense of duty overcame any thoughts of abandoning Gazar. Who was in charge of Gazar now that the eastern peoples were retreating? Why were they retreating? These were questions beyond the reporting capabilities of Vereb, or Mafur, or even Haforn the sea eagle.

Responding to Tesver's summons, Chuluun approached the usual spot on the hill and remarked that in the weeks they had been camped in the clearing, Tesver's skin had taken on a more and more bark-like appearance every day. He wondered as to its texture.

"I have news from Gazar," Tesver began, and explained the message from Vereb.

"The spring equinox is not long from now, only five days." Chuluun spoke in pragmatic facts, but Tesver was able to hear the subtle doubts between his words

"I know that you do not trust Haforn." His eyes had begun to resemble to dark hollows that form in the trunks of old trees, and his movements were turning stiffer with time.

"You move with difficulty, and I fear you will not make the journey." Again, Tesver was obliged to listen to the spaces between the words.

"My Bird magic grows stronger with every hour."

"Tesver, do you remember the story of Golchlon, from the time before the war?"

"I remember Golchlon." Tesver knew where Chuluun was headed with this question, but in a tree-like way, he listened patiently, swaying gently. "His power over Water magic was unchallenged."

"His transformation was rapid, as is yours. When his strength grew more and more towards the Water, it was known that the clear waters of river Gol were his true position in this world. It was not possible to remove him. He was born to fulfil this destiny, to return to the water from which he came. When we go home, you will stay here."

"Thank you, Chuluun."

"You are born to follow this route to the next world. I wish for all Khun to know their path. Mine is unclear, like many who flow through life without knowing. Our paths were darkened by the war in Gazar. You are special among Khun, and we will be sorry to lose your company. Modon Khun you will be known from now. Tree man, man of tree. We will perform the ceremony to honour your transformation."

"The equinox is five days from now," Tesver Modon Khun, reminded Chuluun. "It will be a hard time to wait, with Khuch Chaddhal on his mission."

"He will not make the journey in five days," Chuluun stated bluntly. "And we will make the journey without him. And without Aisling, and Peter."

"He will arrive in the Capital tonight."

"So, he has been caught." Chuluun's voice betrayed no emotion, and Tesver's woody face nodded in jolts. "The return journey is still long. He can waste no time. Do you have news from Orn?"

"Nothing yet."

"It is a pity, I had great hope for the Eagle."

"Do not give up, Chuluun. There is still time."

"He has been looking for a week. It is a foolish task to pursue."

"He will find Aisling."

"We cling to hope."

"Hope is the way of all Khun," Tesver quoted from the Book of Boloi. "You forget that all magic springs from hope."

"Hope is the source of all magic." Chuluun nodded slowly and smoothly to contrast Tesver's wooden movements. "But there is no hope in this land and its people. They live their lives thinking only of the present, distracted by their endless search for Noi and power for their technologies."

"No Chuluun," Tesver rebutted. "It is a type of hope, but it is different to ours. They hope that they never run out of Noi, and that is the problem. Their hope is hidden by fear, whereas ours is at the front of our mind. We see hope in everything, it is the force that guides our lives. The lives here are led by fear, and magic is made invisible. Birds know this. Birds are masters of both fear and hope, and the place where those powers meet."

"Then how is it that our new Khun members have learned magic? If they are so blinded by fear, how is it that they can do the same as we can?"

"The girl is easiest to explain: she joined us young, before the rules of her land could take the hope from her. She joined us with a child's appreciation of all possibilities and without the painful awareness of reality."

A silence fell between them as Chuluun thought over the words. From a distance he might have been talking to a tree, Tesver's transformation was so rapid.

"And Peter?"

"He is harder to explain," Tesver admitted, Vereb nesting in his hair now; hair that resembled twigs and leaves. "I suspect his life contains much tragedy that he has not wished to share. The darker magics have been known to seek out such lives."

"He has affinity for Fire magic."

"Yes, and this could be his downfall. It is those with difficult lives who show the greatest command of Fire." They both reflected, with transformation in their minds. Tesver Modon Khun, master of Bird magic; Golchlon, master of Water magic, the Khun who transformed into Water and whose spirit occupies all parts of the river Gol. "But Fire magic cannot be used without strength of will. Peter harnesses pain within hope. It is dangerous and difficult, and the transformation to Fire master is painful. I suspect it is his difficult past that has given birth to his strong hope: he feels both pain and hope more strongly than us."

"But we cannot know unless he reveals his past."

"In a way, he has already. It is the girl's mother."

"It is not proper for Khun to gossip about the dead." Chuluun warned, then added as he thought about Peter. "Nor the living."

"I will say no more of my suspicions," Tesver acknowledged. "It is curious that the dead occupy the thoughts of some birds. They will talk of nothing else."

"And yet you pushed Bird magic to its limits?" Chuluun was disgusted by the concept. Khun custom prohibited grieving for the dead beyond a certain period, and even talking about the dead was done with care, as it was mostly taboo.

"I have learned very many things from the birds," Tesver answered cryptically. "The Khun life is only a small part of all life. But the birds have no concept of the next world. They live here, now, balancing fear and hope."

"It is a strange way to live, without the next world to guide your action."

"Perhaps. Perhaps not," Tesver creaked. "There are some benefits, but also some issues."

"I can think only of issues."

"My transformation delays my transition to the next world. When I am complete, I will remain rooted here until I am hacked away or the forest burns. I am content with knowing that I sacrifice my journey at my expected time."

"The transformation is a strange thing indeed, no matter which magic has chosen the master."

"It is. I expect I have only a few days before it is finished. Now I suggest you deliver the news of your impending return home to the group. They will be pleased to hear it."

Chuluun patted Tesver on the shoulder in the customary way and noted how prickly he felt on his skin. It was long expected that Tesver would become a Bird master, but the final transformation had been so sudden and complete that it took all of the Khun by surprise. Chuluun positioned himself in the centre of the camp and called all the Khun over. Most were in the midst of their morning activities and making breakfast.

"We will be returning to Gazar on the day of the equinox," he advised the group. Some murmuring erupted.

"The news is trusted?" one older Khun called out from a stool next to his tent.

"It is," Chuluun answered confidently. "Tesver has spent many weeks and months ensuring the network is trustworthy."

"What boats do we have?" Sanakh piped up, her voice cutting across the crisp air. The Khun had a habit of remaining motionless until a meeting finished. No clothing rustled.

"There are the boats originally stored at the place of landing," Chuluun replied. "I suggest that we make preparations to move back to the coast and have all boats ready and prepared for safe crossing."

"How can you know those boats are still in the place?" Sanakh was unconvinced. "It was sixteen years ago." Some sounds of agreement came from the others.

"Then we should go there today, so that we have time to

repair them in case they are destroyed with age. The sea eagle Haforn has advised that the day of the equinox is the day for crossing. We will be on our boats on that day."

"The crossing takes more than one day," Sanakh argued. "Are we to leave here on the equinox or arrive at Gazar on the equinox?"

"It was unclear from the message. Haforn did not take into account the time the journey takes. I think it does not matter."

"Every detail matters," another voice called out anxiously.

"The message from Haforn is that he will ensure safe passage on the equinox," Chuluun replied. "We sail on the equinox."

After some more general questioning, it was decided that the group would travel that day to their first landing place on the beach where they had hidden their boats all those years earlier. They would leave that day to allow enough time for unexpected problems.

"Chuluun," Sanakh asked him after the decision was made and agreed to. "Tesver is unable to walk."

"It is true. He is in transformation now."

"Is he really?" Sanakh nearly smiled, in the way that Khun do. "That is excellent for him, but it is a loss for us. Without his Bird magic to communicate, we will be lost."

"Most of us are able to perform some Bird magic at least." Chuluun laid a hand on her shoulder. "We will manage the crossing even without his ability. And he will help us from here through his network of messengers. Not all is lost."

"I have great hope for us and for Gazar."

"It is our time to return now," Chuluun then repeated it louder for the group and to confirm it to himself because it seemed so unbelievable after waiting for so long. "It is our time to return now."

That night, Chuluun's dreams were hijacked.

"Can you hear me?"

"I think so." The man's question threw Chuluun off guard because they were standing facing each other in a small room. Why shouldn't he hear him?

"I believe I have finally gotten this right."

Chuluun had seen the room many times before, but this time it was more sharply in focus. The man who always appeared in the doorway was not a loose shadow, not just a suggestion this time. Instead, he was a healthy-looking man with a face of about sixty or seventy years old. He had a wispy mane of white hair that reached his broad, bony shoulders. Chuluun studied him, deciding that he didn't look like any of the peoples he had met in his life. He had the same narrow face as Peter's people, but his body was the right height and shape to be one of the Arazi from the north, and his skin was nearly the colour of the Khun. He wore a brown robe, not in the style of any nation Chuluun knew. He had high cheek bones and was terribly thin. It confused Chuluun to look at, and he thought maybe he preferred when the dream man was out of focus.

"You are Chuluun?" He had a voice that was soothing and compelling at the same time. Chuluun's confusion was wiped away and he felt himself again.

"Yes."

"Do you know me?"

"I have a guess." Chuluun was speaking in Khun and the man in another dreamy language, yet they understood each other perfectly well. "I have seen you before, but not for a long time."

"Iwizadi, they call me. This is the first time I have spoken in many years."

"Is it you that I have seen in my dreams all my life?"

"Yes," Iwizadi answered. "I am asleep. It is the safest way to travel the world, but it has taken me too long to be able to speak. Until now, my Dream magic has been enough to bring you to me, but not enough to ask you for help."

"Help?"

"The Dream world is a strange place, and there are not a lot of people I can influence. Only strongly magical people."

"Khun told me Dream magic was impossible. I tried it. I failed. But you are successful. I cannot be called strong."

"After centuries of trying." Iwizadi seemed in no hurry to get to the point, enjoying his moment of victory in creating a new form of magic.

"What help?" Chuluun brought him back to the point.

"There are two things." Iwizadi's voice was so pleasant, Chuluun was eager to hear him speak more. "First, you are correct that it is time to return to Gazar. It is time for Gazar to rise to power and to know a good leader. The country you hide in drains the land of magic, though they do not know it. I have worked hard over these recent years to influence the soldiers to leave Gazar, and now it is the right time for your return. You lead your people well and they trust you. But when you return to Gazar, you will not lead for long. The true leader of Gazar has been found elsewhere. You will lead only until the true leader is in place.

"The second thing: The girl Aisling is to become your daughter by marriage. She is the true leader of Gazar, and the city of Khot, which will be called by its ancient name Libalele. It was foretold that I would return when the true leader is found. My time approaches."

"Aisling? The true leader?" Chuluun was enraged. "She is not Khun! She has not done the initiation! Only Khun can lead Gazar!"

"Libalele belonged to my people long before yours arrived," Iwizadi explained. "It is not only Khun land."

"It is not right." Chuluun shook his head. He could reach out and crush the wizard in his enormous hands. "Lost our houses and families. We waited sixteen years to return."

"I have waited one thousand years!" Iwizadi bellowed, forcing Chuluun to cower back against the wall. He had never experienced anything like the power within that voice, and he immediately felt foolish for complaining about his sixteen years; foolish for thinking he could overcome the wizard with purely physical force. "The reclamation of Libalele has been one thousand years waiting for Aisling and your Khun people will not get in the way of its greatness!"

Chuluun managed to nod, not taking his eyes off Iwizadi.

"It is your destiny to give your people hope, and to lead them back when the time is right. It is your destiny to provide a way for Aisling to lead Libalele: she must marry your son." Iwizadi's voice was back at its normal volume and calm again. "I need you to go to the people in Halasat, tell them the chosen one has arrived. They will understand."

"What about Peter?"

"He has another destiny. It is complicated, but his path diverges from yours now. I have seen his future from a distance. He will see his wife before he follows the path of Fire."

"Maria? She died a long time ago." Chuluun was confused by this, but dreams had a way of playing tricks. If Iwizadi saw Peter with Maria in a vision, it was possible that she was alive, but no guarantee.

"She lives. Now it is time to awaken, Chuluun. You have work to do before setting sail. I will make the seas calm for you when you go."

"Thank you." Chuluun remembered his manners, and the dream began to fade starting with Iwizadi's face, which returned to its shapeless form.

Chuluun was then awake, the dream clear in his mind. Immediately he went a little bit away from the camp and called for Kraka with his best Bird magic. She found him a minute later and he instructed her to deliver the message to the birds that live near Halasat. She went immediately and without complaint. Good, dependable Kraka. Halasat must be at least a week's journey away, and they should be in Gazar by the time she returned. He didn't want to know the reply. He also didn't want to go himself, as Iwizadi had suggested.

Early in the morning on the day of the equinox, the boats were ready and the sea and skies were calm. A current appeared to be pulling to the north-east in the direction of Gazar. The assembled Khun stood nervously on the shore waiting for the final instruction from Chuluun. They had packed a few days' supply of food and all their belongings into the four small boats. The boats were exactly where they were left sixteen years earlier and had miraculously not sustained any serious damage. Just as predicted, Khuch was not back in time, and this made Chuluun feel very ashamed.

Chuluun stood on the beach surveying the sea ahead of him. He felt suspicious about the perfect weather conditions, but allowed his excitement and zeal to push him forward.

"It is too good to be true." Sanakh said apprehensively, her watery voice approaching Chuluun's left side, "How can you trust this? It looks to be a trick."

"Sanakh, my dear." Chuluun put one hand one her shoulder in the customary way. "Gazar is calling us home. What power exists to play a trick on this scale? Only Gazar itself. We are going home, the group agreed together."

"Yes, but…" Sanakh stumbled on her words, considering Chuluun's calm reasoning and his passionate zealotry together. "What if you are wrong?"

"And what if I am right?"

"We cannot know either way."

"Until we try."

Some seagulls barked nearby as they watched the gathered Khun with playful curiosity. Watching them back, Chuluun felt the loss of Tesver from their party. He also felt the tremendous gain for the greater magical power that governed the earth. Birds of all kinds had guided them to this point; Chuluun wondered how their journey would be now without Tesver.

The sea beckoned and the Khun were getting restless. They were eager to get going, since it would take a couple of days to reach Gazar, and they were not sure how long the good conditions would last.

"What if it is a trick, Chuluun," Sanakh said again, "and halfway there, the seas become a storm?"

"Then we will fight the storm."

"We will die."

"Maybe."

"We should go now before we change our minds."

"I think so too." Chuluun gripped the edge of one of the boats and the others did the same. The boats did not look sturdy enough to carry their dozens across the sea, but they were all enchanted to repel water and remain upright. The preparations for the voyage involved long and complex spells to ensure these safety precautions; spells that required the whole group to contribute. Chuluun was satisfied that their spells would hold through the whole trip if the weather stayed good. If water attempted to flood their boats from above in the form of rain, there was nothing to stop it, but if water tried to slosh over the sides of their boats, it would change its mind.

The sea was almost pulling on their boats before everyone was on board.

When everyone was ready, they all pushed off from the beach together, into the beckoning current and the dangerous journey home. Their four boats fell into a single file as they found the current. It felt as if they were being magically tugged home, sent on autopilot, sleepwalking into their destiny.

"It's a sign from Gazar, it wants us to come back," one of the Khun, Ychir, decided. There was nodding from the others on his boat.

"It feels too easy," Sanakh muttered to herself, still not convinced that it was safe to go at all.

"But you are here." Chuluun tried appealing to her hopeful side.

"Yes of course I am here; Gazar is where we belong. Maybe it is never going to be safe to return, but it is our purpose in life to do so."

"You are right. And only by trying will we know if we were right."

They sailed onwards, until after only a short time, their starting point became a distant blip on the horizon. On each boat, one Khun at a time was charged with casting Wind magic into the sails, while another cast Water magic on the boat to propel it forward. There was some uneasiness among the group when they realised that even without either of those essential spells, the boats would still have carried themselves to Gazar.

"It is a trap. I am certain of it," Sanakh confided in Chuluun once more. "I cannot shake this feeling that you have led us here to die."

"You do not trust me?"

"No, I trust you. But I fear that you have put your trust in sources that we cannot verify."

"I trust Tesver."

"As do I."

"And do you trust that his bird spies have told us the truth?"

"Not entirely. Something is wrong. It is too easy."

Chuluun still hadn't told anyone about his encounter with Iwizadi. How he knew with absolute certainty that it was the wizard himself making their voyage possible. Telling them would worry them further and cause all kinds of problems, so it was better to simply tell them he placed his full trust in Tesver.

Before they set sail, news came from the forest that Tesver's transformation was complete. According to the seagulls, who heard it from the sparrows, Tesver had succumbed to the stiffness of the tree life, and was welcomed as a font of magic in the forest. He could no longer communicate directly to humans, only birds.

As silence fell across the boat once more, Chuluun reflected on magic. It was a wonderful thing, but he kept coming back to the same questions: Why did Khun have magic while the rest of the world fought over Noi? Iwizadi had promised Chuluun that he was to be the interim ruler of Gazar while they waited for Aisling to arrive, and that was a lot of responsibility. Sure, he could lead a small group of families. But a country? And why shouldn't he share magic with other people? Magic came from the earth, so why was it kept a secret for Khun alone? There were things in the world that didn't add up, and Chuluun had trouble understanding Iwizadi's plan. Orthodox Khun thinking would reason that all problems either had immediate solutions or none at all. The situation with Iwizadi didn't fit either category and it bothered him greatly.

It was his years of exile and recent meeting with Iwizadi that had given him perspective. Maybe problems could not be all solved as soon as they were encountered. Maybe it was worthwhile thinking about the bigger picture, the questions with no definitive answers.

Why shouldn't he share magic with all peoples when he was leading Gazar? Could he disobey Iwizadi?

He felt for the Book of Boloi, which was stored in his bag, now sitting between his legs. The Book was indeed mysterious: none of the Khun could trace its origin fully, yet it seemingly contained a history of all the magic used in daily life. But the strangest thing about it according to Chuluun was that it didn't mention the Khun once. To be fair, it didn't mention any specific people, but it was most definitely not written by Khun, as they had no legacy of art or literature that resembled it. Since his encounter with Iwizadi, Chuluun had been thinking about the origins of things. Iwizadi had said that the Khun were only taking care of Gazar until the Libaleleans returned.

We aren't taking very good care of it, he reflected sadly.

All the things Iwizadi told him answered the questions that had bounced around his mind for years. His suspicions were right: Khun did not write the book, Libaleleans did. And if the Khun were not originally from Gazar, where were they from? Where did magic come from and why was it kept secret by Libalele? But he could never tell his people. They would lose trust in him.

And that was the next great problem with no immediate solution: When he was temporarily leading Gazar, how could he explain that they should step aside and simply give away their land to a people whom most had never heard of except in fairy tale? Nobody would accept Aisling, even if she was initiated and married to Khuch Chaddhal.

Chuluun was angry with Iwizadi for putting him in this situation, forced to change the whole history of his people. He was only just coming to terms with it himself. And what if Iwizadi was wrong? Deluded? His people were long gone! One thousand years ago! How long did the Khun have to live there before they were natives? Is one thousand years not long enough?

And what was Halasat? What were its people? Why were they so important to Iwizadi and why was he told to go there? So many questions he could not answer. How could he go to Halasat when he had a country to lead? With any luck, they would hear Kraka's message and prevent him from the need to travel.

Despite the anger he felt towards Iwizadi, Chuluun still trusted him. The wizard had gifted the Khun magic in the first place and trusted them with Gazar. Even if it was an eon ago and his motives could have changed, he still offered Chuluun the best hope of answering the questions of his origin and the beginnings of magic.

The second half of their first day at sea was completely uneventful. The boats dragged themselves forward without the aid of Wind or Water magic, and the weather did not change from its perfect cloudless, windless state. They were making such great progress, Ychir calculated they would arrive early the next day. There was a growing excitement among all members of the group, even Sanakh, whose anxiety paradoxically both grew and abated the closer they came to their goal.

As night fell, Ychir and many of the group had trouble sleeping due to a giddy excitement. They were closer to their home than they had been in sixteen years. What would they find there? Would the soldiers still occupy their homes? Would the earth still be scarred and leaking blue where the various occupants had torn open its surface to collect Noi?

Towards the middle of the night, a faint blue glow began to spread upwards on the horizon. A few Khun shed tears and clapped each other on the shoulders when they saw it. Their first vision of home since fleeing from the war. Did any of their family and friends remain? Why had there been no messages from the birds until only recently? Had the birds returned too?

The boats still slunk forward noiselessly through the calm water. Chuluun marvelled at the stillness of the sea and how the boats had hardly felt like they were moving the whole time. Iwizadi truly had power beyond Khun. Perhaps he was right that they were only the caretakers of Libalele, with their inferior magic ability. Chuluun stayed awake through the night watching the deep blue glow of his homeland spread over the horizon, blending the dark sea and the darker sky. His thoughts were full of doubt, questioning everything he had ever known to be true.

Even when the sun rose the next day, the blue light emanating from Gazar was more vibrant than the morning sky. Seeing its distant beauty come into focus gradually, Chuluun set aside his worries and gawked at the magical landscape, as did everyone else. The closer they got to the island, the stronger they felt its magical influence. All the Khun felt more energised, younger, healthier, and much more magically powerful.

As the morning settled in and excitement grew on board, Sanakh spotted a large bird approaching them from the island. They watched eagerly as it came in to land on the prow of their boat and began squawking.

"Greetings. I am Haforn, the Sea Eagle. It is a pleasure to see Khun returning to this land."

"Greetings Haforn," Chuluun spoke. "It is an honour to meet you. Thank you for your messages these last months."

"I have had to fly long distances to feed, and find new outcrops for roosting. The people living here after the Khun left have damaged this place. You are welcomed back by all living things."

"Which peoples are here now?" Chuluun asked with immense gratitude. Many of the others were crying again, very unlike their ordinary stoic behaviour.

"The wars are finished and soldiers gone now, back east. Some Khun are still here, but they are broken. Some other peoples have settled here and live peacefully. Gazar is for Khun again."

Chuluun silently thanked Iwizadi with all his heart. The wizard had been telling the truth. A huge feeling of relief spread through the Khun. Any plots he had to deviate from Iwizadi's instructions were gone. He would go to Halasat without argument.

"Haforn, we are truly sorry for what this land has suffered. We failed in our duty to care for it."

"We can move past this. Birds have started to return too."

"Yes. And we will ask you again for your help. Please spread news of our return back to Mafur the Gull, and to all the birds in that country we hid in. We need all the Khun now to come back, no more hiding. If there are any left."

"I will go with you to the shore, then deliver the good news to the world."

Haforn let forth a triumphant screech and pushed off from the boat into the sky again, gliding gracefully far overhead, announcing their arrival to anything that could hear him. The south-western cliffs of Gazar were coming into view now, their dangerous waves and high drops providing a natural defence against any intruders approaching from their direction. The boats steered themselves east and began to circumnavigate the island, still at a good distance.

Haforn's cries echoed over the calm sea and a flock of birds erupted from the top of the cliffs into the sky. They circled and played through the air as the Khun watched their writhing clouds morph into various shapes. There must have been a million birds in each cloud. Haforn was giving them the hero's welcome, but they felt like they didn't deserve it.

As their boats cruised along eastward around the island, Sanakh's anxiety was replaced with joy, having made the difficult crossing with ease. The eastern coast was gentle, and many of the travellers had memories of swimming at its beaches. The group was talking endlessly about their old homes, wondering what was still there and speculating as to how things had changed, impatient for their arrival.

Finally, around midday, the peak of the great mountain came into view and the Khun were silent at once. It was a sacred moment, one that everyone understood must be remembered for all of their future history. Nothing could take away from the glorious return. The boats turned up into the river Gol and cruised with magical ease directly upstream towards the mountain. Some Khun reached into the magical waters and scooped up a handful to drink.

Nothing could take away from this moment. Nothing could spoil the collective rapture felt by all. Their long-awaited homecoming. They had returned at last.

Chapter 12

Daphne Morris' days always began the same way: she awoke at six without fail and drank a glass of water. She put on her favourite radio station to hear the news and some popular songs. She did half an hour of yoga, and ate a light breakfast – usually a piece of fruit and coffee. She showered, dressed, made herself up, and left her apartment at five minutes to eight. This allowed her enough time to catch the elevator and walk to her office and get some work done before most people arrived.

Work was her life. In fact, she drew a blank whenever she thought about her life before her work with the Department. It was as if nothing was there. But the peculiar thing was that she would instantly be distracted and forget what she was thinking about. The lack of memory never upset her. She had learned all she knew from working at the Department, observing the Participants and trying to copy what they showed. She didn't question her affinity for magic and why other staff struggled to learn spells that she could pick up easily. Everyone in the Department considered that just another question to be answered in time.

Aisling looked familiar to Miss Morris; she even looked similar to her, but if anyone else noticed it they didn't say. She was usually inflexible in her rigid attitude towards work and people. Like clockwork she never missed a beat. But it was strange with the girl, she felt herself inexplicably warming to her, like there was some connection she was missing. She found it unnerving and decided to ignore it, and forced herself to treat her exactly the same as she treated everyone else: with cold, business-like distance.

At exactly eight that morning she entered her office and began work. It was mostly routine things, making sure the other Department heads were satisfied with their work and that funding continued to drip down. It must be hard for the accountants, she thought, to funnel such huge amounts of money to a Department that technically doesn't exist. Whatever magic she was researching, those accountants were the real wizards.

She was surprised to find Jack knocking on her door only a few minutes later. He normally didn't visit the lab unless it was important.

"Good morning, Miss Morris."

"Mister Hargreaves," she replied with strict formality.

"We have a new priority for you today upstairs."

"Upstairs?" That could only mean one thing: someone was in the holding room. "Right away."

They made their way together in silence, Jack sipping on a coffee from time to time. How many times had he done this before? Daphne began to prepare her mind for the usual demonstration of magic that would change the prisoner to a willing Participant. It was a show of trust, a way to manipulate them, a way of saying 'we understand and we care, we're just like you'. It always worked. She wondered what type of magic she would demonstrate today. Usually, Jack only wanted a few drops of water just to show the prisoner, but sometimes it was something different. Truth be told, they had only ever received twenty-something

Participants in the years that the Department had existed, it was truly a rare event when one was found, or even rarer sought them out.

She suppressed a smile, thinking about the importance of her work and the excitement it brought her. She was sure Jack felt the same way, but he was very hard to read. He masked his intentions in theatrics and his mood could go from zero to a hundred in the blink of an eye. He could be frightening sometimes.

Jack paused before opening the door to the holding room.

"The usual?" he asked her. She nodded calmly. They entered the room and saw Peter lying on the bed. He did not stir when he heard them enter, which made Jack scoff and clear his throat.

"Good morning, Peter." When Peter ignored the greeting, Jack pressed on. "I trust you have thought about my offer?"

There was still no response, and Jack moved around the cell to get a closer look, to check if he was asleep, or dead. He saw that Peter was alive, but in a state of meditation.

"Miss Morris, I think we will have a challenge this morning."

"What do you suggest?" She didn't take her eyes off Peter, thinking that he too looked familiar, the same as the girl. It was like a feeling of déjà vu, but much stronger. *What is happening to me recently?* She wondered. *I'm losing it.*

"I believe we will need something more experimental." He reached into his inside jacket pocket and pulled out a small zippered case.

"You're not serious about this?" she asked with apprehension and a small hint of fear. "Substance M has not been approved yet. It should not be allowed out of the lab.

Please return it to me now."

"Daphne," Jack stepped close to her. "I *am* the Department, and this stuff is good."

She stepped back to put some air between them, trying to appear composed, but the small catch in her voice betrayed her. She had never taken Substance M before. Jack continued speaking:

"Look at him. Peter is in a magical trance. We have seen this before. Remember Participant eighteen?" Of course she remembered. Getsiin. She was always uncooperative, refusing to demonstrate even the most basic magics. One day she entered a magical trance and could not be brought to the lab to continue experiments. Nobody could awaken her. She disappeared the next day.

"Can we reach him?" she asked. "In his meditation?"

"You will use Mind magic to find him." He handed her the case and went to sit down, watching as Daphne stood dumbly, unsure how to proceed.

"How can he enter a trance here? What about the anti-magic field?"

"He nearly broke it yesterday," Jack replied, fixated on his brother with something like admiration. Daphne was shocked. She had never heard of anyone showing magic so powerful. Their fields would all need to be upgraded if that were true. She shook her head and tried to give the case back to Jack.

"No. He's too dangerous. Get rid of him."

"It's more complicated than that."

"Complicated how?"

"I know this man. He is Aisling's father."

"So what?" Daphne regained confidence. "He's a risk to the Department as he is, with our fields built the way they are. Get rid of him and we'll upgrade the fields."

"You think the Leader would like to hear reports of us finding a witch of this calibre and just releasing him back into the wild? A danger to the city and to us and to the Leader?" There was a silence. "He must stay. We have an obligation now to detain him. And you will be the one to convince him. He will not listen to me."

Peter was still as a pile of rocks, yet exuded a magical presence that filled the room.

"Take it, and join him in his Mind," Jack ordered, standing up to leave. "You've done Mind magic before; I don't know how to do it. I'll return in half an hour."

"I won't do it," Daphne protested. "It isn't ready."

Jack stepped towards her again, and snatched the case from her. She noticed how broad his shoulders were, how strong his hands, and then she knew there was little that would stop him getting his way.

"You will take Substance M," he commanded, opening the zip and removing one of the prepared syringes from inside. Her eyes were trained on the needle. "The easy way or the hard way?"

"No." She backed away, but he followed, single-mindedly focused on her. The needle was ready. "I won't. I'll report this to the Leader personally."

"So what?" He grabbed her arm tightly. "You think he hasn't tried it himself?"

"That's not right." She struggled and failed to break from his grip and he pinned her against the invisible wall of the anti-magic field. It rippled slightly at their impact. "This isn't the way." She felt him preventing her from moving any of her limbs and in desperation she tried to bite him and missed. How was he so strong?

"Convince him to join," Jack ordered as he inserted the end of the needle into her neck. She yelped as he pushed on the end of it, injecting the powerful drug into her bloodstream. The scream was swallowed by the soundproof room, and didn't disturb Peter from his trance.

Jack released her and placed the needle into a separate section of the case for disposal later with cold robotic precision. Daphne held herself upright and then her pupils dilated, her eyes widened, she felt the effects of pure liquid magic pumping through her body.

"Feels good, doesn't it?" He grinned menacingly. "I'll be back in half an hour."

She wanted to strike him, but she felt itchy all over. Tingly. And so excited. But it was terrifying. She moved her arms and fingers a little just to make sure they were still attached. She felt like she could burst with magic and experimented with a small Water spell. The effects were enormous: her usual drops were magnified to an unbelievable magnitude and a great torrent of water shot forth from her palm across the room. Some splashed onto Jack as he shut himself outside.

Equally amazing was how easily she could stop the Water magic. Normally the effort to stop a Water spell was like damming a river, but with Substance M it was as simple as turning a tap on and off. Incredible. This is what the Department had been working on all these years, finally she tasted her results. And she liked it. *But I mustn't like it,* she tried to remain calm. *That's the drug talking, not me.*

She looked at Peter and focused on the task of convincing him to join. Mind magic was a strange type of magic, one that Participants were reluctant to use, and the Department had hesitated researching. It carried with it the danger of being overcome, absorbed by a target's mind, of seeing things that weren't real, that were beyond imagining. There was the danger of getting lost in the space where their minds met. One of the older Participants told her its use was outlawed on Blue Island. She could see why after having tried it with the Participants before under supervision.

But Substance M filled her with confidence and magical ability beyond anything the Participants had shown her so far. Jack was forgotten as she delighted in the physical, emotional, spiritual feeling of magic taking over her being. How long since this drug was created? How long had she been missing out? *No, this isn't me*, she had to remind herself again. *Never again.*

She sat down and focused on Peter. Her breathing slowed, and she decreased her heartbeat. The entryway to the Mind was ahead of her. She imagined walking through it and fading into a dream.

In the next moment, her awareness was changed and she had entered a state of Mind magic; the same state that Peter was in. Looking around, she thought it was like being outside in a huge field, with a clear flowing river, flowers everywhere that emitted a hypnotic blue glow like Noi but purer. A mountain loomed in the distance with a castle or palace built into its face, and a city spread from its base along the river. She knew this place only from her short educational visits in the past, but it felt like she'd known it for much, much longer.

She had the unpleasant feeling of being watched.

But she had to find Peter and get on with the job. Then she could get back to real life and away from the dangerous Mind. She turned around and saw that behind her and across the river, the blue glow of the flowers was replaced with an orange one. The glow of a raging fire in a dream. She would have felt fear had it not been for Substance M: a witch capable of burning the Mind was something to fear, most certainly. But she felt she could convince him to help the Department. The power they could extract from him would be enough to rule the world. She knew she could do it.

A few dreamy steps floated her closer to the orange sky, and the figure of a burning man came into view. He walked among the glowflowers, savouring their unique light, and playing with the combination of hues that he could create by mixing their blue with the reds that surrounded him. They never burned, despite touching the fires roaring around him. He looked to be at peace with his surroundings, but his fires said otherwise and her false confidence wavered for a moment.

He saw her, and instantly they were standing on opposite banks of the river, barely ten metres apart. She felt the heat of his aura, the brightness of his burning. But it was his eyes that held her prisoner; his red eyes that contained at once all the cosy warmth of a campfire with friends and the untamed ferocity of a wildfire. It was at odds with the peaceful dreamscape. He confused her to look at, but she couldn't look away. The feeling of déjà vu she had when she saw him in the holding room grew stronger, and she felt like she knew him intimately.

The feeling of being watched also grew.

"I already told Jack I won't do it." And again, he appeared distant, far from the river. His voice was familiar too.

"I know you from somewhere," she spoke, but it wasn't her voice. Gone was the cold focus from her work life, and in its place was a soft, youthful voice. He appeared on the opposite bank again, and his flame both shrank and grew at the same time.

"You play this trick on me?" He was as confused as she was. The Mind was dangerous and even with Substance M she wanted to leave. The space around them was turning to a nightmare and she wanted to wake up, but she was not in control. It was not her nightmare to wake from.

"What trick?"

"My wife's voice. My wife's face. Go!" He was again on the horizon, burning strongly while a storm cloud was approaching. Everywhere she turned she could see images from his Mind leaking into hers: faces of the people he knew. Her face. But younger. It was everywhere.

This is the madness they warned me about.

She started to panic as Peter's visions and memories blocked her own and she lost track of how to leave. Substance M was not strong enough to prevent it.

"Get me out of here!" she cried out, again in the young voice that was not hers.

A ghostly young woman was watching her from a little way along the river on her side. The sight of her scared Daphne even more and she screamed for Peter to help. She turned the other way and saw another man distantly watching from all the way in the mountain castle. It was impossible but she knew he was there watching; she knew he could see everything.

The young woman was suddenly next to her, and Daphne saw that they had the same face, only different ages. The dream woman was like her, but much younger. No, she *was* her. Impossible! Daphne was paralysed with fear as the young woman took her hand and guided her to take a step into the river. Her hand was cold and when Daphne tried to hold it, it was like reaching for a cloud. The water was perfectly clear and not deep. They were then standing ankle-deep in the magic water and the ghostly woman lifted a handful of the water and drank it. Daphne did the same, all while Peter's Fire magic lit the horizon orange.

The taste of the water was better than anything Daphne

had ever tried and she felt the ghost woman walk through her, connecting with her, becoming her. The memories came rushing back and her life was made whole again. She knew where she was supposed to be, what happened to her, why she was there.

"Peter!" she cried out again, this time with a different feeling. He appeared opposite her on the river bank again, his colours lighting the air around her.

"What spell is this?" he roared.

"It's me," she softly said, and stepped forward through the water, pausing halfway in the river.

"You died." He stepped into the river, continuing to burn endlessly despite the water. "I saw you die. Jack killed you."

"I have been lost." She was waiting for him to join her in the river. "I lived."

"It's not possible." He walked forward a few steps, his fires shrinking, but not as a result of the water.

"I'm here now." She reached forward for him through the blazing heat and he took her hand. The effect was instantaneous. His fires extinguished and his eyes returned to their normal ashy grey. They stared at each other with amazement.

"Maria."

"Yes."

"It's really you."

"Yes." They kissed, as the water in the river began flowing faster and faster and rising up to their waists. The glowflowers brightened, and all around them everything was blue. Maria felt again the eyes of the man in the castle watching, but it didn't matter then.

"Peter, I need to go on pretending for a while." The Mind magic allowed him to read her thoughts, as her awareness spread beyond her consciousness and leaked into the surroundings. "And I need you to pretend with me."

"Anything," he agreed, refusing to let go of her. "I'll join the experiments. Just please tell me what happened. I was there. I saw you that night. The robbery. When they beat you and took you and left you to die."

"I was not me." Maria explained, looking at the mountain castle. "I lost myself in this place fifteen years ago after they left me. I don't remember coming here. I had no memories after that. I had to learn everything again: who I was. Jack didn't tell me anything about you. Or our daughter. She's a wonderful girl Peter. And a powerful witch. The most powerful I'd ever seen until I saw you."

Their thoughts bled into the air between them and in an instant, they saw each other's memories. They knew all that had happened. Maria knew all about the Khun, about Aisling, about Chuluun and about magic. She knew about his Fire and she cried for him. Peter knew all about the Department, all about Jack and their research. He knew about her losing herself and how Jack had tried to save her, but she couldn't remember a thing.

"We have to leave the Mind now," she sniffed "I'm not a strong enough witch, it's dangerous for me here."

"I'll guide us out." Peter kept her hand in his and they walked upstream through the shallow trickle of water.

"Remember, we must pretend I'm Daphne and you don't know me."

"Anything."

Chapter 13

Since seeing the eagle, Aisling had been expecting something to change. But nothing happened. Two days later it was the same.

She had the same dream again the night before, where Iwizadi in the circular room tried to tell her something. All she could hear from him were the words "hold on," and she didn't know if he meant for her to wait a minute, or if he knew things were going badly in her life

The experiments still hadn't progressed to combining different magics due to some bureaucratic problems that were making Kurt go crazy with impatience. And even though the slow, deliberate practice was making her extremely adept at the magic she could already use well, it was boring. She missed her old life where magic was fully integrated in everything. Magic wasn't a tool; it was how she lived. She still found it weird to heat water and light the room using Noi.

What had the eagle meant? He found the girl. So Tesver is looking for me? Just him or all of the Khun? It must be all of them. Chuluun and Khuch and the others. And where is my dad?

The experiments helped take her mind off her own life, but she still had plenty of hours every night to ruminate and worry. She hadn't seen Miss Morris in a few days either.

Maybe she was sick. She thought that people really suffered without Healing magic and felt sorry for them.

Three days after seeing the eagle, Aisling was stopped on her way to the lab by Jack. He was rarely around, so it was a surprise to see him.

"Good morning, Aisling."

"Hello uncle."

"I've told you, please call me Jack," he reminded her in an effort to appear friendly while hiding the fact that he wanted to remove family ties. "We have something different for you this morning. Tenth floor."

They entered the elevator together. Aisling remembered that part of the building from when she was held in the cell, and when the doors opened, she saw more small offices stretching down a long corridor. Jack led her to a pair of rooms at the end of the hallway and paused before opening the doors.

"You remember what this place is."

"Yes." She was taking it all in: the dim lights, the stale smell.

"I want you to look at these pictures." He showed her two colour photographs. "Do you know those men?"

Aisling squinted and leaned in close to see better. Both photos were of men in identical rooms to the one she was held in when she arrived, an anti-magic cell in the centre keeping them prisoner. In the first photo she saw Khuch, sitting on the bed looking at the door. In the second she saw Peter standing in the centre of the cell and staring at the camera. The flash made his eyes bright red. She tried to hide her excitement and concern.

"Yes of course I know him," she pointed at Peter. "You know him too. Why are you asking me if I know your brother?" She had to think quickly. What would happen if she admitted she knew Khuch? What if she didn't? Jack again looked uncomfortable at the word 'brother'. He pushed on,

"And the other man?"

"I know him," she hesitated to say, not looking at Jack.

"I thought so." Jack seemed pleased. "You are an honest, cooperative girl, Aisling. We all like you here. Your efforts and your attitude in the experiments are really very helpful." She shifted her weight from one leg to the other uncomfortably. Something about being alone with Jack made her very uneasy, like the same feeling she got when confronted with the wolf in the forest all those years before. She wished Khuch was there with her to calm her, not held prisoner in the next room.

"What is his name?"

"Khuch Chaddhal."

"What does that name mean? Is he from Blue Island?"

"Yes." She thought for a moment. "It means something like strength, or power."

"He was arrested a few days ago, not far from your father's old house. Seemingly on purpose I might add." Jack sniffed and ran a hand through his hair. "Like he was in a hurry to get here and knew it was the most direct route. Smart guy, even though he refuses to speak. By the looks of him, he doesn't speak our language. Is that right?"

He came! She felt a warm joy inside. *Was the eagle his?*

"That's right," Aisling lied, knowing that Khuch spoke it perfectly well.

"I need you to interpret for me."

"Okay." She tried to hide from him her excitement at being able to see Khuch again. "What about my dad?" She looked at the photo again.

"I will see him again today."

"Again? How long has he been here?" It was hard to ignore the feeling of betrayal.

"A few days. They arrived around the same time."

"My dad's been here a few days and you didn't tell me?"

"It's not your job to know every detail of how the Department operates," Jack silenced her flatly.

"He's your brother! Why is he still in the cell?"

"He has been offered the same deal as you," Jack answered. "Quite generously, I might add, given his combative attitude."

"How did he get here?"

"He was arrested not far from here after a local man reported him for using magic."

He came looking too… But what was his plan? It was typical of Peter to try something and make it up as he went. But he was usually more careful than that. Either he trusted the man who reported him, or he was trying to get arrested.

"Let's go to see him now." Jack gestured for Aisling to enter the room, "Khuch Chaddhal. Then we will visit Peter and see if he has changed his mind."

"He refused?" Aisling asked while still outside the room.

"Of course he did. He's just like you. Stubborn. Righteous." And Aisling suddenly felt guilty for accepting the deal. Aisling remembered the room's plain decor and inoffensive colours, its boring ceiling panels and beige carpet. Jack placed a firm hand on her shoulder.

"You are my interpreter," he ordered sternly. "You are only here to relay what I say into his language and his answers back into mine. You are not to say anything else. Don't even look at him if it makes it easier for you."

"Okay."

On entering the room, immediately Khuch and Aisling made eye contact despite Jack's suggestion not to, and the strength of their combined magic reuniting was enough to be felt through the anti-magic field. The air in the room filled with a joyful, almost playful energy that made Jack twitch and raise his eyebrows as he observed their reunion.

He made a mental note that this was something to take seriously.

Seeing each other, nothing else mattered. Khuch came up to the wall of the case and put his hands up on it. Aisling stayed by the door, but could not look away from him. Jack broke the silence.

"Khuch Chaddhal." Khuch was surprised to hear his name, and to show that he was listening he lowered his hands, but could not stop looking at Aisling. "You are being held here because you were seen using illegal magic." Jack nodded at Aisling, and she interpreted the message. Khuch nodded once that he understood her and how they could use language to deceive Jack.

"You are also an illegal immigrant from Blue Island, and you are a witch. This makes you an enemy of the state." Aisling interpreted faithfully, and Khuch listened. Jack appeared convinced that she was doing an accurate job to that point.

"I am going to offer you a deal. You work with us for a little while, and in return I can make you a citizen and all your problems will go away." Aisling struggled to interpret the message because there was no easy way to express 'a little while' in Khun. The offer made Khuch wriggle a little.

"What other option is there?" he asked.

"If you refuse my offer, you will either remain imprisoned for using illegal magic, or returned to your Blue Island, where I am told there is still a war and your people are persecuted."

When Aisling told Khuch the offer, he showed the

faintest sign that he knew something Jack didn't and said,

"The war is over. Khun are returning soon." Aisling wished she could hide her emotions the way Chuluun did.

"You have to accept. He won't send you home! He'll keep you in here. We can escape together."

"What are you saying to him?" Jack snapped. "You are only here to interpret."

"I will not go back to Gazar without you. Chuluun and Tesver approve it."

"What is he saying?" Jack was anxious not to let them communicate.

"He says he accepts." This seemed to please Jack.

"Very good." Jack exhaled deeply. "Tell him he should be grateful I saved his life."

"You'll be safe with me if you do what they say. We will go to Gazar together." Aisling decided to use the opportunity to tell Khuch something else because Jack's message was needlessly boastful and unnecessary.

"I love you," he answered, and again the air in the room felt energised, stronger even than before. Aisling felt like her body was going to burst, like Light magic would pour from every inch of her. She knew he could feel the magic between them.

"He says 'thank you'," she told Jack.

"Very polite." If Jack had his suspicions about the accuracy of her translations, he did not mention it. He was preoccupied thinking about the obviously very powerful effect that the interaction of two magic users had on their surroundings. *They damn near broke the field!* But unlike Peter's power stemming from a lifetime of anger, theirs was clearly something different. That was something that could change the experiments and the course of their research. He had to talk to Daphne and that annoying Doctor about it. "I will return with a contract soon." Aisling told Khuch the message, and he nodded.

They left the room and Jack locked the door behind them. He turned to her with a sudden anger and seemed to grow, his snarl intimidating her,

"What were you doing in there? What was that magic?"

"I… don't know." Jack slapped her faster than she could see, and she was too shocked to make a sound.

"You did something in there, together. Even through the anti-magic field there was something. If you don't tell me, I will find out the hard way. I shouldn't trust anyone who speaks that filthy language."

"I don't know…" she repeated, and started to cry silently. Her face stung where he had slapped her.

"I don't want to see that again when we talk to Peter." Jack composed himself. "He is being uncooperative. I need you to convince him to participate. Miss Morris was unsuccessful and she has fallen ill. His magic is powerful and we would be very interested to study him. He would be a great asset to the Department and I'm sure his results would help this country."

Peter was in another room at the opposite end of the hallway to Khuch. Jack opened the door and they entered. Aisling was shocked when she saw Peter, because it was not a problem with the camera after all. His eyes had turned red, and he stood perfectly still, unblinking, uncaring that anyone had come to see him. He was deep in a magical trance. Aisling recognised the look from when she saw Tesver once push his Bird magic powers to their limits: he took on the appearance of a tree then and never fully recovered.

"As you can see, we cannot reach him by ordinary communication," Jack explained. "He shouldn't be able to do that in the anti-magic case, but he is extremely powerful, and hence, extremely dangerous."

"He's not dangerous! He's my dad!"

"Not dangerous?" Jack laughed. "Aisling, you didn't know him growing up! You didn't see how he beat that child half to death when we were at school! You didn't see him box!"

"That's not what he's like!" she yelled back at him, preparing to be slapped again, "You haven't been there for my whole life! Who cares what he was like before? It's important what he's like now!"

"Then look at what he's like now." Jack took over her train of thought. "Look at him. He is a slave to Fire magic. He does not control his anger inside."

"I'd be angry too, if the man who killed my wife was keeping me in a cell."

"What did you say?" Jack whispered through clenched teeth.

"You heard me." Aisling rose up to him, finding a confidence she never knew. It was the effect of Peter's Fire magic radiating through the room that was causing them both to feel confrontational.

"Is that what he told you? You don't know anything." He walked up to the case and pounded on it with a fist, yelling at Peter now. "I didn't kill her! I saved her!"

"Then where is my mother?" Aisling pulled him around by the shoulder, both shouting and crying. "Where has she been my whole life if you saved her? You think you're a hero? Is she in another cell here?"

The rage emanating from Peter outwards through the anti-magic field was so strong that Jack and Aisling were ready to come to blows. Peter stood still as a statue, his fiery eyes terrifying to look at, an embodiment of anger, unaware of the drama unfolding in front of him.

"Ask him!" Jack shoved Aisling back from him and pointed at Peter. "He just found out."

"How can I ask him when he's like this?"

"Mind magic. Go find him in the Mind and ask him yourself. Convince him to come out of this trance, that's the whole reason I brought you in here."

"Why should I help you?" She felt herself flaring up again. "You lie about everything! I can't trust anything you say!"

"Because if you don't help me," Jack tried his best to keep calm, "I'll kill him. Then I'll kill the other witch, Khuch Chaddhal. Then I'll kill you. And I'll make your mother watch."

The threat was serious enough that Aisling stopped. She was tempted to just tell him to fuck off and that dying was better than helping him, but the voice from her dream telling her to hold on was echoing through her head. 'Hold on' was all the voice said, and it was exactly what she needed to hear in that moment.

"Leave me alone with him and I'll do it."

"Good girl." He patted her on the head patronisingly and too roughly, and left before they could fight again. He slammed the door behind him and rested his back to it, sweating and panting, relieved to be free from Peter's anger. Aisling stood in front of her dad, trying to let the warmth of her love for him spread through the room and overpower the pure seething rage that filled the space, but even that wasn't enough. She knew that if he woke up, their love together would contain the anger, but she couldn't do it alone.

"Dad..." She tried to concentrate on opening the way for a Mind spell, but it was hard to concentrate with the air full of anger. Eventually with great difficulty, she saw the way to the Mind and entered.

Aisling entered the Mind and was confronted with a sense of abandonment. Everything looked like it was melting upwards and she found it a little nauseating to look at. The emptiness of the place filled her with loneliness beyond anything she felt before. It was silent, and there were no living creatures, no birds.

She was in a city of some kind. There were cobblestone streets and buildings all around her, but the colours were all running together and bleeding into the sky. Behind her rose a mountain with more buildings built into its face, including a castle or palace of some kind. When she looked at it, she felt sick, like being spun around very fast, and she held out her hands for balance and stared at her shoes for a minute. Opposite the mountain stretched a field of glowflowers and a river that ran from the mountain through the city and out into the horizon. If it had been the real world and not the Mind, she would have thought it was beautiful.

Somewhere distantly in the meadow she could see a pulsating red glow and knew it to be her dad. She went towards him and found the act of walking to be disorienting. Every step took her a random distance from her starting point and it was hard to guess how far she had gone. Things seemed in slow motion.

With some difficulty she progressed towards her dad, noting that his colour grew stronger and bigger. Chuluun had warned her and Khuch of the Mind world. In Khun culture it was not generally permitted to enter, unless one was in the advanced stages of magic mastery. That didn't stop her and Khuch from attempting to visit: they never ventured far but it was frightening and felt wrong to them in a way they could never describe. Chuluun explored once when Tesver was in his trance and he was quiet when he returned, like he was scared to talk about his experiences.

Not that he ever said much anyway. What was her dad doing there?

She saw two figures together in the centre of the red light and recognised one as her dad. The other was a woman with her back to her. She called out to her dad, but he didn't look up. The woman however, turned to face her and Aisling recognised Miss Morris… but she was younger. She looked more similar to Aisling and she thought it must be a trick of the Mind.

"He can't hear you," Maria said, signalling to Aisling that it was okay to come closer. "Let me look at you."

"Miss Morris? What's going on?" Aisling stopped where she could see them and hear them, but not close enough to touch.

"He will become a Fire master soon. We don't have long together."

"What are you doing here? Leave me alone with my dad." Aisling went to her dad and put a hand on his arm, only to recoil from the burning heat of his skin. Maria reached out to comfort her daughter, but Aisling, still thinking she must be a trick of the Mind world, pulled away.

"Don't you recognise me?" Maria asked, allowing her Mind to ebb outward from her body to where it could be absorbed by Aisling.

"Mum?" Aisling realised, absorbing Maria's radiating thoughts from the surrounding air. She was dizzy with confusion. "How can it be you?"

"I lived, but my memories were contained in this world. I had to start life again as Miss Morris. Jack helped me start again." Maria looked at Aisling sadly while saying what happened. "I was trapped being her until I came back to this place and found my old self."

"What is going on?" Aisling still believed this to be a trick, and refused to trust what she was seeing and hearing. She needed Peter to tell her the truth. "Dad?"

Peter's eyes were open the whole time, his face with the same blank expression as it had had in the cell. He unexpectedly turned to Aisling and became lucid, his eyes returning to their normal colour, but the fire surrounding him remained.

"Aisling. I came to bring you back, but they took me too." He sounded miserable, regretful. "Jack gave me a choice between helping him or facing trial. The same as you. But I got the last laugh and a third option chose me. He didn't expect me to follow the path of Fire magic. It won't be long now before I become Fire itself. I'm sorry, I can't put it out now."

"Dad..." Aisling ignored Maria. "What is going on? Why is Miss Morris here? How could your brother do this?"

"I am going to become Fire. It's too late to stop it from taking me, it's going to burn in me until there's nothing left." Peter was hovering a centimetre off the ground Aisling noticed. "And we found your mother."

"This is a trick."

"No trick. Aisling, Maria lived. It was Jack's fault. After the accident he brought her back to the Capital. She was used for an early project of the Department to try to put magic into regular people. They needed people who were about to die for the experiment. They tried to combine a Participant's mind with hers, and it failed. She lost her mind while her body recovered." Peter seemed so calm as he meditated in the fire, but this was shattering news for Aisling. She looked over at Maria, who was watching them, smiling sadly. "I was wrong about that day. He didn't kill your mother. He saved her, but then he lost her again."

"Why would Jack do that?"

"I suspect he wanted me to suffer. He wanted to win."

"That's not what brothers do."

"Aisling, Jack isn't really my brother."

"What are you talking about?" Aisling felt overwhelmed by all that was happening and all she was learning. She was staring at Maria, who was staring back.

"I was adopted. I don't know my real parents. I think that's why he can't use magic like us, because we have different blood."

"Aisling," Maria spoke up, "I am so sorry I wasn't there."

The emotions were starting to overcome Aisling and she had enough of the confusing conversation. It couldn't be real. All of it was a trick! Her dad wasn't turning into fire, she told herself. Miss Morris couldn't be her real mother. Jack was her biological uncle. No, no, no! She turned and ran through the Mind back towards the mountain, drawn there by some inexplicable force. Her steps were hard, like running through deep water, and she struggled to escape her parents' pull. She had to get away from them, she wanted to be anywhere else.

She focused as hard as she could on the mountain and its dizzying appearance. The mountain was like everything else, melting upwards, where its peak connected with a reflection and its colours seemed to drift outwards into a confusing sky.

Suddenly Aisling found herself in a familiar circular room. It had none of the other features of the Mind outside and its walls and contents were stable. It made her feel more at ease. She looked out the window and she knew she was in the castle on the mountain. She looked out over the city beneath her and the field and the river. She could see where her dad was creating a red glow around everything else that was blue and the effect was very weird.

As expected, Iwizadi entered the room. Aisling had seen this many times before, but until now she had not seen his room or his face in clarity. She was surprised to see how young he looked when she expected him to be ancient. After a day of dirty, hard work, sometimes even her dad looked older than him.

"You're getting to be a very capable wizard, Aisling," He greeted her with a smile. His presence made her feel at ease somehow, and she relaxed, feeling like she could talk openly, as if to a friend.

"It's good to see you clearly this time."

"Influencing the dreams of others is not easy," He chuckled. "Besides, you're awake this time. More or less."

"What's happening out there?" She was desperate to know if what she experienced was real or not. Iwizadi could read her mind and got to the point.

"It is true." Aisling felt the blood rush out of her head and needed to hold onto the desk next to her for support. "Peter is about to achieve a transition of magical greatness. He is much more powerful than I could have expected. But I suppose I shouldn't be surprised by it. The true descendants of Libalele still carry strong magic disposition."

"Descendants?" Aisling recognised the name Libalele from the fairy tales.

"I will explain. But first, your father and mother."

"My mother…"

"It is true." Iwizadi went to the window and looked out at where Peter was undergoing his transformation. "Maria, your mother is out there. I've known her a long time. In fact, I would not have found you if it weren't for her losing herself in the Mind."

"What do you mean?" Aisling felt less faint now and sat on a chair. She was still confused by everything, but trusted that Iwizadi would explain everything. It was easy to trust him.

"When Maria came here, she was on the brink of death. But while her body clung to life, her mind was torn away and remained here, lost, forced out by Jack's ridiculous attempt to infuse her with the mind of another. She returned to life as an empty person and wandered the country. She went to Halasat, drawn by its faint magic, and while there a spy reported to the Capital that a woman with no memory and no identity was using magic. Jack saw the opportunity to use her again. It was an oversight of his that she was allowed to return here, where she has now been reunited with herself. You cannot blame her for her absence in your life."

"She's alive now?"

"Yes, when you next see Miss Morris in the real world, she will be only acting the part. It is crucial that you also pretend, no matter how much you want her to be your mother. Jack must not know."

"Okay."

"But it is a curious twist of fate that she had to lose herself for me to find you. When I found her in here, she insisted I try, and I'm glad she did, for many reasons."

"Why did you want to find me?" Aisling was curious and hanging onto every word.

"Because I have been searching for one thousand years for the one who will inherit Libalele and rule it in the next chapter of its history of greatness."

"Rule Libalele?" Aisling was dumbfounded. "I can't rule a city! I'm not a Khun, I haven't done the initiation."

"Aisling, you will not just rule a city. You were born to rule the world." He quickly turned to face her from where he had been staring at Peter through the window, and his face was completely serious. He knew things that she didn't. "Libalele is just a city. But it is built over the seat of all the world's magic. That is why all the peoples of the world are compelled to fight for control of it, though they do not know why. I chose the Khun to be custodians of its power until the true descendants could be found. They have been capable keepers of magic during this time and they will be rewarded.

"Gazar, they called the island in their language, and Khot the city. Since the fall of Libalele, the island has been the focus of war after war after war. The people have no idea that they cannot control it. You see, Libalele calls out for a leader, but it doesn't matter how hard they fight, only the true Libaleleans can rule. Any other power there is temporary while the city searches for its true leader.

"Maybe the Khun told you of a war?"

"Yes. That's why they left Gazar."

"It's true, this recent war has been more violent than previous wars." Iwizadi's voice was both melodious and raspy at the same time. "But I have worked hard influencing the dreams of soldiers to send all those people home. Like I have for every war fought there. The Khun will be returning very soon, on the equinox. I have given them instructions through the birds." He didn't mention talking to Chuluun in a dream.

"They're going back?" Aisling was more excited about this than anything else Iwizadi had said so far. It had been a story she'd heard more often growing up than even the Iwizadi story. It was a legendary story and now finally it was reaching a conclusion. She hadn't yet realised however that the Khun's story of returning to their home was part of the same story of Iwizadi's life, and now also it seemed, hers.

"It has taken me a long time to learn how to influence

and infiltrate the dreams of others. Believe me, I have brought many people to this room, aiming to change their paths. It took me many years of trying before finally the soldiers decided to leave Gazar. And this is the time now for the Khun to return. It cannot wait."

"And what does my mother have to do with this?"

"When she lost herself in the Dream world, she begged me to find you. I did so, thinking that I could practice Dream magic easier on a little girl. And when I found you, I knew you were the one I had been looking for. Your father was born in Halasat to a magical family before being adopted. He is Libalelean. My story is why you have seen this room in your dreams so many times. You are the one I have been waiting for." Iwizadi paused. "So as for your mother, it was for the good of all people that she became lost. Without her, I might have searched another thousand years without finding the true descendants and the rightful leader. It is indeed strange how fate has used me."

Aisling was filled with conflicting emotions. Iwizadi had a point, she could see that her loss was a gain for the greater good. But no amount of reasoning could take away from the pain of absence she had felt her whole life. That was something she could only begin to heal with Maria. Except Jack could not find out, so how could she do that in secret?

"I have given your mother instructions to take you and Khuch Chaddhal to Gazar."

"How is she supposed to do that?"

"Jack is on the brink of unleashing something evil. He will fly one Noicraft to the island with the intention of invading it. Your mother will hide on board with you and Khuch."

"Jack? Evil?"

"Magic comes easily to you, doesn't it?" Iwizadi changed the tone of the conversation. "While the people around you struggle to use it at all."

"I guess," Aisling answered. "But I never really thought about it until they made me do these experiments." Iwizadi nodded.

"They are doing you a wonderful service you know? Whether they realise it or not, they are making you stronger, and that makes you more of a threat to them. But no matter how dangerous they think you are, they still need you." Iwizadi started moving towards the door, as if to say the conversation was ending. "And that gives you power over them."

"Power?" She was suddenly angry and Iwizadi stopped as if he could sense her emotions. "I have no power. They forced me to do this or else I would die."

"I am afraid you fell for a trick. They would have simply let you go. Jack might be blind with ambition, but he would not allow his family to be killed."

"How do you know that?"

"Caution, is not necessarily a bad thing. Taking the safer option has led to great things for you, for your parents, and for Libalele. Just imagine if you had not come to the Capital, the things that would not have happened: Your father finding his old friend, your mother finding her identity, your parents finding each other, Khuch Chaddhal coming to you, telling you he loves you, the Khun returning to Gazar, your father achieving Fire mastery, you being trained in the disciplined study of all magic. You needed to be captured."

Despite being told she held power over others, and she was destined for power, the explanation made her feel more powerless than ever.

Iwizadi continued towards the door, and as he opened it the room started to take on the same dreamy quality as the rest of the Mind outside, where it was hard to tell where one surface ended and the next began. Aisling realised the room only existed when Iwizadi willed it, and she thought of her parents, brought together again in a tragic moment for the briefest time. She tried to run back to join them, to be with her dad again before he completely transformed into fire, but she felt a sharp tugging on her arm and was jolted into consciousness back in the real world. Jack was there with her in the room with the cell, impatiently asking her if she had found Peter.

"Yes, I found him."

"And will he sign the contract?"

"No."

Jack was furious by Peter's refusal. After taking Aisling back to the lab for more testing, he went to his office.

The empty nest at Jack's window was occupied again: the crow had decided to come back and live there for the winter months. He made his presence known when he first saw Jack by rapping on the window. Jack was not pleased to see the crow back.

"Shoo!" He made a fast movement with both arms in an attempt to scare it off.

"I have something to tell you," the crow said. To Jack's surprise he could understand it. He opened the window to hear better.

"What?"

"Something important to tell you about magic people."

"Hurry up and tell me." Jack hid his surprise behind menace.

"They have reached Gazar yesterday."

"Gazar?" Jack thought for a second. "The Blue Island?"

"It is named Gazar."

"I don't care. Why did they go back there?"

"They heard that the war was over." This crow had all the

answers and spoke assuredly. Jack was warming to it.

"How interesting… And how exactly did they hear that?"

"From birds."

"And can you confirm the war is over?"

"War is over."

Jack went to his desk and sat down, resting his head on one hand, with his elbow propped up. Nearly two decades of magic research and the Participants had managed to keep secret the fact that they could talk to birds. It was a huge gap in his intelligence.

But they don't know that I know, he schemed.

"Crow," he turned to the window. "Come inside if you like."

The crow dutifully hopped inside and sat on Jack's desk. Since taking a few doses of Substance M, Jack had noticed the world seemed to contain more possibility. He was more imaginative. Talking to a crow was not so hard to believe.

"What is your name, crow?"

"Svikari."

"Are you the same crow who used to live here?"

"Yes."

"And you recognise me?"

"Yes."

"You've seen me in here, and heard me talking?"

"Yes." The crow hopped about on the desk, never taking its eyes off Jack.

Jack lashed out and grabbed Svikari's legs in one swipe, holding him in place. Curiously he did not flap or peck at Jack and seemed very calm, as if expecting Jack to do something erratic. Svikari did indeed know Jack's behaviour after having watched him for years. Jack loosened his grip but still held Svikari in place.

"I don't want anyone to know I can understand you. It

must be a secret between us. Do you understand?"

"Yes."

Jack released Svikari and started to wonder if he could say anything other than 'yes'.

"You will have a very comfortable life, Svikari, if you help me out and do what I ask. You will be treated like royalty. Now I will leave the window open, you are free to come and go as you like. When I need you, I expect your quick service."

"Win-win," Svikari sang as he flew outside.

Jack walked briskly out of the room and towards the elevator. Top floor. It was time to put their plan in motion. All of their work had been leading to this moment: it was time to invade Blue Island. Those hapless savage witches couldn't stop him, now that he had this advantage over them. All he needed was the Leader's approval.

For most of the population, a personal meeting with the Leader was not possible. Even for employees, it was only a small group who were able to see him with an appointment. Jack was the only employee able to see Abe without notice, though he rarely did. Since the discovery of Substance M, Abe had looked forward to Jack's visits.

The elevator opened and Jack saw that Trina, Abe's assistant was not at her desk. He confidently walked past where he expected to see her and opened the door to Abe's office, glad not to have to tell Trina why he was there.

"Jack!" Abe rose from his desk and went to greet Jack. "What can I help you with?"

"Abe, it is time for operation Blue," Jack said with a serious expression while shaking Abe's hand. Abe's grip loosened and he sat back down and paused. "It's time for us to take the book and the Noi we deserve."

"Are you sure?"

"Yes. The war is over, the witches are returning, and Substance M is ready. There will never be a better time. Those idiots from the eastern countries have been mining for Noi this whole time without knowing the real treasure the Khun were keeping," Jack leaned over Abe's desk and spoke close to his face.

"I was wondering how long before this happened." Abe leaned back in his chair, pulling away from Jack's grim, predatory face. "Tell me, where did you get your intelligence? I have heard nothing of this from the military."

"Substance M." Jack reached into his inside jacket pocket and placed the familiar black case on the desk. "I have discovered a type of magic by chance that they have kept hidden from us."

"What magic?" Abe was eyeing the case greedily.

"They can talk to birds. I have done this too." Jack went to the window and tried to see if Svikari was nearby.

"Birds?" Abe repeated dreamily, staring at the case. Jack's temper flared up and he roughly shoved the case to Abe, where it fell into his lap.

"Oh, go ahead! Just ask next time instead of drooling like a hungry dog."

"Ah, yes thank you." Abe's focus turned to the ritual preparation of the syringe and his arm, and suddenly his aloofness turned to stunning lucidity. "Tell me more about the Bird magic. If I can witness it myself, I will trust your analysis of the situation and we will go at once." He shut his eyes as he felt the needle enter his vein, releasing Substance M into his bloodstream.

Jack went to the window and opened it a crack. He made a sound like a crow, and moments later, Svikari flew up to the ledge. Abe had taken out the needle and disposed of it and held a piece of cotton to his arm where he had penetrated the skin. His pupils were dilated already. Jack purposefully stepped over to where Abe was sitting, Svikari resting on his shoulder, and the crow hopped down to look closer at Abe. Jack couldn't explain why, but he liked the crow.

"What am I supposed to do now? Will he talk to me?" Abe asked, vibrating. He had taken to injecting stronger doses than anyone else in the Department. "Hello crow."

"Hello."

"Amazing!" Abe smiled wickedly. "How is it that we never knew about this?"

"Substance M has only recently been refined to its current pure form thanks to our latest Participant. She is far more powerful and willing than any others we had before. We were undoubtedly missing a lot of things."

"I suppose I have to trust your intelligence is accurate now." Abe turned to Svikari. "Crow, what news from Blue Island?"

"It is named Gazar."

"Whatever."

"Khun have returned some days ago and soldiers are gone."

"And how do you know this?"

"Haforn the Sea Eagle."

"Sea Eagle?"

"Old and wise keeper of skies near Gazar. He can fly very long distances. He told seagulls; they have told all birds here on this country."

"I see. Thank you Crow."

"Svikari," Jack added, though he was not sure why. It didn't matter to him what the crow called itself. He just wanted to be right where Abe was wrong.

"Svikari, thank you," Abe finished. Jack took Svikari back

to the window and closed it after he had flown off.

"So, Abe?"

"So, Jack?"

"Do you now agree that it's the right time?"

"Operation Blue?" Abe was mentally distant from Jack, instead intent on the small spheres of Water he was making dance through the air. "Substance M is just terrific, isn't it?"

"Yes, it is," Jack agreed. Though he had refrained from the sort of dependency that now held Abe, he still very much enjoyed taking the Substance as often as he had spare time. He had also avoided taking doses as large as Abe, due to some of the unpleasant effects the drug had, which Abe seemed to enjoy.

"And we have our deal with the military in place, don't we?"

"Yes, they have Blue unit prepared and provisioned."

"Excellent." Abe turned to Jack and left the room full of floating globs and spoke loftily. "You know, with Substance M in my body, I could kill you before you had time to defend yourself. I could make the water in your cells freeze. I could collect all the water in this room and use it to drown you." The globs started circling Jack menacingly. Jack, aware that Substance M tended to make its users abnormally aggressive, tried to refocus Abe's attention.

"Wouldn't it be better to drown the witches?"

"Yes, you are right, as usual." The globs dissipated, and Abe went to his desk and wrote a note and signed it. "Go see General Osbourne, and give him this. I am ready for Operation Blue."

"Thank you." Jack took the letter. "I have been waiting a long time for this."

"Me too Jack, my friend. With the amount of Noi buried on Blue Island, we will make our country rich beyond measure. And I will be remembered as the man who led this country to the top. We're going to be very rich men, Jack. Rich and powerful. With that book and Substance M, nobody can stop us. Noi might make us rich, but the book will make us immortal."

Jack sneered in agreement, and anticipation that he was so close to recovering the Book of Iwizadi that he had heard about in his dreams. With the book, he would be able to overthrow Abe and have complete power over the Capital and the whole country. He had told Abe about the book and how together they could use it. He told Abe everything he knew. He didn't tell Abe that he had no plans to share it. The book was his undisputed passage to power. Nobody would ever remember the young Jack who needed his brother's help with school bullies, or the gang member Jack who accidentally saw a refugee arrest and knew he needed to join the Department to have access to magic. Jack, who befriended a refugee before betraying their trust, all to meet Department members and start a career.

But everything Jack knew about the book was only what Iwizadi had chosen to reveal to him in his dreams.

It was hard for him to tell how much of the speech was due to Abe's general preoccupation with legacy, and how much was Substance M talking. Either way, he was dangerous, and it was time for Jack to go. Without taking his own dose, he was powerless, and he hated that.

General Osbourne and the experimental Blue Unit were just like Jack, in that they technically didn't exist. They were a group of six soldiers who had signed up – or been signed up – for a special joint operation between the Department and the research arm of the military. They were high-ranking soldiers who had been trained to use and control much more frequent intake of Substance M, and due to the effect it had on human aggression, Jack rarely visited them other than to deliver a new batch. Their barracks was on the eighth floor and required a special pass to enter. A pass like Jack's.

He found General Osbourne's office and saw that the light was on inside. Entering, the General saluted, which Jack did not return. Jack handed him the letter, which was received without a word and read in silence. The General nodded at Jack, who left quickly. There was an atmosphere of magic present on the floor, but to Jack it felt tainted, unlike the pure magic that could be felt when a Participant was in the booth. It was different even to the pure rage that had been filling Peter's holding room for the last week. The magic that filled the barracks just felt wrong, like it shouldn't exist, and Jack didn't like to be there.

Without knowing why exactly, he went to visit Peter. Of course, he knew nothing would have changed since visiting him earlier in the day, or the day before; Peter would still be there. He was always there.

"You know, Peter," Jack said with a gloating tone, "your witch friends have abandoned you. Yes, they've fled the country. Just how you fled our home here, and how you fled your home in that other dirty town, and how you fled that refugee camp you were hiding in."

The setting sun hit the window at the right angle and a beam of light crossed the room, illuminating a spot just next to Peter. He made no sign that he could hear Jack.

"You spent your whole life just running and hiding. And what have you got to show for it? You're here! Captive! And you still try and run away into your mind!"

Maybe Peter could hear Jack, because the energy of the anger floating around the room seemed to increase.

"And you've lost your daughter because you ran away!

Just like you lost your wife! And now you're losing all those witches that you called friends!"

Jack didn't know why he continued, but he felt like the anger in the room grew around him and he couldn't hold back. He couldn't stop. It was like the air itself was a bubbling torrent of pure liquid hatred. Jack was compelled to gloat. Still, Peter remained motionless, his fiery eyes wide open, dominating. The beam of light hit Peter's leg, and he appeared to be steaming in its brightness.

"And now that those pathetic soldiers have finished their war on Blue Island, it's my turn. My turn to take their Noi and to hell with those filthy savages you call friends. We've taken their magic. I've studied it and turned it into a weapon to use against them. To enslave them or kill them, whichever comes first. And when I get that book, I will be in charge here. Powerful, like I've never been before."

In a blinding flash of red light, Jack lost all sense of who or where he was in the world. He couldn't remember why he was yelling, or why he was angry. All he knew was that anger was all around him, and there was nothing that could possibly stop it. When the flash was over, Peter was gone, and in his place was a fire; a fire that burned without fuel, that burned blue and orange at the same time. Jack pounded on the anti-magic case, yelling:

"What have you done! Come back! You always run! You coward! You run now just like you ran from me before!"

His yelling attracted the guard who was stationed outside, able to hear him even through the soundproof walls. The guard burst in, assessing the danger, and Jack grabbed his collar, pointing at the fire.

"Do something about that. Now!"

And he stormed out, leaving the guard to soak up the remaining anger in the room and figure out how to contain

Peter: Peter who had completed his fire transformation by running away from his life, and become an endlessly burning flame of hatred.

That evening, Aisling was planning to escape. It wasn't easy, but she had made progress with Matter magic.

She shrunk herself to only a few millimetres high in the early evening, and snuck out under her door. Without swiping her pass, nobody would suspect she had left her room. Her goal was to get to the roof and find the eagle. The first problem she faced after leaving her room was that at her tiny size it would take all day to run to the elevator.

That's why she left a signal for Janice that morning to find her at the right time and carry her: six tiny apples. Aisling spent all day worrying anxiously, hoping that it would be a clear enough message for Janice. The thought that someone else could find the tiny apples never crossed her mind, and Janice's warning to be more careful had been forgotten.

Which was why Aisling was taken off guard when she saw Miss Morris – Maria – approaching her room accompanied by a security guard. Her immediate thought was that Janice had turned against her. In fact, the timing was purely coincidental. Janice wasn't working that day, and another cleaner found the tiny apples and reported them to Miss Morris directly.

Sensing trouble, Aisling ran as fast as she could back underneath her door and concentrated on performing the spell that would return her to normal size. Just as she was putting the final touches on her hair, she heard a knock on the door.

"Aisling? Are you awake?" It was Maria's voice, but without its usual cold formality. A beep told her that the guard had unlocked the door, and Maria stepped in, the guard waiting at the threshold. She beckoned him inside and closed the door behind them. It was the first time they had seen each other since Maria regained her identity.

"What's going on?" Aisling feigned ignorance, but she was not a very good liar. Maria pulled one of the apples out of a bag, and the colour drained from Aisling's face. As if to calm her, Maria winked. What followed was an act for the guard's benefit.

"We have all seen how powerful you are during the experiments. But it's clear you have knowledge of magic that isn't prevented by our fields, and that makes you a danger to us all." She sat down on the couch and signalled for Aisling to sit with her. She glanced over at the guard, who had already lost interest in what was happening. He was staring at the view out the window.

Aisling heard her mother's voice in her head somehow.

"The fields don't block all Mind magic either, so I can talk to you like this. It's a very difficult magic to negate completely." Then she spoke out loud so the guard could hear. "If we find evidence of illegal magic again, you will be taken back to the holding room and all experiments stopped and your contract cancelled." The guard nodded sleepily.

"We need to get out of here," Maria's voice said in Aisling's mind. "I will get us out, just give me some time. Jack is flying a ship to Blue Island soon; I will find out when. It could be tonight."

"Iwizadi told me something evil is happening. And what about dad?" Aisling wasn't as practised at Mind magic as Maria and her voice was weak in Maria's Mind.

"I'll try," Maria answered, knowing that Peter had completed his transformation already, knowing that he was beyond the point of no return, knowing that Aisling didn't know yet.

"No more warnings," she said sternly out loud. "Now I

need your help with something else: interpreting for the Khun boy downstairs." Everything she said out loud was just an act for the guard.

"When?"

"Soon. I'll come back for you." Maria's voice still had the authority of Miss Morris and Aisling decided she was a formidable actor. In her mental voice she added, "We're going to shrink him like you did to the apples."

She left with the guard.

Aisling, still thinking about escape and too impatient to wait for her mother, went to the window and wondered if she could combine Mind magic with Bird magic. Clearing her thoughts, she sent her most bird-like thoughts out into the sky. It felt foolish, and she sat heavily on the floor, looking out. After a minute, a few pigeons came flapping at the window. Astonished, she heard their cooing as if they were next to her.

"Hello?"

"Um, hello," she answered.

"Do you want to see Orn?"

"Okay, I guess," she agreed, not knowing what was happening. The voices of the pigeons echoed strangely in her mind.

The pigeons left abruptly and Aisling was both pleased and confused. Pleased that she managed to combine difficult magics, but confused what the pigeons were doing. A loud screech shook her back to reality, and an enormous eagle came into view. She recognised him from the last time he visited. He hovered in front of her window since there was no ledge to perch on.

"I am Orn."

"Hello Orn, I'm Aisling."

"What do you want?" he asked without emotion.

"Um, I saw you here before. What were you doing?"

"It was my task to find you. The wizard in the north-east requested it. Now that I have found you, I am free to go home, but I feel a strange duty to you."

"The wizard? Tesver? Is he okay? What about the others?"

"The wizard has become master of birds; he will be always in the forest now." That was too cryptic for Aisling, who unaware of how far along Tesver had come in his transformation. "The others in the party have returned home."

"Home to our village?"

"Home to Gazar."

Aisling was upset to hear that they left her behind. She felt like she was just proved right, that she didn't belong with them, that she was not now and could never be Khun.

"They didn't wait for me... They didn't even come to find me..." The sense of abandonment was too much and she started to cry.

"There is more to this story than we can know," Orn tried to comfort her. "And the young Khun came for you, did he not?"

"Khuch..." she wiped away tears on her sleeve. "He did come, but now he's in prison too and I'll have to rescue him!"

"Then do it."

"Okay, you're right." She picked herself up and felt reassured knowing that Orn and her mother wanted to help. "And what did you mean by duty?"

"I cannot explain it. Something I felt that has drawn me to you, since the wizard begged me for help. Stronger when I found you, it is the force of the world's magic that makes me stay. Perhaps someday it will be explained. It is like the connection my ancestors felt with the ancient protectors of magic."

This answer was too esoteric for Aisling who, raised under the pragmatic outlook of the Khun, searched for immediate solutions.

"What am I supposed to do now? How do I get out of here with Khuch and my parents?"

"There is some movement happening in this building, something evil."

"Evil?"

"Magic where magic should never be."

"What does that mean?" She wondered as to the purpose of the experiments. Were they as dishonourable as Janice claimed?

"We will use it as distraction. You will see me again soon." Orn rose into the sky again and resumed his hiding position in the nest high above her.

Meanwhile, Maria farewelled the security guard who sleepily returned to his desk, then she went to visit Khuch in the holding room. She saw Peter's room down the hall and the door had been marked with yellow tape and a warning not to enter. She wondered how exactly they would contain his essence now that it was sitting in there radiating anger.

But she focused on her immediate concern, which was to find a way to Gazar with the two witches on board a small floating ship filled with aggressive soldiers pumped full of Substance M and trained to kill using magic. It was a suicide mission, but Iwizadi stressed that she must succeed, and somehow, she felt that he would be influencing things to make sure it went well.

She entered the holding room and closed the door behind her. Khuch sat despondently on the edge of his cot, and sighed when he looked up and saw her. Mind magic was by far her strongest ability, and she sent a mental message to Khuch.

"We are leaving today."

Khuch, who was ignorant of the situation with Peter, assumed this was just another trick to try and recruit him. Since his last meeting with Jack and Aisling, he had refused to help. He was mildly surprised that Maria – who he still knew as Miss Morris – could so powerfully enter his mind, but he was more surprised that the anti-magic field hadn't prevented it. He replied to her out loud in Khun, unwilling to demonstrate any magic, even as a response.

"Where?" Khuch had kept one secret from everyone: He could speak Aisling's language easily. It was natural, having grown up together that they learn each other's languages. Yet because Aisling spoke Khun perfectly well, everyone assumed he didn't learn. He never bothered to tell them. Maria had learned the basics of the language from other Participants.

"Blue Island." Maria insisted on communicating mentally, this time sending a message in Khun.

"Gazar? Why?" Khuch still spoke out loud, even more surprised and suspicious to hear his native tongue carry the thoughts of a foreigner.

"Because Aisling needs you with her." This got his attention and he stood up facing Maria.

"What is she doing on Gazar?"

"She is going with us."

"Us? I don't understand your trick."

"There is no trick. You and Aisling belong on Gazar, and I can take you there. You just have to trust me. I know that's asking a lot." The way Maria's voice creaked a little as she said this, and she twisted her body a little, showing embarrassment and humility, reminded Khuch strongly of Aisling.

"How?"

"There is a Noicraft departing soon. We will hide on it."

"Why? Why help us? Why is the craft going there?"

"There is too much to explain, and not enough time. I promise it will make sense soon." She quickly left, hoping that nobody saw her in the corridor. She went back to Aisling's room and knocked quietly.

Aisling opened the door and let her mother in. For the first time, they were alone together. When Aisling shut the door, the silence in the room felt so loud as they stood an arm's length apart staring at each other. They had similar features, and Maria could see some of Peter's mannerisms in her.

"My daughter." Maria held her arms out.

"Mum." Aisling hugged her. They held that position for a long time, neither saying a word. Their experience in the Mind explained all that needed to be explained.

"Here's what we're going to do," Maria outlined her plan in an excited whisper. "You'll shrink yourself, and I'll carry you in my pocket to get Khuch. We'll shrink him too, and I'll carry both of you to the roof, where the Noicraft is waiting-"

"I've never shrunk two things at once... I've never tried to do any magic while tiny either..." Aisling was nervous about the plan, and hadn't even heard the worst part. Maria sensed her daughter's doubts, but knew that without Substance M she couldn't help. She could only use Mind magic comfortably without its help.

"I believe you will be great." It seemed a paltry encouragement. "Sometimes when failure is not an option, we can surprise ourselves."

"I can try," Aisling said unconvinced.

"When we reach the craft, I will sneak on board. Then, I need you to shrink me too."

"What!" Aisling protested. "There's no way! I'm not that strong!"

"It's the only way. Then when we leave this building, you will be able to use magic unrestricted again."

"And what about my dad?" she remembered, realising he hadn't featured in Maria's plan. Maria gulped.

"He is gone."

"What do you mean gone?"

"He's not in the holding room anymore."

"Well, where is he?"

"I don't know," she lied badly.

"Yes, you do. You know!" Aisling saw the lie immediately, still not trusting Maria completely after her experiences with Miss Morris and Jack.

"We will see him again, I'm sure. But he can't come with us this time."

"Where is he?"

"He-" Maria breathed out, releasing some tension in her body and looked at Aisling. "He has become Fire."

"What does that mean? Become Fire?"

"You saw him in the cell, didn't you?" Aisling nodded, angry and confused. She knew the Khun lore about masters. "You saw him in the Mind covered with fire."

"Yes, I saw him." She feared she already knew what Maria was going to say next.

"He is that Fire now."

Aisling said nothing, but went to the bathroom and shut the door. Loud sobbing noises came through the walls and Maria herself was crying. They shared a different grief for Peter.

Maria knew more about the transformation than Aisling after spending time with him in his last lucid days, and she knew that it wasn't the end of Peter's presence. He would continue as a being of pure magic, he told her. Aisling didn't know that. The Khun stories of mastery never included what happened next, and she was so completely paralysed with grief that nothing made sense at that moment. Chuluun believed in an afterlife, but she couldn't think about it then. She couldn't think at all.

She was angry with her mother for so many things, but she was most angry with the way she tried to hide that information from her. She hated the way her mother didn't express her emotions the same way as her. How could she stand there and tell her that her dad died so calmly? What did she mean 'we'll see him again'? He was dead.

Aisling splashed water over herself, believing that it was her fault that this had happened, ever since she used Water magic that day. All those things Iwizadi had told her didn't matter now. Her dad had become fire, or died, she didn't understand exactly. But she did understand that he wasn't coming with them, that he couldn't.

She opened the bathroom door after some time, and saw Maria sitting on the floor against the wall, her knees drawn up to her chest. She was staring at the opposite wall and her makeup had run, and Aisling in that moment realised she had been too quick to judge her. She shuffled toward her and sat next to her, resting her head on her shoulder. She felt the weight of Maria's head relax onto her head in return, and they sat like that in silence for a long time.

"I can do it. I can shrink us," Aisling croaked eventually, realising how thirsty she was. She wanted only to leave the Capital and its misery, and be back with Khuch and Chuluun and everybody where she could be herself again and be back home.

"We have to go now. Iwizadi said there was not much time."

Aisling then managed to shrink herself to a few centimetres tall again, and Maria picked her up and put her in her shirt pocket.

"This is going to be bumpy, hold on tight," her voice boomed down.

A few minutes later they reached the holding room where Khuch was still in the anti-magic field. Maria swiped her pass on a subtle card-reader built into the wall, and the field opened a small compartment where Khuch's food could be passed in through a small opening.

"Khuch, try to squeeze through that opening," she told him. He looked at her like she was crazy, but knowing about their plan to shrink him, he followed instructions. He tried to push his body through, but it was big enough only for his head and one arm. While he was squeezing through, Aisling could see him as if he were a giant, and focused on performing another Matter spell while in her tiny form.

It took some time, but Khuch started to feel like more and more of his body could fit through the hole. He noticed the room growing around him, and found the experience unnerving and dizzying. When he was only a few centimetres tall and still shrinking, he was standing in the opening, waiting for the next instruction. Maria picked him up and put him in her pocket with Aisling.

"The hardest part is coming up. Be strong Aisling," she whispered at her chest.

Maria made her way up to the roof, where she expected to find the Noicraft waiting to go. Her plan was to get on board and hide there before anyone noticed.

But she arrived too late.

When she opened the fire escape door to the roof, she saw the blue lights of Noi floating away across the city. She knew they were too late. Not only could they not prevent Jack's violent invasion, she couldn't even break out of the Capital. And every moment wasted was a risk that they would be found out.

"We're too late," she whispered at her pocket. "Might as well make yourselves normal size now while we think what to do."

A moment later the three of them were standing there in the night sky watching as the blue lights faded distantly into nothingness. There was a flapping sound, and Orn came to a landing in front of them. Maria was stunned, having never seen such a magnificent creature up close like that. Khuch was mildly surprised, and wondered if this might be the eagle Orn that he had heard of many times before. Aisling spoke to him, which astounded Maria, who was ignorant of Bird magic. She looked on as her daughter and the eagle made various noises at each other. Khuch could understand most of the conversation.

"Hello Orn."

"You are troubled, all three of you."

"We were supposed to be on that Noicraft. Now we're stuck here forever."

"I am the king of birds, but I recognise a true leader. I will carry you."

"What true leader?" Khuch asked, confused, but was ignored.

"He says he will carry us," Aisling told Maria.

"Please make your bodies small and I will follow the ship. Where is it headed?"

"Gazar. Thank you Orn."

"Gazar... it is a long time."

"I know it is a long way."

"No, it is a long time since I was there. I will fly with all the speed in the world."

Aisling walked forward and hugged Orn, who at first found it uncomfortable, but relaxed after a second. Then she looked at Khuch and Maria, and together the three of them shrank to the size of small apples, so that Orn could comfortably hold them in his claws.

They shot off into the sky with such ferocious speed that Aisling thought her face was going to fall off. They were sheltered from the wind in Orn's firm grasp, but the experience was terrifying, like being stuck in a garbage can during an earthquake. Maria tried to scream but the air was knocked out of her lungs. Khuch vomited. Aisling nearly blacked out, but her spell required her to be awake. If she lost consciousness, the spell would break, and they would return to normal size, breaking Orn's legs and falling to their death. So, she held on. Their life depended on it.

"Humans," Orn's voice was clear in her mind, "We fly faster than the sky houses. We will arrive in a few hours. We are already over the Mishkash and I can see the great sea on the horizon."

Aisling wanted to acknowledge him, but her tiny voice was impossible to hear above the roaring noise of flight.

Terrified and helpless, they huddled together, waiting for the journey to end

Chapter 14

They had barely been back a week when everything went wrong. Some other smaller groups of Khun had started returning to Khot from the remote corners of Gazar in which they had hidden, and Chuluun was accepted as their interim leader, at least until the city was rebuilt. They were all busy at putting back together the lives they had lost when they were forced out of their homes, and there was barely a moment spent in idle discussion or rest. The recent colonists were reluctant to share the city, but were convinced by the increasing numbers of Khun and their own vulnerable position since the soldiers had left.

The sea eagle Haforn frequently visited, having found himself a nice cliff face near the mouth of the river. It was a very short flight for him to the city and he enjoyed the company of the Khun. Haforn for his part was also very well-liked and respected as a crucial part of their collective story and identity. The Khun recognised that without his network, they would not have known to return at the right time. Everyone except Chuluun of course, who knew otherwise.

Exhausted from their week of hard labour, the Khun had hoped and perhaps naively expected to have a longer break from war before Haforn delivered bad news.

"What do you mean?" Ychir demanded. "How is it possible?"

"The men from the Capital have decided that with soldiers vacating Gazar, it is their turn to come."

"How can you say that so blankly?" Sanakh cried, never being able to get used to the different ways birds feel and express emotion.

"I only report what I have heard from the seagulls." Haforn took a moment to preen his chest feathers.

"So, the Capital has a way to communicate over long distance too," Chuluun stated calmly. "It is something we have overlooked."

"How long?" Sanakh asked Haforn. "How long before they come?"

"They were preparing to leave the Capital when I received news yesterday."

"So that will give us maybe a day?" Chuluun asked for confirmation. Those present mentally calculated the distance and the speed of the government's Noi-powered aircraft. "No, they could reach us by tonight."

A panicked murmur arose from those present.

"How could they know?" Ychir demanded. "Unless someone here has betrayed us. We were safer when they thought the war was continuing." At the hint of a betrayal, the murmur erupted into shouting.

"Quiet!" Chuluun called over the noise. Turning to Ychir he reprimanded him. "If you are claiming there is a traitor here you should be prepared to accuse someone."

"It could be anyone!"

"Or it could be no one here. Haforn spread the word back to that country so that other Khun could find their way back home." Chuluun returned. Haforn listened attentively at the sound of his name. "The news is out there in the world, there is not necessarily a traitor."

"That would mean those people have discovered Bird magic somehow."

"Sadly, this is also my conclusion," Chuluun agreed with Ychir. "It is the most likely scenario. We have lost our greatest secret and advantage."

The crowd drew quiet as they thought about the impact if such a thing were true. For centuries, for the whole history of the Khun, magic had been their most important secret. It was truly a great shame if the Capital had discovered it and learned to use it.

"How could they have learned it?"

"I can think of only one way," Sanakh answered him. "It is from those Khun that have been captured. If they have discovered this magic recently, it can only have been from those that were recently taken."

"Khuch Chaddhal was a strong user of Bird magic." Ychir added, nodding in agreement.

"You accuse my son of giving up our secret to our enemies?" Chuluun stepped in front of Ychir. The two men stared fiercely at each other.

"What about Peter, or Aisling?" Sanakh suggested. "They are not Khun. They have not been initiated."

"Aisling is as Khun as any of us." Chuluun shut her down, clearly missing her and Peter, yet dreading the time he would have to reveal Iwizadi's plan for Khot. "She was raised by us, she speaks Khun like us, she uses magic better than most of us!"

"And Peter?" Sanakh pushed.

"He is Khun too," Chuluun reasoned. "He has been Khun since his first day with us. When no one else would care for him, we made him ours. He knows his place is with us."

"You trust uninitiated people from that awful country?" Ychir pushed Chuluun's chest. "The people that have stolen our Khun and our magic, and now come to steal our home from us? This final insult!"

"You have known them as long as I have." Chuluun pushed Ychir back, much more forcefully and he fell into the crowd. "I trust them with my life."

"Then you be first to greet the invaders tonight! Let them have your life." Ychir spat at Chuluun's feet and left the meeting in the direction of his home.

There was unrest growing amongst those present. Clearly there was no way to prove how the Capital knew Gazar was unoccupied, but the fact remained that soldiers were coming and time was running out.

"Enough," Chuluun addressed the group now and Ychir turned to listen from the back. "We can argue later how they know that the soldiers have left us. We need to prepare the defences as best we can. We are a large group now, but still smaller than any city. Our main task should be to cast Light magic over the whole city, to hide it."

Some people nodded, even Ychir.

"Then have some others wait on the mountains at the edges of the valley."

"Should we capture or kill them?"

"Capture one at least."

The men on board the Noicraft knew that the city was in the valley, on the banks of the river that flowed from the mountain, but they couldn't see it when they came in to land. Unsure of where to go, they flew slowly over the valley in wide circles, trying to decide. Since none of them had ever been there before, they based their directions off what others had told them and what was drawn on official maps.

After some argument between the soldiers as to whether

their mission was genuine, they agreed that the Khun must be playing some kind of magic trick. Trained in magic, they were aware that objects could be hidden through Light magic. But a whole city? Maybe they had underestimated the natives.

They landed the craft on the south bank of the river in the middle of a field of glowflowers, about a kilometre from the foot of the mountain, which rose shockingly steeply out of the flat plain. They exited the ship and looked around for any hints of magic. Even though they were trained to detect traces of magic, their training was rendered useless due to the strength of the magic emanating from the island itself. The glowflowers were magic, and the water in the river Gol contained strong magic too, stemming from its contact with Noi deposits deep inside the mountain.

The men were confused and without clear leadership. Nothing in their training had prepared them for this: finding themselves surrounded by magic and without a target. They began to feel uneasy. Before venturing too far from their ship, they took it in turns to take a high dose of Substance M.

Some Khun were watching from nearby, only about fifty metres away, silently cheering the success of their collective Light magic, but fearful of whatever the soldiers were doing. They had never seen soldiers all inject their bodies with something before an invasion, and it worried them greatly. They sent messages with sparrows to tell all the birds and Khun what they saw. And why was there only one ship? Something strange was happening here, and the Khun were very unsettled by it all.

The whole city and its inhabitants were invisible to anyone not included in the spell, which unfortunately included Orn, Maria, Aisling, and Khuch.

Orn arrived at Gazar ahead of the Noicraft and heard from local birds that the Khun were aware of the invaders. By the time Orn had come to land on a high outcrop West of the valley, the Khun had already cast their protective Light magic over the whole city. So, when Aisling finally released her spell on the group, reverting everyone to normal size, the four of them were confused: Maria and Aisling and Khuch because they assumed the journey wasn't over, and Orn because he remembered the valley from his last visit, but couldn't see the city.

While the four of them learned what was happening from local birds, the soldiers down in the valley faced their first attack. An older Khun named Mori attempted to cast a Movement spell that would fix the soldiers' legs to the ground where they stood. None of the Khun were prepared for the spell to be intercepted and thrown back at Mori. The soldiers had been trained in counteroffensive magic; their strength now amplified by Substance M.

Mori's feet were stuck in place, and his companion Guu desperately tried to relieve him. But her natural ability couldn't compare to the strength of Substance M, and in her horror, she saw the soldiers advancing on their location.

"Impossible!" She whispered to Mori. "How can they know where we are with the Light spell cast?"

"They have traced my spell to this place," He whispered back. "Now run, tell the others what they are capable of."

She ran, taking care to tread silently as she wove through the city. The soldiers, approaching where Mori was stuck, felt as though they had walked through a veil into a hall of mirrors. Mori was plainly visible, as was their immediate surroundings to a radius of about five metres, but the rest of the city remained invisible. It was a peculiar sight and they were clearly impressed.

"So, you have cast a Light spell on the entire city," The Captain addressed Mori. "Very impressive. They said you people were powerful. Why would you attack us though? That's not very nice."

Mori, who could not speak their language, struggled and grunted. The Captain made some gestures and tried to communicate, putting a taste of condescension in his voice.

"Captain," He repeated a few times, pointing at himself. Then, pulling out Aisling's journal from his bag. "You have a book I want."

Mori shook his head, and the message was clear enough. The Captain reached for his pistol and after tossing it between his hands a few times, struck Mori across the face with its butt. He began bleeding from the lip but showed no sign of yielding his defiance.

"They said the natives were uncooperative," one of the other soldiers said blandly.

"This one is useless," the Captain said. "And you, Smith, can't you speak their language? Why weren't you interpreting for me?"

"Sorry sir."

"Let's continue. We'll find their leader when we reach the mountain."

The soldiers left Mori bound in place and began moving blindly through the city, generally following the river. Though they could only see a few metres in any direction, they were possessed by a false confidence that was soon shattered upon realising that the streets of Khot were anything but straight. There was no clear road to the castle, and they were leading themselves into a labyrinth. Adding to both their confusion and confidence, the sight of the river kept their bearings, and they assumed it would only be a matter of time before concluding their mission.

Orn saw the whole scene with his eagle eyes and reported to the three waiting with him.

"Injected?" Aisling asked. Maria looked uncomfortable and thought it might be a good time to tell her companions about Substance M.

It was Khuch, who usually silent, could not contain his outrage:

"You have turned magic into a weapon? The earth has provided us with magic so that we can live here without leaving a footprint, and you turned its pure goodness into a weapon? Wasn't it enough that your people have destroyed the planet digging up Noi, the source of all magic itself, and turned that into a dirty form of false magic? Wasn't it enough that your wars for Noi killed my people and forced them from their homes? And now after everything, you want our magic for war? It's shameful. I am going to help them. Don't follow me."

Khuch stormed down the slope into the valley, leaving Maria slumped on a rock, defeated and heavy with regrets. Aisling ran after Khuch.

"Khuch! Wait!" He did not stop, but he called back.

"You stay back Aisling. You helped them." He continued down the rocky slope, taking care with each step so that he didn't slip and fall. Aisling caught up to him quickly, her light body allowing her to move more easily.

"I'm not leaving you." She wanted to reach out and grab him, but the steepness of the slope made it too dangerous.

"Go! You gave them magic. You are not Khun."

She stopped chasing him, hurt by his words, not knowing what to say back. It stung. She didn't know who she was exactly, but Khun was the best definition she could come up with. "They stole my journal. I'm sorry."

Maria's voice entered both of their minds at that moment,

taking them by surprise. Khuch stopped.

"Both of you listen. I regret helping create Substance M, but I do not regret what it has allowed me to do. I do not regret that in the longest and most fucked up way, it has brought my memory and my daughter back to me."

They turned to look at Maria, still on the top of the hill, with Orn nestled beside her. Khuch looked at Aisling with a face that asked, "Is it true? She's your mother?", and Aisling nodded at him.

"We are stronger together, Khuch Chaddhal, Khun or not. And no matter your opinion, we are here to help stop these soldiers from whatever they are doing here. My daughter is Khun whether you accept her or not, and you cannot erase her life by just saying you disagree with it."

Khuch sat on the ground where he was and Aisling caught up to him. They embraced without saying a word.

Word of the soldiers' magic ability and their mysterious injections reached the other Khun in a matter of minutes. Chuluun was first to draw conclusions and sunk sadly into a chair, speaking to himself softly.

"So, this is what has become of those who were lost… their essence weaponized and turned against us and against the earth itself." He shook himself from his despondency and rose. "It ends here."

"We still have surprise on our side, the Light magic is confusing their path," someone nearby suggested.

"And there are many more of us than them," another voice added optimistically.

"We must be careful, if the message is true," Chuluun hesitated. "They can trace our magic to us and find a path through the Light magic."

They waited nervously for a decision to be made. Would it be best to confront them suddenly and risk being overpowered by their superior, artificially enhanced magic? Or would it be best to scare them off guerrilla style, but risking discovery and retaliation?

"People, this is not like the last time. Last time they overpowered us with numbers and ranged weapons powered by Noi. This time we face a powerful enemy, and we don't know what they are capable of." Something had changed in Chuluun since returning home. Before, he was reluctant to be a leader, whereas now he was eager to act and to do the best by everyone.

"There are only six of them. We can overpower them easily," someone called out.

"It is indeed strange there are not more. Perhaps this means they cannot easily put magic into soldiers. That is also an advantage."

"We have to go now; we have surprise and we have numbers."

"A good leader knows when to follow," Chuluun intoned. "Who of you would prefer to fight head on?"

A clear majority of Khun raised their hands.

"And who would prefer to fight from the shadows and around corners?"

A smattering of hands was raised unconfidently.

"Then we fight now." The group began moving together from their hiding spots. "We will meet them in the Town Square."

Chuluun led them uncomfortably to battle, knowing that no Khun had ever in their history used magic destructively against another human. He expected the Khun to die, but they would die proudly.

After some demoralising trial and error, the soldiers found themselves in an open space in the city: the Town Square. Although their training had taught them to stay out of open spaces, they didn't have a choice. They were unable to see far enough in any direction to decide where to go, and had no clue how to get back to their craft now. In the Town Square, it was disconcerting to not see any buildings around them so they pressed on quickly, hoping to find the next road they could try.

Unfortunately for them, the only road from the Square that paralleled the river was where the Khun expected them to go. So, when they had found the beginning of the narrow road, they were dismayed to find it barricaded. Dismayed, but also confident that going the right way, for why else would it be blocked? They set to dismantling the blockade which was made of piles of wood and furniture and other random objects leftover from previous invasions: a lot of Noi products and even one defunct Noicar.

A bright flash left them temporarily blinded, and they instinctively ran for cover in the nearest alcoves they could find, still unable to see more than a few metres. To make things worse, the air around them started filling with a thick fog, until they could see nothing at all. The Khun added to their torment by casting spells of Sound and Smell magic, which left the soldiers with uncomfortable loud crashing sounds in their ears and rotten smells only they could perceive.

The Khun thought things were going very well, and from their hidden places congratulated each other. From where they were hiding, they could see the soldiers groping through small clouds of fog, trying to find something solid to hold onto.

"You think this is funny?" The Captain's voice broke through the magic, as he shouted above the sounds only he could hear. "Smith! West!"

On hearing their names, the two soldiers furthest from

the Captain sent frightfully powerful bolts of magic back to the sources of their assailing spells, leaving the Khun responsible for the fog and noise unconscious, gasping for air. The smell of rotten flesh remained, but the fog and sound disappeared, and some of the Khun realised they had underestimated their opponents.

The soldiers, having diminished the spell holding the city, were now able to see further through the Light magic, and took in their surroundings.

"Every time you try to stop us, we can see more!" the Captain shouted, not caring whether the Khun understood him or not. Chuluun and a few others did understand him and quickly passed the message along not to cast anything. It was better if they couldn't see through the Light spell.

"We just want to talk," the Captain called out with Smith interpreting. "Who's in charge here?"

There was no answer.

"You know, any aggression against us is an act of war." The Captain found his element and began arrogantly pacing up and down, waving his hands for emphasis. "You don't want to start a war with the Capital, do you? Didn't you just come out of a war?"

This made a lot of the Khun angry, and it was hard for them to refrain from yelling back, though he wouldn't understand any of what they said. Maybe he didn't want to understand.

"I know you're listening," he went on, mockingly. "We want to make a deal. You give us the book, and we let you live."

"No deal!" Chuluun shouted back in the Captain's language, from somewhere he was still invisible. The book? How could they know about the book? The whole time until that point, the Khun were under the impression that the soldiers had come for Noi. But the book changed things. Only Khun could be trusted with it. It was too irresponsible to let anyone else have it. Chuluun, familiar with the duplicitous ways of the Capital's men and their disrespect for the earth knew that it was time to attack.

At once, the six soldiers began sweating profusely and they felt feverish, as the Khun directed Water and Fire magic at their bodies. It was that simple, they thought, to repel any intruders.

Through his rising fever however, the Captain became more and more angry.

"What a great idea. Fire and Water. How very imaginative." His cocky voice echoed through the empty streets. "Higgins, show them Fire. Gibson, Water."

And the nearest of the Khun who was in the middle of casting Fire magic to give the soldiers a fever felt his skin prickling, then saw smoke coming from his hands. Immediately he released his spell, which the soldiers felt better for. But Higgins did not release his spell in return, and shortly afterwards, the tormented screams of that Khun burning alive from the inside sent waves of terror through all the others.

The soldiers' field of vision broadened further, as the Light magic keeping the city invisible was weakened by one caster. They could see maybe ten or fifteen metres away, and the Captain grinned sadistically.

Gibson, meanwhile turned his Water magic to the Khun who was making the soldiers sweat. Cruelly, the Khun's skin began to wrinkle all over, devoid of moisture, and when she tried to move, pieces of it tore in various places like paper, causing her immense pain. Hearing her screams, Gibson knew he had hit his target, and again the Light magic weakened, revealing more and more of the city.

The Captain was very pleased with the result.

From not far away, Maria, Aisling and Khuch witnessed the scene unfolding, horrified, as the Light magic surrounding the city periodically weakened. It still looked like someone had wiped a clear patch in the condensation that gathers on a window on a cold morning, but it was evident what was happening. How the soldiers could commit such acts of brutality was beyond them, even Maria who had known the Department's intentions the whole time. Seeing it in action was regretful.

But Aisling, who was a native magic user from a young age noticed that the soldiers' fluency was limited. They could concentrate only on one spell at a time, and one type of magic, and they used them in rudimentary – albeit powerful – ways. It was unimaginative, and she wondered out loud if they had only been taught a few things.

For her, magic was a language that she could use to express all sorts of concepts and intentions that words couldn't capture. Now, watching the fighting going on between the Khun, who were clumsy in their choice of offensive magic, and the soldiers, who were powerful but limited, she knew she had an advantage.

"Substance M was designed to open a person to magic," Maria explained. "It alone can't teach someone. The training relied on what we were able to replicate from the Participants."

"Great..." Aisling sulked a little. "So, everything I've done in that booth-"

"They can probably do it too. And what they could learn from your journal."

"But there must be things you haven't shown them?" Khuch hoped.

"Yeah. There's a lot," Aisling said. "And they only wanted

one thing at a time."

"So, you have one advantage of having kept some magic secret at least, and another in combinations of spells," he said.

"Right."

"We never changed size in the experiments," Maria added hopefully.

"Matter magic," Aisling and Khun said together.

"So as far as we know, they aren't aware that it exists," Maria concluded. "Our best defence against them is magic they don't know."

"Exactly. And any magic they do know, we can do better. Right Khuch?"

"Right."

The three of them exchanged nervous glances while brainstorming.

"What if you shrunk them all?" Maria asked. Aisling shook her head.

"No, I can shrink their bodies, but their magic power will be the same, like when I was tiny and I could still cast spells. It's not helpful, it just means we won't be able to see them as easily." Maria accepted this, but pushed on with the same thinking.

"What if we change the size of other things around them, or make us bigger, as a way of frightening them?"

"We can, but what good will it do?" Khuch answered. "Will that really frighten them?"

"Can you cast anti-magic?" Maria changed her ideas.

"I've never tried it," Aisling replied, looking at Khuch, who shrugged.

"What if we were able to create a field to contain them?"

"I guess it might be possible." Aisling considered the idea. "Let me try something small here first."

She looked at Khuch, who smiled supportively, and remembered the feeling he gave her in the forest that day. Their forest had become a city, and their wolf a pack of soldiers. She focused on a patch of grass in front of her, and allowing the memory of the warmth to fill her mind, a transparent box about ten centimetres to a side appeared. Maria picked it up and examined it, awestruck. It was light as air.

More of the city and the Khun came into view, meaning the soldiers had killed someone else. They were filled with hurt and anger, and hurried to produce a solution.

"You've done it!" Maria said excitedly.

"But which magic does it prevent?" Khuch asked. "Aisling, can you make one of these around me?"

She nodded, and in seconds Khuch was encapsulated in a transparent box. He looked like he was straining with effort for a while before finally giving up.

"I can't do any Fire, Light or Water in here. I think it's going to work."

Aisling felt buoyed up by adrenaline, but creating that field was tiring. She removed it quite easily, but noted how tired she felt, and rested on Khuch's shoulder. They could see how draining it was to perform such demanding spells, especially after her extraordinary effort at keeping them tiny during their flight. Khuch, who had lived with magic and Aisling his whole life, understood there was something about the way she used magic that was stronger than any Khun. Maria, whose experience with magic was limited to the lab experiments, Substance M, and her proclivity towards Mind magic, understood that her daughter's ability was far more powerful than any other user she had seen, perhaps even more powerful than the soldiers down in the city. They had a great hope that they could win this fight, or at least contain the soldiers.

Down in the Town Square, the Captain was still mocking the Khun defending their home. The soldiers could now see far enough to see the detail of the Square and almost as far as from one side to its opposing side.

"Don't you understand? You can't stop us. Now give me the book!"

But what his bravado didn't reveal was that the effects of Substance M were wearing off. If they didn't reach a conclusion to their mission in the next half hour, they would either have to take another dose or they would suffer the unpredictable effects of withdrawal. All of them carried extra doses with them, but in the heat of battle it would be a challenge to use. The Captain already considered all this, but believed the 'diplomatic' mission would be concluded in time, before Jack arrived.

"Come and talk so that we can agree on something. We only want your book; we don't care if you stay here. We don't care if you die either. Just get out of the way and give us what we came for."

Maria concentrated from where she was hidden on casting a Mind spell. She wanted to warn Chuluun – who Khuch had mentioned would be able to spread the warning – of their plan to contain the soldiers. She sent her spell towards the city, but because they still couldn't see properly, she had to search for Chuluun.

Unfortunately, Maria's plan backfired when Smith caught the trail and recognised the magic in it. Before she realised, he had hijacked her spell and his voice was in her mind.

"That was a mistake."

And she felt herself heating up. Smith had traced her spell back to her body and seen where she was hidden. Maria struggled to release her spell, which was holding her tightly, and panicked as the heat in her body turned painful. Smith was going to kill her.

The ends of her hair started sizzling and she broke into a fever and she reached out for Aisling to say goodbye.

"Put a box around him!" Khuch ordered, while trying to cast a spell both to cool Maria and heal her burns.

Aisling was about to seal the soldier in an anti-magic field, when something happened that shocked everyone. Maria burst into flame, succumbing to Smith's Fire spell. But rather than scream, she looked comforted, and rather than the expected yellows and oranges, she was engulfed in a brilliant flame of blues and greens. Aisling too felt strangely comforted by it, and didn't flinch when Maria took her in a big hug.

"I told you we'd see him again," she whispered in Aisling's ear, both of them enjoying the feeling as if Peter was there hugging them too, telling them he loved them.

Then she understood. Khuch watched on in confusion, but recalled what little he knew about mastery and had to guess that he was looking at Peter, protecting them. He felt in that moment convinced that Peter was undoubtedly Khun. Galyn Ezen he would be called from then on: Man of Fire.

Smith meanwhile had been unable to release his Fire magic. Not understanding the complex culture of magic like the Khun did, the soldiers were unaware that all types of magic came with their unique side-effects. In this case, Smith's anger grew and grew until the Fire that he thought he controlled turned around to burn him with its insatiable appetite. The last thing he saw was a being of blue and green fire standing before him, reflecting all his anger inwards. Then Smith was just a pile of smouldering ash and a burning smell.

For the first time since arrival, the Captain was nervous. The other soldiers briefly paused what they were doing when they saw Smith crumble into ashes, and looked to the Captain for instruction. They had not been warned of this during any of their training.

"Take another dose now," the Captain ordered, ducking into a covered area.

"Sir, it's too soon," West advised.

"We need more power. You will follow orders." The Captain already had his needle in hand and was preparing a dose for himself. The other four soldiers all looked anxious. It was too much. It was too soon to take another dose, and none of them knew what effect it would have on their bodies and minds.

They didn't need to wait for long to find out, because they too had started preparing their doses, and were injecting themselves with more Substance M.

"We are facing a very powerful enemy," the Captain told them as his pupils dilated almost fully. "More powerful than we expected."

All the soldiers waited while they felt the drug enhancing their perceptions of the world. They felt like gods.

All the Khun as well as Aisling, Khuch, Maria and Orn were watching them, and Aisling knew then that if she took Substance M, she would be unstoppable. That was the key to winning this battle.

"Mum, do you have any more of it?"

"Aisling! You can't!" Khuch protested. "You don't know what it will do to you! It isn't natural!"

"He's right Aisling. It isn't safe. I can't let you do this."

"If I have some, I can contain them all," she spoke quietly and seriously, knowing the dangers. "I can't make a field big enough or strong enough for all of them. And they all just took more."

"They'll be unstoppable…" Maria pondered, tempted to give in. She saw reason to what Aisling proposed. They had to fight fire with fire, literally.

"She's right… They'll kill everyone," Khuch admitted, wishing none of this had ever happened. But it was the Khun way to see a situation and overcome it. Khuch learned from an early age that complicated problems have easy solutions if you look hard enough.

Sharing a mournful look with the other two, Maria slowly took out her own little black case, which contained one dose of Substance M. All three of them looked at it with revulsion, disgusted by everything that had happened to lead to its existence, and by the perversion of nature it represented.

Aisling opened it and looked at the needle and shivered. She was afraid, and asked her mother:

"Will you do it for me?"

Reverently and in silence, Maria prepared the syringe and tightened a band around Aisling's arm to raise the vein.

More of the city came into focus as another Khun was murdered.

Aisling's breathing got faster and shallower, and her palms were sweaty. Khuch held her hand and she was relieved to feel his warmth flowing into her, like she often remembered. Love magic, she called it then. What else could it be? It was all his love giving her strength. And just as she thought that maybe Love magic was enough for her to overpower the soldiers, she gave a little yelp and she felt the needle pierce her skin. She felt faint and wanted to vomit. She felt the discomfort of the Substance M being introduced into her body, and through the strong feelings of love and fear found an unnatural courage.

Maria removed the needle and cleaned the place it entered Aisling's arm, her hands shaking with regret for everything.

"Are you okay, Aisling?" She asked softly, stroking her daughter's hair.

"I feel weird," she replied dreamily, gripping Khuch's hand tightly.

"It feels weird to start. Then it feels to me like your whole body is opening up so that the magic can enter, and also like you want to explode with power from every part of you."

"Mm-hm," Aisling agreed, unable to find the words to describe it. Her face muscles were all clenched. She was glad she had her mother there to help her, for the first time in her life. Khuch watched and tried to remember every detail so that he could tell the others later. He had a terrible feeling that the soldiers on that day were just the first ones they would have to fight as the Khun struggled to keep their home. He continued sending Love magic into Aisling, helping silently.

After coming to terms with the immense feeling of power, Aisling stood up and with huge black eyes looked down at the city. During the initial discomfort, Orn entered her thoughts and she felt a huge influx of Bird magic. She knew where he was and could see what he saw as he circled overhead. Now when she looked at the city, she could see things that were far away in great detail. She could see through the Light magic too, and for the first time could see the city of Khot in its ruined glory.

She could see its abandoned homes and buildings. She saw its huge size, big enough for thousands of Khun. She could see the castle on the mountain, and recognised the scene from the Mind and from her dreams. She knew the room where Iwizadi waited. The city called for her and she called back.

"I'm going down there and I'm going to stop them," she calmly announced, and began to run, her feet landing slightly above the ground with each step. Maria tried again to reach Chuluun with her Mind magic, and Khuch continued sending Love to Aisling.

Some Khun noticed Aisling running towards the city and knew something was wrong. Nobody should be able to see them, and they frantically sent messages to each other with sparrows and with Mind magic if they were able. They saw her run purposefully towards the Town Square and stop where she could see the soldiers and where they could see her. Some Khun recognised her and were happy to see her. Others didn't and assumed she was going to be more trouble.

West was unconscious after his second dose of Substance M. It was too strong for his body to handle: the feeling of magic flowing through him tore his Mind apart and he collapsed. His Mind became lost. The other soldiers were not far from it either, but managed to push through the uncomfortable period in which the drug took effect.

They made sure West was alive and propped him up against a wall out of the way. Then they decided together that it was in their best interest to seek out and kill any Khun. Substance M raised their aggression beyond normal levels.

But they were barely upright when the Captain turned around and saw Aisling standing in the Square.

"You're not Khun." He started walking towards her, followed by his remaining three soldiers. "But FINALLY, someone has come to talk."

"No, I am Khun," she corrected him, which confused some of the other Khun who could see this unfolding. "And no, I haven't come to talk."

Before he could think of anything to say, the Captain was paralysed as magic held his legs to the ground and his arms behind his back. The other soldiers noticed something going wrong and rushed to help him, but they too were bound by Aisling's spell. The soldiers whispered to each other that a real witch had come to stop them. The Captain, drunk with the effects of Substance M began to laugh madly.

"A real challenge!" He struggled against the spell and managed to free his arms. The other soldiers were weaker and could not break free. The Captain touched a radio transmitter on the strap of his backpack, and spoke into it. A crinkly reply came through that only he could hear, but he seemed pleased with it. "Maybe this is where our mission ends, little witch, but this isn't over-"

His speech was cut off when a transparent box materialised around him. Each soldier found himself trapped in a similar box, even West, who would never remember what he was doing on Gazar. The Captain beat against the box with his free hands before realising the complexity of the magic Aisling had summoned to contain him. He was captured, defeated by a witch half his age.

It was an embarrassment that Jack would find unacceptable when he arrived.

Chuluun rushed forward to Aisling from his hiding spot and scooped her into a massive bear hug. She passed out a moment later, exhausted from Substance M and all her efforts of the day.

"Last time we saw each other, I told you it was not goodbye." He laid her down gently as a crowd formed and the Light magic protecting the city was released.

As the Khun celebrated their victory, Iwizadi felt that it was time to re-join the people. He decided that now, after the centuries of sleep in which he had orchestrated and influenced the actions of all the nations of the world, things had finally reached a point where the future of Libalele looked good. Even through his sleep he could feel the magic of Aisling arrive at the island. He knew the Khun had defended it and seen her on their side. It was time.

In a cave hidden among the rocky cliffs off the south coast of Gazar, only visible at low tide, the legendary wizard's eyes slowly opened and adjusted to the darkness. Before moving any part of his body, he scanned his surroundings and remembered the cave. There was no other living creature inside because of its inaccessibility. There was the dampness of lichen and mould, and the soggy smell of seaweed. He was clothed in the same loose robes he had always known, as was the fashion in Libalele one thousand years earlier. He was barefoot. Time asleep in the cave had done no damage to him, protected as he was by a magical barrier of his own creation. Indeed, had someone been lucky enough to find the cave, they would not have been able to see him, and would have immediately forgotten why they came at all and been desperate to leave. Such was the power of his protective spell. He knew that he intended to sleep for a very long time, and had to be sure that he was safe.

He did look the way he did in the dreams: a man in his sixties with grey hair that flowed like a mane around his shoulders. He was very tall and very thin. His face was ordinary, with some slight wrinkles, but otherwise without blemish. His nose was unremarkable, his jaw sharp and his cheekbones raised. He could have blended in anywhere in the world. The only thing that set him apart were his eyes, which tended to change colour at random.

Seeing his cave and remembering the feeling of being awake, Iwizadi wriggled his toes. The cave was smaller than he remembered, but then again, it had been an exceptionally long time. It must have been high tide when he awoke, because the exit was underwater and the air smelt stale.

He moved his arms slowly. His joints felt like rusty gates. He slowly straightened his legs in front of him, moving out from the cross-legged position he had been holding. His hips ached with the movement, but he pushed through. The place he had chosen to sleep was a kind of rocky landing at the top of some naturally formed steps, and it was here that he stretched out, easing his posture forward and reaching towards his feet.

He cleared his throat, which felt raw, but still remained moist due to the dampness of the cave. He flexed his fingers, then reached up to touch his face and hair. He made some more noises with his mouth, as if testing out a new musical instrument, then his face broke into a smile.

After spending so long in dreams and minds, it was a pleasure to feel reality again. His joy at experiencing things as they really were seemed to radiate outwards and he glowed faintly. He set about testing some magic by sending some light into every corner of the cave.

His command of Light magic was so powerful that rather than sending small globs floating around the cave, he lit the cave itself. Anyone else would have trouble understanding where the light was coming from, compared with the way the Khun performed Light magic. Iwizadi stood up and gently walked from one end of the cave to the other, remembering the feeling of weight. It was all coming back to him quickly, and he relished in the pleasure that sensation brought him, whereas everything in the unconscious world was just a trick.

Iwizadi looked down at where the sea water entered the cave and lapped at its interior. He was feeling stronger with every breath, and waved a hand at the tide. He played with it for a few moments, swishing his wrist and sending the water left, then right. Smiling confidently, he strode out towards the water and with both hands carved a path for himself, defying the tidal power of the sea and the current. While others would have been trapped, unable to even find the cave he was meditating inside for the hundreds of years, Iwizadi simply walked out.

When his height was fully below sea level, his pathway through the water opened before him and closed behind him, and remained covered on the surface, so that anybody looking down at the water would see it as it normally was. Underneath, Iwizadi casually strolled along his shifting pocket of dry seabed as the world continued moving around him. *It was always like that*, he reflected, *that the world moved around me*. Sometimes it was because he made it do that.

The mouth of the river Liba, or Gol as they called it now, was quite some distance from the cave, and Iwizadi would have taken several days walking at his pace. Instead after some minutes, he jumped on the spot, and his dry pocket jumped with him off the sea floor, and when it was at full height he thrust his arm forward, driving the pocket forward at great speed with him in it.

He reached the river in a few minutes, and could feel its magical current spilling out into the sea. Truly, it was a natural wonder and hardly surprising that wars were fought over the land. The river's surface was calmer than the sea, and someone looking at the right place at the right time might have been able to see him walking upstream underwater. But nobody looked. Their attention was focused on the aftermath of their great battle.

Eventually Iwizadi reached the city of Libalele, and decided to leave the safety of the water. He was not afraid to make a spectacular entrance. His air pocket floated up and he continued walking upstream on the surface of the water, not leaving even ripples where he stepped. The Light magic had been lifted since the battle, and it was a pleasure to see the city he loved, even in its state of destruction.

He was halfway through the city, close to the mountain and the castle when he was seen. But he did not break his slow, regal pace as he fixedly moved toward the castle. He knew exactly where he was going: the river flowed down from the peak of the mountain and after a magnificent fall, collected in a secluded basin, which the castle included within its walls and used as a private port. That was where he expected a greeting party; being seen was part of the plan.

He was first seen by some Khun who were milling about, discussing how to clean up their city. Then by the Captain and the soldiers, still contained in Aisling's fields. He was impressed by her work. He reached into the field and removed the Captain's last dose of Substance M, drawn by its tainted magic aura. He examined it and looked at the Captain, who was suffering from the nasty withdrawal of Substance M. He tucked the needle into his robes for later, considering trying it himself if he didn't need it for something else already.

The river which wound through the city was an ideal path for gathering attention, and by the time he reached the port the whole Khun population had been collected. Aisling, Maria, Khuch and Chuluun, who were in the middle of their own reunion were drawn to see what all the fuss was about, thinking perhaps one of the soldiers had escaped. Aisling was recovering from Substance M and doubted if she would be able to create another anti-magic field. Orn, meanwhile chose not to attend, but rather went off to the mountains in search of a good home. He had chosen to stay on the island.

The crowd made room for them as they made their way

to the front, and any confusion they had was instantly dissipated when they saw him standing there; an average man who stood on the surface of the river, with robes flowing gently, with eyes that were blue one moment and orange the next. There was no mistaking him.

"Chuluun." His voice was soft and high-pitched, yet somehow filled everyone's attention with its demand for respect, sounding above the pounding of the waterfall behind him. He spoke Khun with a native accent. It was a fearsome sight in its relaxed command of magic; magic that was beyond the ability or imagination of anyone present, except perhaps Aisling. "Just the man I wanted to see. And you, Aisling. I'm glad you made it here with Khuch Chaddhal."

"My Lord Iwizadi," Chuluun greeted him, bowing his head. Some Khun followed suit but Iwizadi politely stopped them before they got carried away.

"None of that please. It is you who is charge here, Chuluun. Isn't that right?"

Chuluun felt guilty, still not having told anyone of Iwizadi's intentions with Libalele. He felt like Iwizadi could see into his soul and was sure his thoughts were not private. He felt violated. Why wouldn't Iwizadi just take over? Surely, he was powerful enough?

"You haven't told them yet, have you?" Iwizadi asked Chuluun directly, who bowed his head again in shame.

"Told us what?" Khuch asked his father.

"There was never a good time," Chuluun lamely tried to excuse himself to Iwizadi, ignoring Khuch's question at his side.

"No good time? How about now then?" Iwizadi wasn't looking at anyone else, it was as if for him the crowd wasn't there.

"Gazar is not for Khun," Chuluun mumbled so that only Khuch standing right next to him could hear.

"What was that?" Iwizadi asked. "Gazar is not for Khun? Maybe you should explain that more clearly. Or would you prefer if I tell your people their fate?"

The crowd faced Chuluun with a mixture of anger and confusion. Aisling took Chuluun's hand and spoke gently to him.

"What is he talking about, Chuluun?"

"Everyone!" Chuluun yelled out to be heard above the waterfall. "The great wizard Iwizadi visited me in a dream not long ago and told me his plans for the future of our Gazar." At once the crowd turned its anger towards Iwizadi. How dare another outsider try to plan the future of their land? Chuluun saw their reaction and knew that he had not yet lost his people's respect as leader.

"He told me many things. He told me I was to lead, as I have led many of you through our years of exile." Some small cheers could be heard by Chuluun's closest supporters. "But he told me also that my leadership would not last for long. It is his plan that the girl at my side, who many of you know from a baby, will lead this land and its people."

There were outraged cries from some people present, particularly those who Aisling did not know, but including Ychir, the sight of which filled her with embarrassment. Chuluun's news was shocking to her, yet somehow looking at Iwizadi amidst the rising clamour she knew it was the right path for Gazar.

"She isn't Khun! How can you let an outsider rule us again!" Ychir yelled out angrily. There was a menacing atmosphere as the crowd became more and more angry, though they were not sure if they were angrier at Chuluun,

Aisling, or Iwizadi.

"Then we will do the initiation!" Chuluun roared to be heard, which seemed to settle some of the noise.

"But Chuluun," Iwizadi's voice was perfectly audible to all. "You haven't told them the best part." The crowd quieted itself and listened eagerly.

"The wizard has informed me that this land does not belong to us Khun."

The crowd surged forward as a ferocious beast now, outraged beyond reason and still hyped up from their battle. Chuluun grabbed Aisling protectively and turned from the crowd to shelter her, but it was not her they were swarming. The mass of angry Khun rushed forward to where Iwizadi was still standing on the surface of the river out of their reach, hurling abuse at him, shouting that Gazar was home to the Khun for a thousand years, and they would not stand for any more invaders.

Iwizadi heard their outcries and grinned at them all. Their anger rose and rose until one foolish Khun threw a magic fireball at Iwizadi. It fizzled pathetically on impact, and it seemed to be the signal Iwizadi was waiting for.

He waved one arm vigorously at the front of the crowd and they all toppled backward. But this wasn't enough to deter them and they surged forward again, with some now wading into the river in an attempt to capture him by force. Iwizadi pointed at those Khun in the water and with a flick of his finger sent them tumbling downstream. The crowd however, did not let up in its abuse. They had had more than enough of outsiders controlling their land and their destiny, and it was time for them to take matters into their own hands, releasing their years of collective suffering.

A bright flash of light and a deafening bang like a lightning strike brought things to a halt. All the Khun in the crowd were suspended in mid-air, temporarily blinded and with a horrific ringing in their ears. When they came to, they were unable to move or speak. Chuluun released Aisling from his protective hold, and Maria and Khuch stood back, listening and watching. Iwizadi spoke to Chuluun, so that all could hear.

"Your people respect you Chuluun. This is a good thing. They respect the land. But you and I know that Khun are just another temporary people occupying this place. You will lead your people to victory, wherever you choose to go next."

"What if we choose to stay?"

"You are welcome to stay, but you stay as guests." It was possibly the most insulting thing the Khun had ever heard. "This is Libalelean land. It always has been. The Khun have only been keeping it, and our secret, safe."

"For a thousand years."

"Yes, you're welcome. For the gift of one thousand years of magic. And I'll be needing my book back; it isn't finished yet. Or maybe I'll start work on a second volume."

Chuluun, remembering the other part of the instructions asked, "And what of Halasat? What is its importance?"

"You Khun were never very lateral thinkers, were you? I suppose that's what made you such good caretakers of magic. Good servants. Halasat is where the people from Libalele migrated to, after the city's collapse one thousand years ago. Its people must now return here to their true home."

"And why would I go there to bring them back?" Chuluun laughed at the absurdity of it. "Why would I give up my homeland and personally welcome my coloniser?"

"Because you don't have a choice," Iwizadi replied. The floating Khun suddenly started gasping and clawing at their throats. The sound of them collectively suffocating was horrific, and Aisling screamed at Iwizadi to stop. "Should I stop, Chuluun? Do you understand now?"

"Stop! Stop!" Chuluun ran to the nearest Khun and tried to pull them back to the ground. "I'll go! I'll go to Halasat!"

"Good boy." Iwizadi released his magic and all the Khun fell to the ground breathing heavily and hatefully. "Now, if you need anything else, you know where to find my study. Aisling, come with me, we have things to discuss. Thank you for taking care of my book, Chuluun. Now if you please?" The Book of Boloi came sailing through the air and landed in Iwizadi's hands. Chuluun knew he couldn't stop it. He couldn't stop Iwizadi from taking their most precious item, the book that he had guarded with his life, as had countless generations before him. He couldn't stop him from giving their home away to the people from Halasat. He felt powerless. It was all for nothing and none of his efforts mattered.

Aisling twitched and Maria ran to hold her. She hugged her mother, then kissed Khuch quickly, and let Iwizadi lead her to the familiar round room of her dreams, dreading what other horrors she would see that day.

Haforn flew down to Chuluun's feet and stood as tall as he could.

"I have word from a crow named Kraka." Chuluun listened intently. "The people of Halasat do not understand her voice. She failed to deliver the message." Devastated, Chuluun knew this meant he would have to go in person. His future was not in Gazar.

Jack walked through the deserted streets of Khot. When he saw the soldiers held captive in Aisling's anti-magic fields, he stopped to admire the craftsmanship. The Captain might have been one of the most highly-trained and deadly men on the planet, but seeing him held prisoner and suffering the withdrawal effects of Substance M reminded Jack that power came with a price. In this case, it was humiliation. He felt no compulsion to release the men. He was focused on something more important, and they could wait.

Looking at the mountain ahead of him, he considered a plan of attack, and decided that surprise was his greatest asset. He stood still for a moment before casting a Light magic spell on himself to hide in plain sight. Though he had no way of telling, Iwizadi nearby giving his speech to the Khun registered Jack's spell and knew he had arrived. Just as planned.

While the Khun were hearing all about how the future they had fought for was being taken from them, Jack made his way stealthily through the city, and then the castle. He saw the crowd gathered at the base of the waterfall, and heard their outrage. He saw Iwizadi floating above the water and he realised he had not considered this outcome at all. The wizard was supposed to be asleep, or just a myth, or a nightmare, but there he was, exactly the way he appeared in Jack's dreams. Instinctively, he ran up the stairs, seeking out the room that he had seen a hundred times before. If the book was anywhere, it would be there, and he would rather not face Iwizadi in person.

He opened the door and was struck with déjà vu. He knew every detail of the room. He had explored it many times. He had practised magic in it. He had been shown the book, and he had been told his destiny.

Still invisible, Jack closed himself in the room and carefully began looking in drawers and cupboards. If he could not find the book within the next few minutes, he would have to run.

But before he succeeded, he heard a melodious voice

from outside. It penetrated the walls of the room and felt as if the speaker was whispering in his ear: 'I know you're in there'.

After Peter left the Capital, young Jack learned to be the strongest in every room. He learned that people respond to authority. He carried that lesson all through his adolescence and career. Yet for the first time since his childhood, he felt afraid hearing that voice, like he was not the strongest man in the room, and he didn't like it at all.

The door began to open and Jack froze, hoping in vain that Iwizadi couldn't see through his Light magic. But he knew of course he could.

Aisling entered first, unaware. Iwizadi followed. Their eyes met as soon as he came in, and Jack heard his voice fill the room.

"We are not alone in here Aisling." And with no effort whatsoever, Iwizadi negated Jack's spell. "I suppose you've come for my book." He tossed it nonchalantly onto the desk.

"Uncle?" Aisling froze.

"Yes. I've come just as you told me," Jack answered Iwizadi. Turning to Aisling, he added, "But I did not expect to see you here."

"You told him to come?" Aisling asked Iwizadi, feeling betrayed.

"Yes, I have visited the dreams of many people."

"Can I have the book now? I would like to go home and start ruling the world now. Like you promised. I did all this because you promised." Jack was losing patience.

"Rule the world?" Aisling turned to Iwizadi angrily. "What about Libalele? I thought I was supposed to rule."

"You?" Jack scoffed.

"Indeed, I have told you both some things that do not

add up." Iwizadi sat at his oak desk and watched them. "Not everything in life is tidy. Nor do I control destiny. I can only reveal it to some people, just as it was once revealed to me."

"What are you talking about, old man?" Jack reached out for the book, but Iwizadi withheld it.

"There can be only one ruler. I have seen both futures, and it was my destiny to bring you both here, so that you can decide." Iwizadi reached into his robe and removed the needle he had stolen from the Captain. They instantly recognised it when he placed it gently in front of him on the desk. The pure craftsmanship of the natural oak contrasted with the hard clinical sterility the needle represented. "Only one ruler will leave this room."

Jack immediately snatched the drug greedily, thinking it would be easy to take it and overpower his niece. Aisling meanwhile was distracted by some movement outside: Orn was hovering at the window. His voice entered her mind, telling her to hold on, and she couldn't tell if it was Orn, or Iwizadi, or simply her own memory. Iwizadi and Orn shared a look, Aisling noticed. They knew each other.

Her uncle had finished his preparation and began to feel the drug moving through his body. His mind opened to all magic, and he looked at Aisling menacingly, deciding on the best spell to use. He looked at Iwizadi and through the aggressive side effects of the drug thought he might just kill the wizard too.

Jack directed a spell at Aisling to encase her in a bubble and drown her, while Iwizadi sat impassively watching and judging. She tried to defend herself, but Jack with Substance M in his body was too powerful and she found her head underwater. She held her breath. And eventually when she couldn't hold any longer, and she knew it was time to die, she looked at Iwizadi imploringly, and saw him wink. Her lungs gave way and she inhaled, accepting death.

Except she drew in air normally.

Across the room, it was Jack who spluttered and coughed. It was Jack who spat water and whose face turned blue. The unnatural blue of Noi. He released the spell and Aisling shouted at Iwizadi.

"Help! He's dying!" But Iwizadi did nothing as Jack continued drowning from his own spell. Nor did Orn attempt to break in and save him. Aisling, horrified, turned her desperation to anger.

"Why won't you do anything!"

Iwizadi stood up and walked over to where Jack was on the brink of death and examined his face closely. He was definitely drowning, though there was no water anywhere, and Iwizadi celebrated his own success at tampering with Substance M. Aisling saw her uncle die, and despite all the evil he had committed and the fact that he was never present in her life, she still felt his loss.

"Congratulations," Iwizadi said, as she knelt over Jack's body.

"You did this," she spat at him, realising the wizard had hidden motives and distrusting him. "You made it backfire."

"Yes."

"Why? What if I took it instead?"

"Jack was going to take it. I have seen this moment." Orn's voice entered the room.

"Listen to the Eagle. This moment had to happen for you to fulfil your destiny, just as I have now fulfilled mine. All that is left is for you to marry Khuch Chaddhal and become ruler of Libalele."

"You made Jack come here. It wasn't destiny. You made it happen!" Aisling blamed Iwizadi for everything that had gone wrong. He opened the window and Orn came in and nestled into Aisling, comforting her. "Why?"

"Why? Everything happened so that you could be brought here, trained in magic, and prepared to lead. Jack had to have a reason to come here so that he would establish the Department and capture you; capture that led to your command of magic. Jack had to invade the island so that you could save it; save it so that the people believe in you as a leader. That reason was the book."

"I don't believe it." She shook her head. "You set this up so long ago. All so that I could be here now. Why me?"

"I told you I was searching for the ruler for one thousand years." Iwizadi sat back down. "Your father told you he was adopted. Did he tell you he found his birth parents?"

She shook her head.

"They were from Halasat."

The name meant nothing to Aisling. She had only heard of Halasat that day.

"Halasat is where my people fled, after the city's destruction." Things were starting to click into place. "Aisling, we are related. You were born to lead this city. This is your inheritance. I did this all for you."

A short while later, Aisling ran out of the room and back down to find the others. She found them on their way to the Town Square, as they solemnly trudged away from the mountain, wondering what might happen to them if they chose to stay. She caught up to them and her words stumbled over each other as they raced out of her mouth. She tried to tell them everything that had happened, but she had trouble explaining it all. Orn drifted alongside them and came to rest on Khuch's outstretched arm. Chuluun put a hand on her shoulder, the same as he would do to her dad. The same as he would do to any other Khun.

Aisling didn't feel grief over losing her uncle, but it was

many days before she could put a name to why his death was so distressing.

"I feel sorry for him," she told Maria as they helped Sanakh repair her home. "The way Iwizadi used him for so many years."

"Me too," Maria said. "But I hated him too. You didn't know him. He made choices that affected us all for the worse. It's because of him that you lost me. Should I feel pity for him, when for the lifetime that I've known him, he has only over used people to benefit himself?"

"Maybe-"

"He pushed everyone away. It's because of him that your father is gone now."

"I have long suspected that Peter Galyn Ezen would follow the path of Fire," Sanakh said in Khun, listening in. She was able to understand Aisling's language after living together for so long, but wasn't able to speak it. "I believe that he would have done so regardless of his brother. Mastery chooses its Khun, it is a mysterious thing."

Aisling translated Sanakh's speech for Maria, and the three women reflected on mastery for some time while they worked on the house.

"And I feel so betrayed by Iwizadi; he only ever tells half the truth. How can I believe anything he says? I feel so foolish for trusting him," Aisling complained.

"He helped me find you when I was lost," Maria offered. "But I don't trust him either, after learning how he poisoned Jack's mind with the promise of power. That's why I feel sympathetic for Jack; he was blind and Iwizadi exploited his weakness."

"He helped me too. He says he did this all for me," Aisling said. "But I'm worried that he only did it to help himself."

"You might be right."

"Then what should we do? Is there any point trying when he's controlling everything from a distance?"

"I have known you since you were tiny, Aisling," Sanakh spoke up. "Maybe it is a good moment to remind you of the way Khun respond to challenges. What would your father do?"

"He would want more information," Aisling realised. Maria was rapidly learning about Khun culture and felt a resonance with their way of life. "I need to know more about Iwizadi before I can know what to do."

"There is always a point in trying," Maria answered the other question. "Your father taught me that, a long time ago when we lived in the Capital. He never stopped trying for a better life, even when everything was going wrong."

"But that's what got him killed- I mean, turned to fire."

"He never gave up trying for you. For us both"

"If he gave up, he'd be here with us now."

"And I would still be lost in the mind."

They realised it was a hopeless game of 'what if?', and though they were starting to understand the reverence Khun held for the masters, it did little to heal their grief. They wished that there was another version of the story; a version where Peter had gone home with them to Gazar and they lived happily ever after as a family.

But there are no happily ever afters in real life.

The Khun held a small ceremony to honour Peter Galyn Ezen, just as they had done with Tesver Modon Khun only one week earlier. Peter's ceremony was more traditional by comparison, since they had the waters of the Gol at hand.

Eryyl led the ceremony. As Peter's closest relative, Aisling waded into the Gol with her and as it soaked her skin, she felt rejuvenated and imbued with Healing magic. She remembered the hideous river from the mind, and knew then that its resemblance to the Gol could not have saved Peter.

The Khun who knew Peter all followed into the river to knee-depth. Eryyl began to burn deliberately, even as she stood there dripping wet. The other Khun in the river did the same, and the collective strength of the spell made Maria and Orn shiver. The Khun who did not know Peter remained on the banks, and stood as statues watching the ceremony.

Aisling was the last to catch alight. She stood surrounded by flames of all colours; colours that only she could see. She felt the anger of Fire magic reach into her as if to control her. She let it find the part of her that wished Peter hadn't been so stubborn.

And he answered.

She felt his presence in her private fire, and knew then that he wasn't gone. Tears were streaming down her face but she didn't move to wipe them, and for the first time since losing Peter on that day they went to Nelasive, she felt like she was in the right place. She knew that wherever there was Fire magic, her dad was there too.

The world seemed just a little brighter.

The Khun let their spells fade, releasing the fire's grip on Aisling gradually, until she was left standing in the river, staring dumbly at Maria with a rapturous grin and wet face. Khuch waded over to her and put a hand on her shoulder to guide her out, and she followed like a child.

There was a growing feeling of uneasiness in the city. The Khun were still of a survival mindset. They hardly dared to make plans for their future, especially since learning of Iwizadi's plans. Iwizadi for his part, retreated into his private study, emerging only rarely. If he was even there at all, nobody knew, for they didn't dare disturb him. Some of them would have liked to imagine that he didn't exist.

The Khun were distrustful of Aisling, too. As he always had been, Chuluun was her greatest ally, troubled though he was by his own situation.

"I can't lead Khot, Chuluun," she confessed to him, after the ceremony.

"But you will."

"I have to, don't I?"

"Yes." They looked around at all the Khun present. In addition to their small original group, there were dozens of new faces, with more arriving each day. Word had spread around the world that Gazar was free again, and Khun were coming out of hiding. Chuluun agreed that he would continue to lead Khot while there were still so many arrivals. Aisling dreaded the day when they stopped coming. Then he would be going to Halasat.

"Many who don't know you admit that you are Khun now," said Chuluun, understanding Aisling's hesitation.

"Really?"

"You have convinced strangers that you deserve to be here. They have seen your magic, how you fought to save Khot, and slowly they have come to see the trust that we have in you."

"Chuluun, on the day this all started, my dad was going to talk to you about me doing the initiation."

Chuluun laughed like a wild boar.

"*Tsenkher*, there is no need for that."

"What?" She felt like he was laughing at her.

"You have fought in battle for Gazar and there is no magic beyond your ability. You have lived with Khun and speak our language like we do. Even our most traditional Khun accept you as an adult and a leader. What is there left to initiate?"

Aisling knew then how Khuch often felt, talking to his father. She knew his frustration at always facing an unwavering wall of reason. She knew Chuluun was right. She felt silly for not realising it herself, but now that he spelled it out, it was obvious. She was Khun, and she was right where she belonged.

"You are welcome to perform the ceremony, but it will not change a thing."

Yet in the back of her mind, a small seed of doubt had been planted by Iwizadi. She was Libalelean too, and he had said that Gazar was not for the Khun.

Two weeks later, the mass influx of Khun slowed to a trickle and Khot was bustling with activity. It was truly a beautiful city, Aisling noted. She could only compare it to the cities she knew – Nelasive and the Capital – and those cities seemed like festering wounds in comparison. Khot shone; it glowed with magic and a feeling of welcome. The Khun loved their land in a way that the people of her homeland would never understand. The care they showed to their city and to each other made her remember the dirty streets of Nelasive, the abandoned buildings of the Capital, the soulless, sunken faces she saw, the oppressive atmosphere and the overwhelming distrust of the people towards their neighbours.

Maria learned Khun very quickly with the help of Sanakh, with whom she had formed a strong friendship. She also spent as much time as possible with Orn, after learning Bird magic.

"Khun weddings are very formal and usually short meetings for families to ask each other questions," Sanakh explained. "It is a ritual to recognise the joining of two families and establish the expectations and relationships.

For Aisling and Khuch Chaddhal, it will be a little longer than normal, I suspect. It will be the first Khun wedding in sixteen years and we all have great hope that the joining of our families will end our suffering. I am sure that there will be many questions."

"I thought most Khun had agreed that she has earned your respect now," said Maria.

"Yes," Sanakh confirmed. "They are ready for a peaceful chapter in their story. You should be proud that your daughter will lead them in that direction." Sanakh had readily accepted Aisling as her new leader, but not every Khun felt the same way.

Maria swelled with pride, but the sadness that followed reminded her that she had missed Aisling's childhood. She promised to make up for the lost time.

"They are still quite young, aren't they?"

"Khun have no standard age for marriage," Sanakh answered. "All initiated Khun are eligible."

"She wants to marry him."

"And he wants to marry her."

"Thank you, Sanakh."

"For what?"

"You were more of a mother to her than I ever was."

Sanakh laughed, "It seems like you naturally tell sad stories like a Khun. Are you sure you are not one of us?" Maria laughed too. She frowned sarcastically and stiffly put a hand on Sanakh's shoulder. They laughed harder and Maria embraced her warmly.

During this period, Khuch grew distant from most others. He was deeply troubled by Iwizadi's involvement in all of their troubles, and was convinced that he could not be trusted. He often walked in the hills that surround Khot, stewing with worries over their future.

Orn had roosted in the craggy mountains north of Khot, where he had a good view over the Lele valley. Though his perception of human affairs – even earth people – was not the same as humans, he too felt deeply wary of Iwizadi. It was shameful that he, the sky king, had been so easily manipulated. He and Maria bonded over their assessment of the wizard, and Orn agreed to spy on him.

"Are you ready?" Khuch asked Aisling.

"Yes." They stood knee-deep in the Gol together, facing each other, holding hands. Chuluun stood behind Khuch and Maria stood behind Aisling. Hundreds of Khun stood watching from both banks.

"You never told me how you made the stone," Aisling said. "The one that's always the colour I most want to see."

"Yes I did," he replied, and they kissed. The Love magic they shared was visible to everyone watching: bright sparks of every colour swirled around them in patterns like birds in formation. The sparks started from their hands up to surround their whole bodies, then doubled back to each other. Several Khun became uncharacteristically emotional. Even Sanakh's heart melted as the Love magic was amplified by the Gol and she thought of her husband.

Chuluun and Maria were covered by the sparks too. When the kiss was over, they threw handfuls of the magic water into the air above themselves. Chuluun and Maria gripped each other's arms and there was a different type of Love magic between them too.

"It's time to lead, Aisling," said Khuch finally.

"I'm ready," she replied.

Epilogue

Abe Brown writhed on the floor of his office, his jaw and fists clenched painfully tightly. He had shut down the Department after the disastrous mission to steal the book, but knew that it would put an end to his supply of Substance M. He knew that he was taking more than anyone else, and more often. And as his supply dwindled, he began to dread the day it would eventually run out.

But when he shut down the Department, he hadn't counted on the withdrawal from Substance M dependency being so violent. Rather than wait for the long, slow withdrawal to consume him, he decided to enjoy what remained as fast as possible.

Now, as he lay gripped in a seizure, he realised that he had gone too far. This was the end. There was no recovering this time. There would be chaos in the Capital when they finally found him.

Acknowledgments

There are a lot of people to thank. Bridget, for lots of things: being my sounding board for ideas, giving feedback on the drafts, creating brilliant illustrations and cover designs, asking questions about the characters and finding holes in the plot. Mel, for your feedback on the first draft, which helped immensely to shape the final version of this story. Rob, for donating a humongous stack of books for me to read, which ended up being just the right inspiration. Authors Wilbur Smith and Ken Follett, for your styles, which have influenced me a lot. All my friends, who when I told them I was quitting my job to write a book told me it was a good idea.

About the Author

A. C. Smith is a nerd with a background in linguistics, political science and psychology. He is fascinated by the interplay between these fields, and the roles that language and personal choice play in regards to power. Originally from Sydney, Australia, he has also lived in Spain and The Netherlands.

In the Iwizadi Trilogy, Smith explores how words can be used and abused, and examines the spaces where different truths overlap.